## Praise for the Ghost Hunter Mysteries

### *Ghouls Just Haunt to Have Fun*

"M.J.'s back and reluctantly ready for her close-up in the latest funny, yet chilling, adventure by gifted storyteller Laurie. . . . Goose bumps and ghosts are plentiful in this creepy, utterly entertaining murder mystery."
—*Romantic Times* (4½ stars)

"[A] fun, suspenseful, fast-paced paranormal mystery. All the elements combine to make this entry in the Ghost Hunter series a winner."
—The Romance Readers Connection

"A hair-raising tale that will keep readers engrossed in the ghost-driven action. *Ghouls Just Haunt to Have Fun* has as much dark and danger-filled action as ever, and introduces a wonderful new character that readers will be hoping to see more of in the future. This is a must read in the series!"
—Darque Reviews

"A lighthearted, humorous haunted hotel horror thriller kept focused by 'graveyard' serious M.J."
—Genre Go Round Reviews

### *Demons Are a Ghoul's Best Friend*

"Ms. Laurie has penned a fabulous read and packed it with ghost-hunting action at its best. With a chilling mystery, a danger-filled investigation, a bit of romance, and a wonderful dose of humor, there's little chance that readers will be able to set this book down."     —Darque Reviews

"M.J.'s first-person worldview is both unique and enticing. With truly likable characters, plenty of chills, and even a hint of romance, real-life psychic Laurie guarantees that re                               hrilling ride."
—*Romantic Times* (4½ stars)

*continued . . .*

## What's a Ghoul to Do?

"A bewitching book blessed with many blithe spirits. Will leave you breathless."
—Nancy Martin, author of the Blackbird Sisters Mysteries

"Laurie's new sleuth, M. J. Holliday, is a winner.... Laurie makes everything that her characters do ring true, which can be a feat in a paranormal story. This highly entertaining book has humor and wit to spare."
—*Romantic Times*

### Praise for the Psychic Eye Mysteries

"Victoria Laurie has crafted a fantastic tale in ... [her] latest Psychic Eye Mystery. There are few things in life that upset Abby Cooper, but ghosts and her parents feature high on her list ... giving the reader a few real frights and a lot of laughs. ..."          —Fresh Fiction

"Fabulous.... Fans will highly praise this fine ghostly murder mystery."          —The Best Reviews

"A great new series ... plenty of action."
—*Midwest Book Review*

"An invigorating entry into the cozy mystery realm.... I cannot wait for the next book."    —Roundtable Reviews

"A fresh, exciting addition to the amateur sleuth genre."
—J. A. Konrath, author of *Dirty Martini*

"Worth reading over and over again."      —Bookviews

# GHOULS GONE WILD

## A GHOST HUNTER MYSTERY

# Victoria Laurie

AN OBSIDIAN MYSTERY

OBSIDIAN
Published by New American Library, a division of
Penguin Group (USA) Inc., 375 Hudson Street,
New York, New York 10014, USA
Penguin Group (Canada), 90 Eglinton Avenue East, Suite 700, Toronto,
Ontario M4P 2Y3, Canada (a division of Pearson Penguin Canada Inc.)
Penguin Books Ltd., 80 Strand, London WC2R 0RL, England
Penguin Ireland, 25 St. Stephen's Green, Dublin 2,
Ireland (a division of Penguin Books Ltd.)
Penguin Group (Australia), 250 Camberwell Road, Camberwell, Victoria 3124,
Australia (a division of Pearson Australia Group Pty. Ltd.)
Penguin Books India Pvt. Ltd., 11 Community Centre, Panchsheel Park,
New Delhi - 110 017, India
Penguin Group (NZ), 67 Apollo Drive, Rosedale, North Shore 0632,
New Zealand (a division of Pearson New Zealand Ltd.)
Penguin Books (South Africa) (Pty.) Ltd., 24 Sturdee Avenue,
Rosebank, Johannesburg 2196, South Africa

Penguin Books Ltd., Registered Offices:
80 Strand, London WC2R 0RL, England

First published by Obsidian, an imprint of New American Library,
a division of Penguin Group (USA) Inc.

First Printing, March 2010
10  9  8  7  6  5  4  3  2  1

Copyright © Victoria Laurie, 2010
All rights reserved

OBSIDIAN and logo are trademarks of Penguin Group (USA) Inc.

Printed in the United States of America

Without limiting the rights under copyright reserved above, no part of this
publication may be reproduced, stored in or introduced into a retrieval system,
or transmitted, in any form, or by any means (electronic, mechanical, photo-
copying, recording, or otherwise), without the prior written permission of
both the copyright owner and the above publisher of this book.

PUBLISHER'S NOTE
This is a work of fiction. Names, characters, places, and incidents either are the
product of the author's imagination or are used fictitiously, and any resemblance to actual persons, living or dead, business establishments, events, or
locales is entirely coincidental.
   The publisher does not have any control over and does not assume any
responsibility for author or third-party Web sites or their content.

If you purchased this book without a cover you should be aware that this
book is stolen property. It was reported as "unsold and destroyed" to the
publisher and neither the author nor the publisher has received any payment
for this "stripped book."

The scanning, uploading, and distribution of this book via the Internet or via
any other means without the permission of the publisher is illegal and pun-
ishable by law. Please purchase only authorized electronic editions, and do
not participate in or encourage electronic piracy of copyrighted materials.
Your support of the author's rights is appreciated.

For my cousin, Hilary Laurie,
the funnier half of the Tee-Vee Variety Show

# Acknowledgments

Most of my novels are inspired by some paranormal event that I've personally experienced or heard about and this particular story is no exception.

About four years ago I had the scariest and most "real" dream I can ever recall. I vividly remember being in a cold, damp house that was rapidly decaying. The walls were gray and crumbling, the floor was littered with debris, and the atmosphere was so oppressive it felt claustrophobic.

I don't quite remember the beginning of that dream—how I came to be in that exact spot—but I do remember my sense of panic. I knew I had to get a mother and her two children out of that house, but they were hidden away in a room that I couldn't find. I could hear them, though—the laughter of the children at play, and their mother's voice in the background—and my panic worsened.

About the time that I finally found the door to the room they were in, someone came into the hallway where I was. It was a woman and evil wafted off her in thick heavy waves. I remember being acutely afraid of her, and I shouted in alarm for her to leave the children alone. I know she thought very little of my efforts to warn them; in fact, I knew intuitively that she thought very little of me in general.

And her presence only made my own panic mount. The mother and her children seemed completely unaware of her presence and I just *knew* the little ones were in danger.

But I wasn't able to warn them—because in the next instant, I woke up. It was the middle of the night and my heart was still racing from the dream. I can remember thinking, "That was bizarre!" and I probably chalked the whole thing up to the bean burrito I'd had for dinner. But the dream lingered in my thoughts, and I never really did get back to sleep.

The next night I was watching one of my favorite shows—*Most Haunted.* It comes on Friday nights usually around ten p.m. and it is one spooky hour, let me tell you! The premise of the show is that a team of British paranormal investigators travel around Britain to the most haunted locations they can find and document anything that's willing to go bump in the night on camera.

This particular episode was a two parter—I'd missed the previous show, but they ran a few clips of what had taken place. The team was at a remote farm and there were two separate buildings that they were investigating. One was an old crumbling barnlike structure; the other was an abandoned house. A family lived in another house nearby—a father, a mother, and their two young daughters—and they were quite frightened by the negative energy that seemed to permeate the two crumbling buildings and the surrounding grounds.

The night I tuned in, the team was investigating the abandoned house. The barn was said to have been the place where a coven of witches killed the small children they'd kidnapped from the surrounding countryside. The head of their coven was said to be a particularly evil and cruel woman, and it was thought she liked to torture the children before she sacrificed them.

I remember a shivery chill going up my spine as the clips of the previous night's investigation rolled across the TV screen—but that was nothing to what I felt the moment the *Most Haunted* team entered the abandoned house. The camera zoomed in on the crumbling gray walls, the debris-littered floors, and the claustrophobic feel that permeated the place.

I remember staring wide-eyed at the television—not believing what I was actually seeing. It was an *exact* replica of the house I'd been trapped inside the night before in my dream!

I then quickly muted the TV and called my close friend (and agent) Jim. I explained everything that had happened to me in the dream the previous night and how I was looking at the very same location on the television as in my dream. "What should I do?" I asked him, pacing the floor and eyeing the screen nervously.

"I know exactly what you should do," he said with confidence.

"What?"

*"Stop watching that show!"*

☺

Ah, if only it were that easy. I don't know how or why I ended up having that experience, but I truly believe there is a lot more to this paranormal stuff than meets the eye. And it was such a powerful experience that I knew someday I'd get around to telling the story. Or at least an idea inspired by that experience. (And on a quick side note, the village of Queen's

Close is a complete fabrication, just in case any of you were thinking of taking off for that particular part of haunted Scotland.)

Like with all creative projects, there is always more than one input. And again, this particular novel is no exception. So it is with great pleasure and profound gratitude that I would like to thank the following souls for their generous help to this novel.

First, my agent, friend, and muse, Jim McCarthy: Jim—I've said it over and over, but seriously, dude, I heart you somethin' fierce! Thank you for all that you do on my behalf. The encouragement. The enthusiasm. The occasional insult . . . but only when I need one, right? ☺ And of course, thank you soooo much for those wonderful Gilley lines!

My new editor, Sandy Harding: Sandy, all I can say is WOW! You came in, hit the ground running, and never lost a stride! I can't tell you how much I appreciate all the fabulous feedback and wonderful insight. *Merci, merci, merci!*

Claire Zion: Words cannot express how grateful I am that you worked so hard to find me such an amazing editor. Thank you for taking such wonderful care of me, Claire. It's most appreciated.

Michele Alpern: As always, my fabulous copy editor . . . YOU RULE!

Betty Stocking: Betty, thank you for allowing me to bounce all things British off you. I adore you and I'm truly grateful!

Also, allow me to thank the many folks who assist with taking care of me on a regular (sometimes daily) basis so that I can focus and write these books!

My cousin Hilary Laurie: Tee, you're so amazing and so special and you always say the perfect thing!

You have given me some amazing perspective more times than I can count, and you've made me laugh just as often. Love you, *mia carina*.

Profound thanks to the rest of my family, but especially to Elizabeth Laurie and Mary Jane Humphreys. Aunties, *what* would I do without you?!!!! (I'd be a crumbling ruin, that's what!)

And of course a huge thank-you to my peeps and close friends, who are amazingly understanding when it comes to the disappearing act I pull every time I write a new manuscript, not to mention the boundless enthusiasm they display when the latest and greatest hits the shelves. In no particular order they are Nora Brosseau (and the rest of the Brosseau family!), Karen Ditmars, Leeanne Tierney, Silas Hudson, Thomas Robinson, Jaa Nawaitsong, Jennifer Casey, Tess Rodriguez, Shannon Dorn, Christine Trobenter, Pippa Stocking Terry, David Hansard, and of course my very own security detail and the person responsible for controlling the *massive* (cough, cough) crowds at my book signings, Katie Coppedge.

Love you guys. MEAN IT!

# Chapter 1

I'm not really put off by the skeptics out there: people who believe that, for me to call myself a psychic medium, I must be something of a fraud. They see me sitting across from a client, struggling to come up with the name of a deceased loved one or a relevant and specific detail related to that loved one, and it's easy to believe I'm making the whole thing up.

But they don't know what I know. They don't feel what I feel. They don't hear what I hear or see what I've seen. And they never will. Well, at least until *they* cross over, of course. There are no skeptics on the other side.

Case in point, one of the best readings I ever did was for a woman who had just lost her father, and by *just*, I mean earlier that very morning. When she came to me, desperate to know that her dad was okay, I took pity on her and fit her into my schedule right away. When we sat down together, her father came through immediately, and all he kept saying was, "Holy cow! This stuff is real!"

Turns out that, for seventy years, he'd been the biggest, loudest atheist you'd ever want to meet, and been convinced that people like me were total shams. So imagine how surprised he was when he died and discovered a whole new world—*literally*.

And really, because of that experience, I no longer worry about the snarky little side comments I get from folks who think what I do is a big charade. They just don't get it, and maybe, they're not supposed to until they too drift off into that great night.

But none of that is going to slow me down or even give me pause. There's *way* too much work to do for me to linger on what other people think.

I've got my regular work as a medium—connecting the living with their deceased loved ones—and my other job as a ghostbuster for a brand-new cable-TV show.

It seems that there's a growing fascination among television-viewing audiences for watching the things that go bump in the night. And, truthfully, our world is chock-full of those poor souls that haven't made it across yet. I'm talking about grounded spirits, better known to most as ghosts. There are millions and millions of them out there, wandering aimlessly about—and some places are more heavily populated than others.

Take Europe, for example: You can't walk a mile anywhere on that continent without bumping into a ghostie or two. . . . They're *everywhere*. Which is why our production company wanted to fly us "across the pond," so to speak, and plunk us down somewhere old and spooky.

My two partners and I were part of a ghostbusting team recruited by a small production company headed by this guy named Gopher. Well, that's not really his name. His real name is Peter Gophner, but everyone calls him by his nickname. I often wonder if that's because sometimes he can be a real rat.

Anyway, with Gopher's assistance we'd landed a major contract with the Bravo cable network to develop a ghost-hunting show called *Ghoul Getters*. Bravo wanted ten episodes to air every Saturday night beginning in January. If all went successfully, my team and I would be rich and famous in no time.

My ghostbusting squad was made up of my best friend and the team's technical guru, Gilley Gillespie, and Heath Whitefeather, a brilliant medium in his own right and someone whom I'd recently worked another bust with.

I'd known Gilley since I was in first grade back in Augusta, Georgia. I'd found him on the first day of school by himself on the playground with a pair of G.I. Joes he was pretending were having a make-out session. Even back then Gil was featherlight in his loafers. We'd become instant BFFs.

After high school, and to get away from the dysfunction of my father's house, I'd followed Gilley out to Boston, where he landed a full ride to MIT.

It was around that time that my psychic-medium skills had really sparked, and after three years Gilley quit school to help me run my business. He'd set up a Web site for me and managed my personal clients, and things ran smoothly until I got burned-out.

It was Gil who'd come up with the rather genius idea of opening up our own ghostbusting business. Unfortunately, the general public didn't find the idea so genius, and we'd barely managed to eke out a living.

Then, about four months ago, Gilley had answered an online ad on my behalf to participate on a reality-TV show called *Haunted Possessions*—sort of an *Antiques Roadshow* meets *Most Haunted*.

I'd reluctantly agreed, but that had actually turned

into the current opportunity with Bravo TV, so things had worked out in the end—at least financially.

And that first TV show had also been where I'd met Heath Whitefeather, who was a genuinely good guy.

Heath was an amazing talent as far as mediums go. He was American Indian, raised on a reservation in New Mexico, and he could communicate with the dead as well as anyone I'd ever met. Physically he sort of resembles Ashton Kutcher, but with darker, longer hair, and more-olive skin. His chin is also a little more square, but his body is just as finely chiseled . . . er . . . not that I've noticed or anything (ahem!).

Okay, so the truth is that if it weren't for the fact that I was currently attached, I'd likely fall for Heath in a heartbeat.

Gilley and Heath were really geeked about the idea of venturing overseas. But I wasn't so stoked, mostly because of whom I'd be leaving behind.

My sweetheart, Dr. Steven Sable, would have to stay in Boston and work, and lately, Steven and I hadn't been doing so well. A lot of our issues had to do with our crazy work schedules. He worked days, and I worked nights, so lately we hardly saw each other.

Intuitively, I knew that what we really needed was to spend more time together and strengthen our relationship, but when I signed the contract with Bravo, there was little chance of that happening.

So, not only was I about to put my romantic relationship on hold, but I'd have to leave behind my beloved African Gray parrot, Doc, who would be looked after by a trusted friend while I was away.

Doc and I have been together for over twenty years and in all that time we'd never spent longer than a week apart. The filming schedule had our crew out of the country for the next eight to ten weeks, which was what had me so glum about the prospect of leaving. And it must have been obvious because as I sat in my office waiting on a client, Gilley came bounding in, took one look at me, and said, "Don't pout, M. J. You'll develop frown lines."

I sighed. "Way to cheer me up, Gil."

"Are you still moping about the trip?"

"Doc's going to think I've abandoned him," I said moodily.

Hearing his name, my bird gave a loud wolf whistle from his play stand in the corner and said, "Nice bum! Where you from?"

"He'll be fine," Gilley insisted.

"And I think Steven's not real thrilled that I'm leaving either."

"Distance makes the heart grow fonder," Gilley sang, patting my arm sympathetically before showing me a small box that had just been delivered. "Look what came FedEx!" My partner tilted the box, which he'd opened, so that I could see the contents. Inside was a DVD.

"What's that?" I asked.

"Location footage," Gil replied. "Remember when you insisted on approving each location before we committed?"

"Yes, and I thought I already approved all of them." I distinctly remembered the three hours Gil, Heath, and I had spent viewing each location that'd been chosen by the production company to film each episode of *Ghoul Getters*.

Gilley nodded enthusiastically as he came around my desk, popped open my laptop, and slid in the DVD.

"Gopher called me yesterday," he explained, referring to our producer/director. "He found a new spot he thinks we should investigate first. He said the location team that scouted it is still freaked-out about what they saw, and he says we can't pass it up. It's the scariest place on earth!"

"Great sales pitch," I grumbled, still moody over leaving home for so long.

Gilley ignored me and hit play. My computer screen filled with the image of a drizzly gray landscape. Old brick buildings lined a narrow cobbled street as rain dripped off thatched roofs and collected in puddles.

Someone off camera began speaking in a lovely Scottish brogue. "Before us is the infamous Briar Road, the most haunted lane in all of Europe and maybe even the world—while below our feet are the world-renowned caverns where countless hundreds lost their lives to the Black Death, starvation, fire, and murder. Pain lines this street and seeps up from deep underground. Here, the earth is so thick with it that nary a beast will tread down these cobbled stones. No bird, stray cat, or dog will venture here. Only humans are fool enough to walk this road."

I wanted to roll my eyes at the theatrics, but before I even had a chance, a man appeared on-screen holding a cute, cuddly charcoal-colored puppy, shivering in the rain. The man, dressed in a long black raincoat with a black bowler, wore something of a wicked grin and I immediately disliked him. "What's he doing?" I whispered as the guy came forward and held up the puppy to the camera so that we could get a better view of the adorable face.

"Aw, it's a pug," Gil said. "M. J., you love pugs!"

Gil was right, I did love the puggies, but something

told me this guy was up to something, so I didn't reply with more than a nod. And sure enough, in the next instant the man set the little pup down on the ground. Securing a leash to its collar, he announced, "I've selected this adorable pup from a local shelter to demonstrate what happens when an animal finds itself on Briar Road."

And with that, the man turned and began to trot down the narrow street, leading the puppy behind him. At first the pug was all too willing to follow, but then, about ten yards into their walk, the pug stopped abruptly and tried to sit down. The man looked behind him, smiled, then stared keenly into the camera. "They all attempt to resist in exactly the same spot," he said.

I hoped it would end there, but it didn't. The man pulled cruelly on the leash, dragging the puppy along, as it began to squirm in earnest, and the farther the man tugged it down the street, the more terrified the puppy became. Its eyes bulged wide and it began to bite at the leash and growl and whimper and snarl. Five more feet had it resembling some sort of rabid animal—it was so terrified that it was nearly unrecognizable as the same dog that'd been held up to the camera only moments before.

"That rat bastard!" I growled as I stared in horror at the computer screen. I could feel my hands curl into fists and I wanted nothing more than to reach into the image and punch that guy in the nose. But he managed to anger me even further when he picked up the puppy, who was wriggling and squirming and snarling, and held it suspended for a moment while the camera moved in for a close-up.

Gilley and I sat there in stunned silence; I couldn't

believe the cameraman was cooperating with this clear-cut case of animal cruelty! A moment later the man began to walk slowly back toward the camera, and the second he got to within about five feet of the cameraman, the puppy suddenly calmed down and settled for just dangling in the man's hands, shivering pitifully from nose to tail.

I closed the computer screen and rounded on my partner. "Get Gopher on the phone!" I snapped. *"Now!"*

Gilley was already dialing and after three rings sounded through the speakerphone, we were rewarded with Gopher's enthusiastic, "Hi, Gilley! Did you get the DVD?"

"What the *hell* was that?" I yelled, not even bothering to announce that I was in the room with Gilley.

There was a pause, then, "Hi, M. J."

"Don't you 'hi' me, Peter Gophner! How could you let them *do that* to an innocent puppy?"

"It wasn't my idea," he began, but I wasn't interested in excuses.

"Of all the stunts you've pulled, Gopher, this has to be the lowest, most underhanded, most ridiculous. . . ." My voice trailed off and I began to pace the room. "You're lucky I don't quit over this, do you hear me?"

For a long moment Gopher said nothing, which was probably wise, and I knew that he was likely waiting for me to calm down long enough to hear him out. Finally, Gilley said, "You didn't have to use the dog to get us to agree to the location shoot, Gopher."

We heard Gopher sigh before he said, "You're right. But I swear to you, using the dog wasn't our idea. I sent Kim and John over there to do some more scouting, because I wasn't really excited about our first pick. They found a few spots that were just okay, but when they got to this little village on the outskirts of Edinburgh, Scotland, they called to tell me they'd hit the jackpot.

"I guess the guy you saw on the footage is some local who does these ghost tours and he picks up a new dog or cat every week from the pound to demonstrate what happens when you try and walk an animal down Briar Road. From there he took John and Kim down into the tunnels and caverns right below and the footage gets even freakier. Did you guys happen to watch the whole thing?"

"No," I said, still angry about the pug. "And I'm not planning on watching it, Gopher. That was just sick, do you hear me? *Sick!*"

There was another long pause, and another sigh from Gopher before he said, "Okay, I understand, M. J. We'll stick to the original plan and fly your team to Yorkshire."

That got my attention. "No," I said firmly. "Now that I know what's happening there, we're absolutely doing Edinburgh first."

"We are?" said Gil and Gopher together.

I nodded. "Definitely."

"Fantastic!" said Gopher, and he began to say something else, but I cut him off.

"We'll go to Edinburgh on one condition," I said. "And that is that you call ahead, and find out where that puppy is and if he's okay."

"Er . . . ," said Gopher.

"Further, that you let that ghost-tour guide know that I want a meeting with him, specifically."

"Ummm," said Gopher. "M. J.?"

"What?" I snapped, reading his tone.

"Are you sure that's a good idea?"

"Positive," I said. "Get me that meeting, Gopher."

"Okay," he agreed. "I'll do that, but watch the rest of the footage, okay? There were some really amazing and creepy things happening belowground that I know Kim and John are still really shaken up about. It'll help prepare you for the shoot."

"When was the footage taken?" I asked, still worried over the trauma the puppy had experienced.

"This past weekend," said Gopher.

I didn't reply and Gilley took the lead. "Sure thing, Gopher. See you tomorrow at the airport."

After Gilley had hung up, I hit the eject button on my computer and handed him the DVD. "Burn this," I ordered.

"To another disc?" he asked.

I smiled. Only to a computer geek would the words "burn this" not include the thought of fire. "No, honey," I said. "Destroy it. Make it into barbecued brisket or chop it up into a million pieces. I never want to see it again."

"But Gopher said to watch the footage," Gil whined, refusing to take the disc from me.

I scowled at him and walked around to my shredder, where I fed it into the grinder. It made the most satisfying noise as it was gobbled up. "I guess we'll have to go in blind."

Gilley looked at me skeptically. "I never like it when you say that."

I smiled. "Come on, honey, let's go pack."

We landed in Edinburgh in the pouring rain, which was fitting, since we left New England in a torrential storm. And the temperature wasn't much different either: friggin' frigid, by my estimate.

It was also two a.m. local time, or eight p.m. our time. I tried calling Steven to let him know I'd landed safely, but it went straight to voice mail. I left him a message and wondered where he could be. We'd been playing phone tag for the past two days, and I hadn't actually talked to him in all that time.

"You okay?" Heath asked as we piled into the van Gopher had rented.

"Fine," I said. I knew he'd probably caught the frustrated look on my face when I'd snapped my phone closed, but I couldn't help it.

"You sure?"

I forced a smile. "I'm sure. Thanks."

Gopher drove us to the village of Queen's Close, which, by the map I was given, was a good distance away from the heart of Edinburgh. It took us about forty minutes to get to a quaint little inn where we all checked in. We then went directly to our rooms to catch some shut-eye before an early-morning start. I did a lot of staring up at the ceiling wondering about the boyfriend I'd left behind, my birdie, and the little pug puppy that I hoped was okay.

The next morning Gopher knocked on my door, waking me from the short sleep I'd finally managed to fall into. "M. J.?" he called. "It's time for breakfast. You'll need to come down in the next ten minutes if you want to eat before we leave for the shoot."

I mumbled something unintelligible, and I believe he took that as a sign that I was up and moving, because nothing further came from his side of the door. With a sigh I sat up and shivered. My room was freezing and the coverlet left a lot to be desired.

This spurred me to get dressed and get downstairs in search of a nice hot cup of coffee, pronto.

I met up with the rest of the crew in the dining room, which included Meg, our personal assistant and makeup artist; Kim and John, our location scouts; Gopher, our producer/director; Jake, our camera guy; and Russ on sound.

Also at the table were Gilley and Heath. "Hey there," Heath said as I sat down, rubbing my hands together.

"Coffee?" I asked hopefully.

Gilley reached over and poured me a piping cup from a carafe on the table. I curled my fingers around it gratefully. "Don't they heat this place?"

"Welcome to Britain," Kim said. I noticed she was bundled up in a layer of sweaters, a thick scarf, a down vest, and fingerless gloves. "They're a bit hardier here in Scotland. They don't turn the heat up past sixty-five anywhere around these parts."

I looked at Gil. "I'll need warmer clothes, honey. I can't tune in if I'm a Popsicle."

"We'll send someone out for you," Gopher assured me, and he looked pointedly at Meg. "Can you get her some sweaters, gloves, a scarf or two, and a warmer coat?"

Meg nodded and jotted a note into her iPhone. My eyebrows rose in appreciation. I could get used to this.

After I'd ordered breakfast, Gopher placed a map on the table and discussed the filming schedule. "There are two main areas that I think we should focus our attention on: This street," he said, pointing to a small line on the map marked *Briar Road*, "is supposed to be one of the most haunted streets within Queen's Close. So we'll start there and see what you guys can pick up.

"Next," he said, indicating a shadow that ran parallel to Briar Road, "I want to get some footage down here."

"Down where?" I asked, squinting at the map.

"This is a cavern that runs right underneath Briar Road," he explained. "It connects to a large grouping of other tunnels and caverns that wind under most of the village and make up the close."

"What's close?" Gilley asked.

Gopher smiled. "That's what they call a grouping of caves and tunnels here in Scotland."

Gilley's eyebrows shot up. "Oh! I get it. The village of Queen's Close! It's named after the underground caverns."

"Exactly," said Gopher. "Anyway, these caverns are alleged to be teeming with strange noises, mysterious shadows, and disembodied voices. In fact, legend has it—"

I cut him off with a wave of my hand. "Hold on, Gopher," I said. "It's better if you don't tell Heath and me anything about the history. We're better off going in blind and telling you what we pick up."

Beside me Heath nodded his head. "M. J.'s right," he said. "It'll look more authentic if we can get it on our own."

Gopher smiled. "Okay, have it your way," he said. "But remember that the network wants something scary at each shoot. The name of the show is *Ghoul Getters*. We're searching for malevolent spirits here, so if you find any, try and invoke them into doing something creepy, like throwing something or lashing out in some way."

I held in a sigh. Heath and I had had this conversation with Gopher before. Bravo wanted us to push the envelope at these haunted locations because we were competing against other already-popular ghost-hunting shows. The network honchos felt that if our show could ratchet up the creepy factor, we'd be able to hang with the other more-established programs. Gopher had taken that to mean that we should purposely antagonize any nefarious spirits we encountered. What he and the network just didn't understand was how dangerous that game plan was.

Heath and I had privately agreed we would attempt to make contact with any spirit we encountered, and we would work to give accurate histories about those spirits to the viewing audience and encourage them to communicate with us through knocks or whispers or by showing themselves on camera, but we were *not* about to paint ourselves as targets for any violent reaction by an evil spirit. That was just stupid.

Still, we knew it was pointless to argue about it with Gopher. He just didn't get how risky his directions were, so I bit my tongue, glancing sideways at Heath, who looked like he was doing the same, and we both simply nodded.

"Oh, and I got you that meeting with the ghost-tour guide," Gopher told me after my food arrived.

"Today?"

Gopher nodded. "Yep. Right after breakfast. I'd like to tape it if you don't mind."

I did mind, but I understood that I'd signed a contract and that right now Gopher pretty much owned me. "Okay," I said with a side glance at Gilley.

"Is there any word on the pug?" Gil asked.

Gopher nodded at Kim, who said, "We found out which shelter he's in. It's a small, privately run place not far from here."

"Tell the tour guide we're going to be late. I want to run by the shelter first."

Several people at the table squirmed in their chairs, and Gilley made a face that suggested I'd spoken out of turn. "Um, M. J., can I have a word with you over there, please?"

I frowned, wondering why everyone was acting weird. I followed Gilley over to a corner in the large room and he leaned in to whisper in my ear. "Can you maybe lay off the demands a little?" he asked.

My eyes widened. "Excuse me?"

Gil shuffled his feet nervously. "Look, I'm not gonna beat around the bush with you, but sometimes, M. J., you can be a bit of a pill, and these guys are all starting to think you're sort of a diva."

My jaw dropped. "Are you kidding me? *How* have I been acting like a diva?"

Gilley sighed. "Where should I begin?"

I folded my arms across my chest defensively. "Um . . . *any*where?"

"Okay," Gil said, "how about starting with your insistence on approving all locations prior to shooting?"

I shook my head, completely confused. "Gilley," I said reasonably, "I did that because I didn't want to walk into any surprises, I mean, who knows where these bozos could have set us down! Some rickety old castle that's falling apart and could be a death trap for us?"

"It says that you lack faith," Gil said gently.

I took that in for a minute. "Fine," I conceded. "What else?"

"Demanding to meet with the tour guide."

Again my jaw fell open. "You saw what he did to that puppy!" I nearly shouted. "And you want me to sit back and not say anything?"

Gil placed a gentle hand on my shoulder. "Of course

that's not what I expect, M. J., but maybe insisting on it first thing was a bit over-the-top? And now you're trying to change the schedule again, honey. I mean, have you heard yourself lately?"

I blinked at my partner, opening and closing my mouth as I tried to form words. I wanted to argue my point, but the truth was that I knew Gilley already understood it, and that he still thought I was being a little too demonstrative was sobering. Finally I sighed and leaned against the wall. "Fine," I said after a lengthy pause. "I get it."

"Do you?"

I closed my eyes. "Yes," I said grudgingly. "I'll lay off the attitude."

"Let me do the asking from now on, okay?"

My eyes opened and I flashed him a smile. "I've already formed a reputation, huh?"

"A bit," he said, returning my smile.

"All right. You win. But see if we can fit the pug in sometime today, will you?"

"Consider it on the agenda."

I looked over Gil's shoulder and saw that my breakfast was getting cold. New attitude in hand, I got back to the table and smiled politely at the crew. "Wonderful day for a ghostbust, don't you think?" I asked a bit too cheerfully.

That won me several nervous smiles. I decided to quit while I was ahead and just eat.

After breakfast we loaded into the huge van Gopher had rented and headed toward town. We arrived very soon afterward at a street I recognized from the footage I'd seen on the DVD Gopher had sent us.

It had stopped raining, but there was a cold mist in

the air that chilled me to the bone despite the warm coffee and hearty breakfast. We unloaded from the van and were met by the guy in the bowler hat who had pulled the poor defenseless pug down the haunted street.

He smiled at us as we got out of the van, appearing delighted to see us. His smug expression made me even angrier, and I couldn't wait to put him in his place.

The man in the bowler was introduced as Fergus Ericson, which fit. He looked like a Fergus to me and as the cameras came out and Gopher pointed to me, he said, "And this is our star, M. J. Holliday. She's a psychic medium from America and the one who specifically asked to be introduced to you."

Fergus puffed his chest out. "Oh, a medium, do you say?" he asked Gopher before stretching out his hand toward me. "Lovely to make your acquaintance, miss," he said jovially.

I stared moodily at his hand before shaking it with only one pump and letting it go. "Tell me, Mr. Ericson, do you make it a habit to traumatize poor defenseless puppies?"

This won me an odd reaction. Fergus laughed merrily. "Why, no, miss, sometimes I like to traumatize the kittens too."

I narrowed my eyes at him. "I'm not joking, Mr. Ericson," I said evenly.

Ericson's smile broadened. "Aye," he said. "I didn't think you were."

I glanced at Heath, who was frowning and balling his fists in anger. "*Why* would you feel it necessary to torture small animals?" Heath asked him bluntly.

"Because they make such good little canaries, don't you think?"

"What?" I asked him. "What do you mean, they make good canaries?"

Ericson waved at the cobbled street and motioned for us to walk forward. Without thinking about it, I fell into step with him. "Don't you remember your mining history?" he said. "When the miners went down into the shafts, they took a canary along with them. When the birds dropped dead, they knew they needed to get back up top, and be quick about it."

"What does that have to do with what you're doing to these poor animals?" I demanded.

"They let me know where the ghosties are, Miss Holliday. And as it's the way I make my trade, I couldn't very well get along without the little darlings, now, could I?"

Ericson's soft voice and seductive brogue were at complete odds with how detestable I found him. I had no idea how to react to someone who so obviously didn't care whether I judged him, and I was at a loss as to what to say next. I looked over at Heath for support, but his head was down and his shoulders were hunched. I suspected he was concentrating on keeping his own temper in line.

I took two more steps and walked into hell. Or, to this day, what I'm convinced hell actually sounds like. My energy felt as if it was being assaulted from all sides; screams and wailing and a torrent of terror hit me like a battering ram.

I stumbled back and grabbed my head. "Agh!" I moaned. Someone gripped my arm tightly and tried to pull me forward, but that was toward the horror that was surrounding me. I became completely disoriented, nauseous, and terrified. The noise around me felt like it was happening both inside and outside my head, like it was permeating through me, and the volume kept turning up, and up . . . and up.

"Make it stop!" I shouted. But it wouldn't. Instead, it got worse. "*Gilley!*" I screamed in agony. "*Get me out of here!*"

I couldn't see and I couldn't hear above the noise, and I couldn't feel anything besides the terror running up and down my spine. Finally I was aware that I was moving, and in another moment I was able to lift my head up. I realized that Gilley was half carrying me, half dragging me down the street. "Get Heath!" he shouted to someone nearby.

And that's when I realized that I was still hearing screams, but they came from only one source. Gilley set me gently on the ground next to the van. He lifted my chin and looked at me with grave concern. "M. J.? Can you hear me? Are you okay?"

My head bobbled on my neck. I felt sick as a dog and like I was being sucked down, and down, and down, as if I were melting or fading away. "Water," I gasped. "Gil, give me some water!"

The screaming stopped and as Gil rushed to get a bottle of water out of the van, I saw Heath's limp body being pulled between two of the crew over to where I sat.

Gopher eased him down to the ground and held Heath's head between his hands. "He's out cold!" he said, then looked at me, his expression frightened and concerned. "*What* happened to you two?"

Someone chuckled behind Gopher and wearily I looked at the maker of the offensive noise. "They've had a taste of Briar Road, is all," said Ericson, standing just behind Gopher.

I swallowed hard, and considered whether I could

lean far enough forward to throw up on his shoes. "You . . . total . . . dickhead . . . ," I managed.

Gilley came back to my side and held up the bottle of water. "Here, honey," he coaxed. "Drink this."

I took a small sip but continued to glare at Ericson, who was thoroughly enjoying himself at our expense. "Let that be a lesson to you," he said to me with a shake of his finger. "And next time, perhaps you'll think twice about crossing the Atlantic to issue me a lecture."

With that, he turned on his heel and strode casually away.

# Chapter 2

Heath came to about ten minutes later. And even though he was soon fully conscious, he remained pale and withdrawn for the rest of the morning. "Tell me what happened," Gopher said gently while the camera propped on Russ's shoulder made the softest whirring noise.

I wiped a stray hair out of my eye and huddled a little deeper into the blanket someone brought me. "I don't know how to explain it," I said, looking over at Heath, who merely shook his own head.

"I've never come across anything like that," he said. "Never."

"Was it a ghost?" Gilley asked me.

I nodded. "Yeah, but it wasn't just one, Gil. It was *thousands*."

"And they were all screaming," Heath added with a shudder, "in tremendous pain, like they were each being subjected to some kind of torture."

I looked back up at Gopher. "It was overpowering. So much trauma and pain and terror in one small section of land . . . my God. It's a wonder *anyone* can walk down that street."

Gopher turned to Gilley. "Did you feel anything?"

Gilley shook his head. "No," he said. "Well, except maybe a little light-headedness, but nothing too extreme."

Gopher sighed. "What should we do?" he asked.

I shivered again. "I don't know what you could possibly do, Gopher. I mean what can anyone do? There are thousands and thousands of tortured, grounded souls on that street, and you will never get me to set foot there again."

"I'm with M. J.," Heath said. "No way, man. Briar Road is off the agenda."

"Should we abandon the entire location?" Gopher asked.

I looked at Heath and smiled contritely. "Maybe going blind into this wasn't such a great idea."

Heath shrugged. "M. J., there's no way you could have known what we'd encounter. I mean . . . that was just *unnatural*."

"This is going to be expensive," Gopher said gloomily. "And I don't think the network's going to like it."

I frowned and eyed Heath again. He shrugged in silent understanding and nodded. "I suppose we could take a look at the caverns, Gopher," I said.

Gopher brightened and gave me a pat on the shoulder. "That's the spirit!"

I wondered if the pun was intended. "Hold on, guy," I added. "If we get down there and it's anything like Briar Road, we're not going to be able to continue. And someone's going to have to make sure we come out quick if we get into trouble."

"No sweat," Gopher agreed. "We'll have your back, M. J."

Next, I focused on Gilley. "Honey, can you please do some research and find out what exactly happened on Briar Road? Some great catastrophe had to have taken place there to cause such turmoil. Also, see if whatever happened on that road also happened in the caverns below. We'll need to know what we're getting ourselves into and if it's worth the risk of heading underground."

Gilley saluted. "I'm on it," he said.

I turned again to Heath. "We need a sea-salt bath and we need it soon."

He nodded dully. "Yeah, good idea."

"Why a sea-salt bath?" Gopher asked as I got wearily to my feet.

"To help clean and repair our auras," I told him. "It's sort of like getting a vitamin B shot. It should help us feel better in no time."

"Do you need me to get you some sea salt?" asked Meg.

"Yes," I told her. "I mean, yes please, Meg, that would be really great."

She blushed and slung her purse over her shoulder. "Any particular kind?"

"Natural sea salt is the best," I said. "And lots of it. Something tells me we're going to be taking a lot of baths while we're here."

Several hours later Heath and I were fresh out of our respective tubs and sitting in the inn's main parlor, warming our feet by the fire. "I feel like we're way out of our league, here," I said.

"I don't know if I can do this, M. J.," he confessed, and I knew exactly what he meant.

"We need some serious protection," I told him. "Crystals, maybe some magnets, something to help combat the effects."

Heath leaned back in his chair and stared up at the ceiling. "My grandfather would know what to use."

"Is he gifted like you?"

"Was," Heath said. "He used to know a lot about the spirit world. Sometimes he'd drift off into a trance, and there was no waking him from it. He'd be completely out of it for hours, and then, all of a sudden he'd be back and he'd talk about all the dead people he'd walked with out on the plains."

"Does he ever come to you?" I asked.

Heath eyed me from his chair. "Sometimes," he said. "Every once in a while he'll show up in one of my dreams."

"Do us a favor and try to contact him," I said in all seriousness. "Maybe if he sees that you have a need, he'll come visit you while you're sleeping tonight." Heath looked doubtfully at me. "Worth a try at least," I reasoned.

He smiled. "It is," he conceded. "Okay, I'll call out to him before I hit the hay. Maybe we'll get lucky and he'll respond."

"And I'll do some scouting around for someplace we can get some crystals."

Gilley came into the room at that moment, followed closely by the camera and sound crew. He seemed to be enjoying that fact, or so I gathered from the constant smile on his face every time they were around.

"Hello, dahlings!" he said with a grandiose hand flourish.

"Gil," I said.

"Guess what?"

I sighed tiredly. "You've discovered something riveting in your research?"

Gilley rocked back and forth on his heels. "I did!"

"What is it?" Heath asked.

Gilley looked around at the many available seating surfaces, and finally moved over to sit next to a lamp where he positioned himself just so on the couch, before glancing up at Jake, the camera guy. "How's my lighting?"

"Fine," Jake said in a way that told me he was sick of answering that question.

Gilley turned up the wattage on the made-for-TV smile and said, "I found out why Briar Road knocked you guys on your keisters."

Heath leaned forward. "What'd you find?"

"Sooo much," Gil said. "For starters, that road is one of the oldest in the village. It dates back to the middle of the tenth century, in fact. And it's seen its share of tragedy too. There have been at least five major waves of bubonic plague that have run rampant through this village over the millennia."

I eyed Gilley skeptically. "I don't think so, buddy," I told him. "I mean, yeah, I would expect a place as old as this to have its fair share of spooks, but the intensity of that street, Gil . . . I don't even know how to describe it! It was like my skin was on fire and the level of panic was out of this world." I turned to Heath and he was nodding his head vigorously.

"It was beyond description," he said, "but M. J. comes pretty close to what it felt like."

Gilley nodded as if he knew just what I was talking about. "I get it," he assured me. "And I really think I understand why it hit you two in exactly the same way. See, in the mid-sixteenth century the plague came through here with a vengeance. At that time, Briar Road was part of a densely populated quarter of this village, filled to bursting with lots of small shops and residences. Most of the village's poor lived on or near Briar in cramped close quarters. Problem was, with all that traffic and humanity packed into such a small space, the Black Death had plenty of victims to choose from, and it wasn't long before the entire street was lined with dead bodies.

"About two weeks into the height of the plague, and in a poorly thought-out attempt to contain the spread of it, a few of the village's noblemen decided it was a good idea to set up barricades at each end of Briar Road, which they did, blocking the residents in. And then, the noblemen set fire to it."

My jaw dropped. "They burned the whole street with all those people trapped inside?"

"Yes," Gilley said somberly. "And then they repeated that action a few years later when the plague returned."

I was horrified. "But *how* could they do that? I mean, Gilley! How could they burn all those people alive? It's barbaric!"

"Welcome to the Middle Ages, M. J.," Gil said. "Back then, they were a bit less concerned with preserving the lives of the less fortunate."

There was a long silence that followed. I didn't know what to say, and I was so torn between my disgust over what had happened to those poor souls and a grim comprehension of what had hit Heath and me on Briar Road. "Now we know why it felt like our skin was on fire," Heath said, mirroring my thoughts.

"Good God," I whispered. "Gil, please tell me that we're not going to encounter that in the cavern below Briar Road."

"You should be fine once you get underground,"

he assured me. "I couldn't find anything close to that tragic for the caverns. It looks like it was used primarily as a refuge for the village poor once they caught on to the fact that the noblemen were likely to set them on fire if they appeared sick."

At that moment Meg came into the inn carrying a bundle of packages. "Hey, guys!" she sang when she saw us.

"Hey." I nodded absently at her, my mind still on the victims of Briar Road.

Meg dropped several of the packages at my feet. "I got you some stuff," she said happily, and this pulled me back to reality.

I sat forward and attempted a smile. "Thanks," I said. "I really appreciate it."

Out of the corner of my eye I caught Gilley giving me a small thumbs-up, which irritated me no end because I actually *can* be nice when I want to. I just have to want to.

Still I worked to pump up the smile as Meg sorted through the many bags by my feet. "First up," she said, her voice still filled with enthusiasm, "is this little bundle right here."

I watched Meg reach into a large brown duffel and pull out something small, black, and furry. "Ohmigod!" I squealed as she held up a wriggling puppy triumphantly. "You found him!"

Meg grinned from ear to ear. "Yep," she said. "And he's a little rascal, let me tell you."

Eagerly I wrapped my arms around the squirming little guy, who was snorting and licking his nose and mine just like pugs do. "He's adorable!"

"And he's for rent," she said.

"Rent?" Gilley asked. "What do you mean, he's for rent?"

"I found him at this small shelter called A Paws Sanctuary. Sarah Summers is the owner, and to help offset the cost of caring for the local strays, she rents out some of the animals to anyone interested in a little puppy or kitty lovin' for the day."

"Hold on," I said as I tugged my sleeve out of the pug's mouth, which he must have found delightfully chewy. "You mean to tell me that this woman is *renting* animals to people?"

"It's a great idea when you think about it," Meg explained. "Sarah says that by renting out the animals for a few hours a day, she can keep a steady flow of donations coming into the shelter as well as offer the chance for a real connection to form between man and a dog or cat. It helps convince those folks who might be on the fence about bringing a pet into their lives whether or not they're making a good decision. More often than not, they rent Fido or Fluffy for the day, then come back and claim they're in love and want to adopt. It's win-win for everyone involved."

I frowned. "Unless you're this pug and the guy who's rented you is some sadist who gets his jollies by tugging you down a haunted street."

Meg's eyes dropped. "Yeah, I mentioned that to Sarah. She knows it's wrong, but Fergus rents several of her pets a week and he's her biggest contributor. She says that she never rents the same strays to him twice, and that the pets may come back frightened, but not permanently traumatized. She believes that it's for the greater good of all that a few have to endure the experience."

I felt my temper flare, worked hard to rein it in . . . and failed. "Sarah's an idiot!" I snapped. "And anyone who believes that these dogs and cats aren't being treated with undue cruelty needs to have their head examined."

"M. J.," Gil murmured, adding a look that said, "Chill, please."

I sighed. "Sorry, Meg. I know you're just repeating what Sarah told you, but Heath and I can fully attest to the fact that the experience on Briar Road was something you don't soon put out of your mind, even if you're only a dog."

"Oh, I get it," Meg agreed. "But, M. J., you didn't see this shelter. I think Sarah puts every spare penny she has into it, and she really is trying to do her best by these animals. It's a tough situation for her to be in. I mean, Fergus contributes about fifty pounds a week to her cause."

Heath and I exchanged a look. "You thinking what I'm thinking?" he asked me.

I smiled. "Down the middle?" I asked. Heath nodded. "And let's increase it by twenty-five."

Again, Heath nodded. "Meg," he said. "When you take this little guy back, can you tell Sarah that M. J. and I will be more than happy to take over Fergus's generous weekly contributions, and increase the donation by twenty-five pounds to a total of seventy-five pounds a week."

Meg's eyes lit up. "That's going to make her day!" she said.

Heath held up his finger. "But there's a catch. We'll only give her the allowance if she stops renting her shelter animals to Fergus."

Meg shrugged her shoulders like that wasn't an un-reasonable request at all. "Everyone comes out ahead," she said. "I can't see her turning that down."

I stroked the pug's head and asked, "When do you have to take him back?"

"I rented him for twenty-four hours, so not until noon tomorrow."

I picked up the pug under his shoulders and he dangled there limply in my hands with the most ador-able buggy brown-eyed expression before licking my nose. I then looked meaningfully at Gilley.

"Uh-oh," Gil said with a shake of his head.

"What?" Meg asked.

Gil pointed to me. "I know that look. You want to keep him."

I swiveled the pug around so that he could face the group gathered round the fire. "Of course I want to keep him!" I exclaimed. "I mean, wook at da widdle guy!" I then turned the pug back to me and cradled him in my arms. He farted noisily and Meg, Heath, and I laughed.

Gilley rolled his eyes. "Here we go."

But I knew that any logical argument he was about to lob at me was already moot. "I'm going to call him Wendell," I said. "And I'm totally keeping him."

Gil made a *tsk*ing noise. "What about Doc?" he asked.

"Oh, he'll be fine," I reasoned. "I mean, it's not like I'm bringing home another bird."

"Getting that guy through customs isn't going to be easy," Heath cautioned.

"Oh, I think it works," said a voice from the hall. We all looked up to see Gopher coming into the room with his hands positioned in a square, like he was look-ing through a camera lens. "I mean, we could use a mascot, and Wendell would definitely pull in some viewers. Plus, we could tie it in to the earlier footage we shot with him and Fergus on Briar Road. You know, *Ghoul Getters* steps in to save a helpless puppy. I smell an Emmy for Best New Cable Show, people!"

I made an "I told you so" face at Gilley, who gave me another eye roll.

Meg turned back to the pile of packages. "Well, I also bought you some warmer clothes and long underwear, M. J., along with a down coat for the night shoots, but I'll need to go back out if you're keeping Wendell and pick up some supplies like a dog bed, a crate, and some food."

"That'd be fabulous," I told her. "Thanks, Meg."

She smiled broadly at me, and I felt bad for treating her so poorly earlier. "No problem," she said. "I'll just take these up to your room and be on my way."

I watched her gather up several of the bags when I heard Gilley clear his throat and give me a pointed look, then motion to Meg struggling with the bags. "Um," I said quickly, "why don't you leave those, Meg. Gil and I can take them upstairs."

Meg looked unsure, but Gilley came over to her and gently took most of the load out of her hands. "Leave it to us," he assured her.

Gil helped me with the packages up to my room, complaining the whole way that he'd turned into a pack mule. I did my best to ignore him while I walked Wendell down the hallway on the short leash he'd come with. "Renting a dog is actually a genius idea," I said when we got to my door and I worked to unlock it. "I mean, for people who can't have a dog in their apartments but still want some puppy love, it makes perfect sense."

"Except when they act impulsively and adopt the thing on the spot."

I gave him a withering look as I walked into my room and set some of the bags on the bed. "Subtle, Gil. Subtle."

"You coming out to eat with us?" he asked after he'd brought the others in.

I yawned and stretched. "Naw," I said tiredly. "I think I'll try and take a nap here with Wendell."

"Okay," he agreed. "I'll do a little more digging on these caverns and try to find us a good spot tonight for the shoot."

"Keep it well away from Briar Road," I cautioned.

Gilley winked. "Will do," he promised.

After he'd gone, I gave Wendell a little of the food Meg had stowed in the duffel, then took him back outside, where he watered and fertilized the lawn. Then we came back in and I ended the afternoon with him curled in my arms, snoring softly.

The gentle gurgling rhythm put me to sleep within minutes.

I slept soundly for a while, but soon my slumber was disturbed by the most unsettling dream. I was cold, chilled to the bone in fact, and I was in a very dark, damp place. Somewhere nearby the wind moaned in a disturbing way, and I swore there were voices riding the currents of air that added to the eeriness of the place in which I'd landed in my dream.

I shivered, and felt an awful presence. A phrase floated through my mind, *Something wicked this way comes. . . .*

My head swiveled right and left, searching out the source of the malevolence, but for the longest time the only way the sinister presence made itself known was by the heavy weight in the atmosphere. I had the urge to move—in fact, I had the urge to run—but my feet felt leaden and stuck to the floor. With tremendous effort I pulled myself forward one step at a time, but it was difficult.

I also struggled to keep my eyes open. My lids felt heavy and it was difficult to see. I knew I needed to get out of this place, but I didn't quite know how I would manage it.

And then, from somewhere behind me, I heard the sound of wicked laughter. Something, it seemed, found my efforts to escape delightfully funny. "Who's there?" I called out.

The laughter increased. It became shrill and set goose bumps all along my arms. I felt the hair stand up on the back of my neck, and the chill in the air intensified. "What do you want?" I demanded, my breath quickening as the adrenaline continued to course through me.

Something moved in the shadows just off to my right. There was a rustling of clothing almost like the swish of skirts before the laughter surrounded me, as if it were coming from all sides. "Come for a visit, lass?" said someone with a thick brogue.

I fought to keep my eyes open, but my eyelids seemed to have a mind of their own. I felt almost as though I'd been drugged. Every movement was an effort and all I wanted to do was sink to the ground and give in. There was also an intense buzzing sound happening all about my head, like I was wearing a bonnet made of bees.

In the back of my mind I realized that this dream had all the characteristics of an out-of-body experience.

My astral body was reacting lethargically because it was caught between worlds—half in the physical plane, half in the astral one. "Clarity *now!*" I shouted, and immediately the buzzing stopped and I felt the lethargy leave my limbs.

This was good in a way, but bad in another because it also brought my environment into full focus . . . and let me state for the record—it wasn't pretty.

The cold dampness that I'd felt made sense because I saw immediately that I was, in fact, in some kind of cave. The flickering shadows that I'd caught out the corner of my eye appeared to be cast from a torch set into the wall, the flames making swooshing sounds as they were battered by the cold wind swirling about the chamber I was in.

And then, right in front of me, dangling in the air, as if suspended by invisible wires, was a wicker broom that looked like something right out of *Harry Potter*, but way scarier.

It was jet-black, with a knobby handle, and thick branches made up the head, and these ended in jagged angles. I doubted that there was a floor in the world that this broom could clean. To make it even more menacing, it hovered in the air without moving for a moment right before it began to twirl in a tight circle. It moved slowly at first, then faster, and faster, until it became a swirling blur.

I watched it, growing increasingly dizzy under the sort of hypnotic spell it was creating, when, without warning, it spun away from its location and came straight at me.

I had no time to duck; in fact, I barely managed to close my eyes before it swatted me full in the face. I felt the sharp twigs that made up the bottom of the broom scratch my cheek and forehead, and the force of the blow from the broom sent me sprawling to the ground. I landed hard on my right knee and elbow, and I know I either grunted or shouted out in pain because someone nearby shouted, "Stop this!" and everything changed.

I rolled over and sat with my back against the wall, able to open only one eye while my other eye throbbed and leaked tears. "Who's there?!" I demanded, terrified out of my mind by the ferocity of the assault.

To my surprise, as I forced my good eye open, I realized I was no longer in the cave but now leaning against a huge oak tree in the middle of a beautiful field of wildflowers.

Gone was the damp air and its chilly temperature. It had been replaced by a soft breeze that brought the sweet fragrance of fresh-cut grass and springtime flowers to my nose. "Where am I?" I mumbled, and put my hand to my mouth. "Oh, great," I muttered. "My lip is bleeding."

"You're lucky that's the only thing bleeding," said a gentle male voice that startled me.

I realized there was an old man with a long mane of silver hair wearing a white linen tunic and matching pants standing right in front of me. "Holy freakballs!" I exclaimed. "Where did you come from?"

The old guy laughed. "Me?" he said casually. "I've been here all along. The question is, M. J., where did *you* come from?"

I looked around. "You might be right." I tried to stand up, but my knee hurt something fierce and my elbow was throbbing. Still, it seemed rude to sit while the older man stood.

"Stay where you are," he said gently when he saw

me trying to get to my feet. "I'll sit and we'll have a talk."

A blanket with a beautiful Southwestern pattern appeared underneath me, and the old man sat down next to me, also leaning against the trunk of the tree. "That was cool," I told him, referring to the blanket.

"I have a few tricks up my sleeve," he said with a wink.

"So . . . not to be rude," I began, "but *who* are you, anyway?"

That won me a chuckle. The old guy reached out his hand and said formally, "I am Samuel White-feather."

I took his hand and eyed him curiously. "Any relation to a friend of mine named Heath Whitefeather?"

Samuel nodded. "My grandson."

I could see the small resemblance in the nose and maybe around the eyes. "Heath's a great guy," I told him truthfully.

"Yes, he is," he said proudly. "I was glad to see him partner up with such a talented spirit talker as yourself. Although, why you two want to go meddling around in foreign lands dealing with evil like that . . . well, I just don't understand."

I wiped my sore eye gingerly and managed to open it a fraction. "'Evil like that'?" I asked. "You mean the bully that just whacked me with the broom?"

"Exactly like that," Samuel said gravely. "She's a wicked one, M. J. You and Heath are going to have to watch each other's backs."

I rolled up my pant leg to inspect my knee. There was a long gash in it and the beginnings of a pretty good bruise. I blew on it and said, "Want to let me know who we're dealing with?"

"The Witch of Queen's Close," Samuel told me. "In life she went by the name Rigella. That's important," he added. "Remember that names have power."

"'Kay," I said, not really knowing where all this was leading.

Samuel regarded me critically for a long moment, and I felt like I was somehow coming up short. "You'll need help," he said. "From the Spirit World."

"Don't tell me you're volunteering," I said, only half-joking.

"I don't know that I have much of a choice. Rigella's way out of your league, kiddo. And she's up to something."

"What's she up to?"

"Something bad. Vengeance."

"Vengeance? For what and against whom?"

But Samuel only looked up at the sun, which was quickly sinking on the horizon, before he reached into the folds of his white tunic and pulled out a small charm with a green crystal. He leaned forward and secured this around my neck before he said, "Do your homework. You'll find out soon enough. In the meantime, you'll want to get some peroxide on that knee."

I shook my head. Samuel wasn't making much sense. "Some perox—" and that was as far as I got. There was some sort of a snapping noise, and all of a sudden I felt a strong tug backward. The next thing I knew I was sitting up in bed, Wendell stirring near my lap right before a pounding sounded on my door.

# Chapter 3

The person making all the racket was Gilley. He and Heath had come to my room to fetch me for dinner. But the moment I opened my door, they both took a step back and sucked in a breath. "What the hell happened to you?!" Gil demanded.

I blinked hard at him, and when I did, I felt a soreness around my eye. "I was sleeping."

Gil reached out and put a finger under my chin, inspecting my face. "Okay, Mr. Tyson, while you were sleeping, did you go a few rounds with the lamp or the bedpost?"

My own hand flew to my face. I could feel the heat coming off my left cheek and my eye was definitely puffy. I turned and walked back into the room, and as I did so, I could feel my knee throb—something I hadn't noticed when I'd bolted out of bed to get the door. "This can't be real," I said, moving quickly to the mirror. But the evidence was right there in my own reflection. My cheek was red and swollen, as was my eye, and there was a small cut on my puffy lip.

Gingerly I pulled up my pant leg to reveal my knee, which was bruised and marred by a small gash.

"M. J.?" Heath said, coming around to stand right next to me. "What happened?"

I sat down in a nearby chair and Wendell whimpered from the bed. Gil moved over to pick him up and sit him in his lap. "Tell us," he said gently.

I shook my head. I had no idea how to explain it, and the fact that I'd encountered something on the astral plane that had injured my physical body was really blowing my mind. I glanced up at Heath and decided to start from the beginning. "You know about astraling, right? Having out-of-body experiences?"

Heath nodded. "I have OBEs all the time," he said.

"Have you ever been hurt or injured on the astral plane?" I asked. "I mean, have you ever encountered anything evil that maybe took a swipe at you?"

Heath cocked his head to the side curiously. "No," he said. "The worst thing that ever happened to me was that I got stuck half in my body, half out, and I got so sick that when I finally managed to get myself back into my physical body, I threw up."

I nodded. I'd had a few similar experiences myself. "M. J.," Gil said from the bed. "Are you telling us that you just had an OBE and something on the astral plane *hurt* you?"

I looked meaningfully at him. "That's exactly what I'm saying," I said. And then I went on to explain that the Witch of Queen's Close had given me a wallop with her broom.

"But how could that hurt your *physical* body?" Gilley said. "Don't OBEs happen in a completely different dimension? I mean, that's why they're called *out of body*, right?"

Heath and I exchanged a look. I knew he understood. "It's not totally unheard of," he said. "There are recorded instances of people being injured on the astral plane and when they come back here, they've got the physical evidence to prove it. But the power needed to cause you real injury would be tremendous."

"It would be," I agreed. "And it was." I then chronicled my experience by telling them about my encounter with Heath's grandfather.

When I began describing him, Heath exclaimed, "That's totally him!" I smiled and continued my story, telling Gilley and Heath everything Samuel had said.

"Whoa," Gil said when I was done. "That is too cool."

"So Gramps is gonna help us?"

I nodded. "He said we'd need some backup. I guess this Rigella woman is really bad news."

"What do you think he meant by, 'She's out for vengeance'?" Gilley wondered.

I shrugged. "I've no idea. But my guess is that it's nothing good. Gil, can you do some digging into this witch and see what you can come up with?"

"I'm on it," he said. "But first, let's see about getting you cleaned up, okay?"

"Gil's right," Heath said, eyeing my shin. "That cut's going to need some peroxide." I looked at him in surprise and laughed. "What's so funny?"

"Your grandfather said the exact same thing."

Heath grinned. "He was big on peroxide. Used to keep a big jug of it under the bathroom sink, which was smart because I was always getting banged up on the reservation."

As Heath turned to the door, I called him back for a moment, "We're also going to need to check into some charms."

"Charms?" said Gil. "What kind of charms?"

"I won't know until I see it, but Heath's grand-father gave me one when we sat together. It had a specific design and the moment he placed it around my neck, I felt safer. I think it was a message. We'll need to arm ourselves before we risk going into those caverns."

Heath and Gilley exchanged an uncomfortable look. "It's six thirty, M. J.," Gil said. "All the local shops are pretty much closed."

"Okay," I said. "Then we'll hit them first thing in the morning."

"Gopher wanted us to start filming tonight," Gil reminded me.

I took that in for a minute. "Crap."

"We can see if he'd be willing to postpone it," Heath suggested.

I looked to Gilley, who seemed doubtful. "We're on a really tight schedule," he said. "But maybe we could stall a little by insisting we do a baseline of the cav-erns first?"

"That's a good idea," I told him, getting up to rummage around in my suitcase. I kept a bottle of prescription-strength ibuprofen handy in case I had a bad case of cramps, and my head was starting to hurt enough to warrant popping one now. After downing one of the pills with a little water, I said, "We should also load up on the magnetic spikes while we set up the still cameras and meters. If we're armed, nothing should bother us tonight."

"Great," Gil said, getting up off the bed and hand-ing me Wendell. "You sit tight. I'll go clear it with Go-pher, and Heath can see about getting you some first aid."

\*    \*    \*

Several hours later, Gil, Heath, and I and the rest of the crew were standing at the entrance to one of the creepiest-looking caverns I've ever seen. And it was even more unsettling because it so closely resembled the one from my OBE.

We were standing in the cavern that ran directly under Briar Road, and at least there was one good thing about it—Heath and I weren't feeling the distress of all those burned souls from above. Still, the place didn't feel pleasant. It felt oppressive.

We'd had to descend two separate sets of stairs to reach this underground web of tunnels, caverns, and corridors, and even though I had meditated for an hour beforehand, coating my aura with a form of reflective and protective energy, I still felt the goose bumps rise along my arms. Next to me, I heard Gilley audibly gulp. "Ick," he said. "This place is ick."

I completely agreed. "It makes the haunted houses on our side of the pond seem like an amusement park, huh?"

"It's just so intense!" Heath said. "I mean, it's like radiating something bad from every crevice."

I was fully conscious of the fact that there was a camera recording our reactions, and I wondered what the viewing audience would think about these not-so-brave ghostbusters standing frozen in fear at the entrance to a simple underground tunnel. "Okay, boys and girls," I said, trying hard to keep the quiver out of my voice. "Let's get this party started."

Heath and I stepped forward alone, and when we'd gone a few paces, we both realized that no one was following. I turned to look over my shoulder and I saw every member of the crew holding fast to his position. "Gil?" I called.

Gil's eyes were wide with fear. "I don't wanna go in there," he admitted.

"You've got your sweatshirt on," I reassured, referring to his specially made sweatshirt with glued-on magnets from the cuffs to the collar. "Nothing can come near you while you're wearing that."

Gil's eyes continued to stare wildly at me. "Uh-uh," he said, shaking his head no. "I think I'll head back to the van and set up the equipment from there. I'll record and monitor your progress where it's safe."

I felt a smile pull at the corners of my lips. Gilley was scared to death of things that went bump in the night—and for good reason. He'd seen a lot of crazy spooky stuff over the years, and he'd never grown comfortable with chasing after the ghoulies. He preferred the safety and comfort of a ghost-free zone—like our van back home or the one we'd rented here. "Okay, Gil," I conceded. "But the rest of you are coming with us, right?"

I directed my comment specifically at Gopher, who also appeared rooted to the spot. Jake and Russ looked at Gopher as if waiting for him to order them forward, and after a minute's silent contemplation, he did. "Um, yeah," he said. "Yes. Let's go, guys."

Reluctantly, our sound and camera crew followed their producer and together the five of us entered the close.

I kept my sixth sense wide-open, with one hand on a canister that held a magnetized metal stake. We call these grenades, because their effect on grounded spirits is rather explosive.

When a powerful magnet is introduced into the electromagnetic field of a ghost's energy, it can severely alter that energy and make it impossible for the spook to stick around. The magnetic spikes act like a blaring fire alarm amped up one hundred decibels, and they make it exceptionally uncomfortable for any grounded spirit to continue to occupy the area. The minute the canister is opened, the electromagnetic frequency changes and the ghosts typically flee.

My grenades have been tested against even the most powerful of malevolent spirits—and so far, they've worked every time.

For the first part of this ghost hunt—what we called setting a baseline— we were intent only on laying out our equipment in certain hot spots—or those areas where Heath and I were sensing a lot of activity. We intended to place our meters and thermal gauges and night-vision cameras in those locations where he and I felt they might capture poltergeist activity when we weren't around. And as we edged into the tunnel, I knew almost immediately that we could pretty much plop our equipment anywhere, and something somewhere was likely to capture and record the activity.

"Can you feel that?" Heath asked me. "It's like it's just radiating out of the walls!"

"I can," I told him with a slight shiver.

"What are you two picking up?" Gopher asked, and he made a not-so-subtle gesture toward the camera.

"Lots and *lots* of people died here," I said to him. "Right now, it feels like Heath and I are wading through a sea of grounded spirits. It's incredibly intense."

"As bad as up top?" he asked, eyeing us nervously. I knew Gopher was counting on us being able to explore the close, so I was quick to reassure him.

"No," I told him. "I mean, there are a lot of grounded

spirits here, but it doesn't have the same intensity. It's not nearly as terrifying."

"In other words, it's bearable," Heath said.

At that moment and from just behind us we heard a loud series of knocks, like someone rapping their knuckles against the rock. "What was that?" Gopher whispered uneasily.

"Hello?" I called out. "Is there anyone who wishes to communicate with us?" There was no reply. "If you would like to talk with us, please knock on the walls to make yourselves heard."

For a moment, nothing happened, and then all around us came hundreds and hundreds of knocks. The sound was loud, and powerful and intense and freaking scary. *"Ahhhhhhh!"* screamed Russ.

*"Shiiiiiiiiiiiit!"* screamed Jake.

*"Holy Christ!"* screamed Gopher.

And as if all three of them had the exact same thought at the exact same time, they collectively shouted, *"Run!"* and bolted, leaving Heath and me standing in the middle of the cavern all alone.

"Stop!" I yelled at their departing forms.

In hindsight what happened next was pretty amusing; our brave crew didn't stop, but the knocking did. "Good job," Heath said with a playful smile. "Way to scare away the crew, M. J."

The situation was so ridiculous that I began to laugh. Heath snickered, then chuckled, then began laughing in earnest too, and before long we were leaning against the walls for support as tears leaked down our cheeks and we took turns pantomiming the terrified crew who'd just abandoned us.

When we'd collected ourselves again, I heard Gilley's

concerned voice sound loudly into my ear. "M. J.?! Are you there? Over."

I giggled and clicked my headpiece's microphone on. "Hey, Gil," I said. "I'm here. Over."

"You guys okay?"

"Fine," I assured him. "And I take it the crew has made its way back to you?"

"Yes," he said. "And they're totally shaken up. What happened?"

"M. J.'s been working the crowd," Heath said with a laugh.

"What?"

"Nothing," I told Gilley. "I'll explain it to you later. Listen, in my duffel is there a camera?"

"Yes," he told me. "You and Heath both have four night-vision cameras in each of your bags."

I set down my duffel and fished around inside, quickly locating the cameras. "Fabulous," I said. "I've got them." I motioned to Heath and he also set his duffel down to retrieve a camera. "Tell Gopher that we'll record things from here. I doubt the crew will want to come back into the close tonight, right?"

It was Gilley's turn to laugh. "Russ and Jake have already quit," he told me. "Gopher's trying to talk them out of it as we speak."

"Figures," I said. "Okay, well, we'll get to work. You monitor from your end and make sure you're getting readings from all our equipment."

"Roger that."

I swung my duffel bag back onto my shoulder and motioned Heath forward. "Keep your senses alert," I cautioned. "If this gets too intense, we'll set off a grenade and push back the energy."

"It already feels intense," Heath said quietly.

I knew exactly what he meant. I felt bombarded by energy coming at me from all sides. It was a bit like entering an unseen crowd that was pulling on your clothing or whispering in your ear. At one point I even batted the air next to my head when I felt a cold breath blow the hair around my neck.

It was hard to get focused and think clearly. Hell, it was even hard to move. To distract myself, I reached back into the duffel and pulled out an electrostatic meter. I turned it on and immediately it began to register activity. "We're in a hot zone," I said.

"You don't need a gadget to tell you that," Heath said.

I smiled ruefully. "Well, it helps to see it on the meter sometimes." I put the gadget on the floor of the long cavern near the wall. "Gil?" I asked. "Are you picking up the readings?"

There was a whistle in my ear. "Man," Gil said. "Where *are* you guys?"

"In hell," Heath answered, and I had a feeling he wasn't really kidding.

"Readings are off the charts," said Gilley. "Your meter's already in the red. M. J., you might want to secure a camera to the wall where you're standing. It seems like it's a good spot to pick up some activity."

"Copy that," I said.

With some help from Heath I was able to secure one of the small cameras to the wall, and then I stood in front of it and backed slowly away so that Gilley could tell us if he had a good picture on his monitors. "A little to the left," he told Heath, who was in charge of adjusting the lens.

After a few tweaks Gilley was satisfied and we continued to move deeper into the corridor. "How's your breathing?" I asked Heath at one point, only because I felt the air all around us had gone from damp and chilly to hot and stifling.

"I'm having a hard time catching my breath," he admitted. "Also, I think I'm running a fever."

I placed a hand on his forehead and he did in fact feel warm. "Oh, man," I said.

"What's the matter?" Gil asked.

"Heath's sick."

"Does he need to come out?"

Heath shook his head. "I'm okay," he assured us. "Just a little queasy, but I can push through. Come on, let's get this baseline done already."

We continued for about another forty-five minutes and my concern for Heath's condition mounted. He looked pale and shaky, and he'd broken out into a cold sweat. He also appeared to be having difficulty swallowing and I swore the lymph glands around his neck looked thick and swollen.

"That's it," I finally said to him as we encountered another hot spot and I got out the seventh camera. "This is the last camera we're putting up. I'm calling it a night."

Heath didn't argue with me; instead he just blinked drowsily. "Okay," he agreed as if saying the word took effort.

As we were struggling to fasten the last camera in place, I heard Gilley's voice burst into my ear, "What the freak is *that*?!"

Gopher's voice joined Gilley's in the background. "Holy shit! Did you *see* that?!"

"What's going on?" I demanded.

Heath winced and pulled his headset off. "They're too loud," he whispered.

"M. J.!" Gil shouted. "Ohmigod! You're not going to believe what we just captured on film!"

At that moment I was struggling with the camera, which wouldn't stay still against the slippery rock. "I'm a little busy, Gil. Can you tell me later?"

"No," he said. "I can't."

I sighed and stepped away from the rock with the camera still in hand. "Fine, what's going on?"

"Something big and black just dashed across camera one," Gil said excitedly.

"Human?" I wondered.

"Definitely not," Gil said.

Gopher's voice took over—he'd obviously donned a headset. "M. J., it was like some sort of smoky shadow just flew by the camera."

"What'd it look like exactly?" I asked.

"It didn't really look like anything. It was sort of like a big blob of dark mist moving through the air really fast."

"And it's gone now?"

"It is," Gilley confirmed.

"Okay," I said, returning to trying to mount the camera. "Let me know if it comes back."

I'd just gotten those words out of my mouth when both Gilley and Gopher shouted, *"Whoa!"* in my ear.

I winced just like Heath had and dropped the camera. "Hey," I yelled. "Volume, guys!"

"M. J.!" Gilley squealed. "The shadow!"

"Is it back?"

"Yes and no," Gil said, his voice holding a tremor.

"What does that mean?"

"Yes, it's back, but it's not back in front of camera one. It's hovering right in front of camera two!"

The hair on the back of my neck prickled and a chill raced up my spine. "It's on the move?" I asked.

"Well, if by 'on the move' you mean it went from camera one to camera two, then yes, but right now it seems to be holding steady right in front of . . . oh . . . wait! There it goes again! Okay, it flew off and out of sight."

I eyed Heath, who was looking dully at me and holding his right arm out at an odd angle. "What's wrong with your arm?" I asked him, momentarily forgetting about the camera and the shadow.

"My armpit hurts," he said. "And I feel like crap."

I set the camera on my duffel and moved over to him. Taking him by the arm, I coaxed him over to a small boulder and sat him down. I felt his forehead again, which was even hotter than before. "Honey, we're gonna have to get you out of here and into bed."

Heath nodded and began to tug at his sweater and then his shirt. "My armpit *really* hurts," he said. I helped him raise his clothing and the moment he had it up to his chin, I sucked in a breath. "What is it?" he asked me without any hint of alarm. "Is it swollen or something?"

The area right under Heath's arm was indeed swollen and a huge black boil emerged that was so ghastly-looking that I took a full step back. "Gilley," I said into my microphone, forcing my voice to sound calm. "We have a situation down here. Heath's in really bad shape. I think we need to get him out and to a hospital. Immediately."

But at that moment both Gilley and Gopher erupted

in a fit of noise and shouts. For several seconds I couldn't understand what they were yelling about, but then I clearly heard Gil say, "It's at camera three! M. J.! It's moving in your direction!"

My heart began to race. Heath and I had laid six cameras along our route, which twisted and turned along the main corridor of the close. If the shadow that was making its way along the tunnel was in fact following our trail, it was only about three hundred yards behind us.

"What's it doing?" I demanded. The shadow was obviously a spook, but at this moment I didn't know how powerful a spook it was, and I had Heath to worry about.

"It's just hovering," Gilley whispered. "It's like it's looking right at us!"

"How big is it?"

"Full-body size."

"Is there any clarity to the shape?"

"You wouldn't believe me if I told you," Gil moaned.

"Try me."

"It looks like a woman riding a broom," Gopher said. "M. J., it looks like the ghost of a witch!"

I closed my eyes and held my breath. That was the last thing I wanted to hear. "Rigella," I whispered.

Gilley said nothing, but I knew him well enough to know he was thinking the same thing. After taking a quick moment to gather my courage, I opened my eyes again and squatted down to rummage through my duffel. "Gil, tell me the moment she moves away from camera three," I said urgently.

"Roger," Gil said.

After digging through my bag, I located the map of the close we'd each been given, and inspected it. I had my grenade and fully intended to use it, but I couldn't be sure it would buy us enough time to get out of the close. There was *so* much paranormal activity within the cavern we were in that I had a feeling the great bulk of it would reduce the impact of the grenade. Rigella was toying with us, and I also had Heath to worry about. I couldn't risk an encounter with her when he was in no shape to help me.

"What's happening?" Heath asked me.

"Trouble's coming," I told him honestly while my finger traced the path we'd come on the map. "And we need an exit, pronto."

"What's coming?" he asked, and I glanced up to see him looking back down the cavern.

As if in answer, Gilley shouted, "She's on the move again!"

I stood up and swung the strap of the duffel over my head before reaching under Heath's good arm and gently lifting him to his feet. "Come on, guy," I said urgently. "We gotta go!"

Heath's ragged breathing felt hot against my neck and he stumbled several times as I guided him forward. "What'd you see under my arm?" he asked.

"A lump," I told him, leaving out the gory details. I remembered my European History class from college well enough to recall that black boils that formed in the armpit and high-grade fever were two of the telltale symptoms of the bubonic plague that had run rampant all over Europe in the Middle Ages. I was pretty sure the disease had been eradicated in modern times, but what I'd seen under Heath's arm and the heat coming off him were quite alarming.

"Lump? What kind of lump?" he persisted.

I didn't answer him; instead I fought to push us

both forward while keeping one eye on the map so we didn't get lost.

"It's at camera four!" Gil shouted.

"Keep me posted, Gilley!" I commanded.

"Where are you?"

"Heading toward the southeast exit."

"How far away are you from there?"

I glanced down at the map, noting a fork in the cavern that we'd just passed. "I'd say about five hundred yards."

"Oh, my God!" Gopher shouted, and I had a feeling that things were about to go from really bad to extra awful. "M. J., the shadow's got company!"

"What kind of company?"

"Two additional shadows have joined Rigella's ghost, and they all have the silhouette of witches on brooms!"

"And they're moving!" Gil yelled urgently. "I think they're heading to camera five!"

Heath moaned next to me, as if he was in pain, but there was no way I was stopping. Instead I took hold of the map with my teeth and reached over to remove his grenade from the belt he was wearing. "Hold this," I said through gritted teeth as I placed the canister in the hand draped across my shoulder. Heath gripped the canister and I tugged up on the cap; freeing the lid, I tossed it to the ground.

"Three shadows at camera five!" Gopher shouted. "And they're not stopping! M. J., I think they're picking up speed!"

I adjusted my hold on Heath's middle and gripped his arm tightly while ordering, "Hold on to that canister, and don't let it go until I tell you to!" Heath mumbled something unintelligible, but he held fast to the canister.

We made it another two hundred yards when I heard Gilley say, "M. J., Gopher's on his way to meet you at the exit and something just whizzed by camera six!"

I was panting heavily as I struggled to bear Heath's sagging weight and move us along as fast as possible. I'd left the seventh camera on the floor of the cavern after not being able to mount it, and that camera was a mere two hundred yards away from camera six. And *that* meant that Rigella and her crew were only about four hundred yards behind us, and closing in fast.

"Gil!" I said, gasping for breath.

"Yeah?"

"Are you getting a reading from the meter on my belt?"

"Yes."

"Tell me when it spikes," I said.

"It's spiking now."

"Tell me when it *really* spikes!"

Gilley made a small squeaky sound. "Jesus, M. J., hurry, okay?"

I wanted to tell him I was doing my level best, but I was too focused on moving forward. Heath continued to stumble and lean heavily on me. "Almost there," I told him, spying the exit just fifty yards away.

"You're spiking!" Gilley shouted.

"Is it in the red zone?"

"The needle's at the top of the graph, honey! *Get out of there!*"

"Heath!" I shouted as he tripped over something that crunched under his feet and nearly pulled us down. I groaned, stumbling over what looked like a small radio that we'd just crushed under our feet, but with Gilley yelling in my ear to run for it, I didn't give it a second thought. Instead I shouted to Heath, "Drop the spike out of the canister!"

I heard a loud *ping* on the ground next to us and with great relief I noticed that all that awful energy that seemed to constantly be pounding against us vanished.

We moved forward several steps with ease, and even Heath's footing felt more secure. In the back of my mind I was grateful that the somewhat constant noise level that had been assaulting us from grounded spirits everywhere was gone and we moved nearly twenty-five yards without incident. And then, just as the door to the exit opened and Gopher appeared in the doorway, something with tremendous force crashed right into us and sent Heath and me sprawling to the ground.

# Chapter 4

I landed hard and smacked my bad shin on the ground. Heath tumbled just to my left, rolling over twice before coming to rest on the opposite side of the cavern. Near the exit I heard Gopher scream bloody murder, and then the slam of a door told me he'd run off for the second time that night.

I'd lost my headset, but somewhere nearby I heard Gilley's distant voice shout, "M. J.?! Come in! Come in! *For the love of God, what's happening?!*"

With a groan I tried to get to my feet, but the moment I rose, I felt a tremendous kick to my abdomen that literally lifted me off the ground and knocked the wind right out of me.

For several panicky moments I couldn't even breathe, and I crawled forward on hands and knees, trying to coax my diaphragm back to its normal rhythm. "Get away!" Heath moaned. "Get away!"

The most sick and twisted cackle I'd ever heard sounded loudly about the cavern. "Sacrifice!" I heard someone say.

I took a ragged breath and closed my eyes, willing myself not to pass out. My fingers fumbled at the canister tucked into my own belt while I struggled to take just one breath.

Something sharp raked across my back and I winced in pain, but still I worked at getting the canister free. "Stop!" Heath begged. "Stop them!"

With tremendous effort I finally managed to take a small breath, but it wasn't enough air to revive me, and when I opened my eyes again, all I could see was stars and darkness closing in. With the last bit of strength I had, I tugged the canister free, and pushed the lid up with my thumb. A second sharp pain raked across my back, followed by another cackling laugh in my ear.

The cap on the canister wouldn't budge, and I knew I wasn't going to have time to get it free before I passed out. "Breathe," whispered a calm, soothing voice. "Just breathe, M. J."

Immediately I was able to suck in a full lungful of air and the stars and black edges vanished from my vision. "Good job," said the voice. "Now twist the cap." I gripped the top of the canister with renewed strength and tugged. There was a popping noise and the metal lid came off. With painful slowness I tipped the canister and slid the spike out. As it emerged, I heard a shriek, a curse, and the swish of skirts, and then everything went quiet.

I sat still for the longest time, clutching the metal spike and focusing on getting oxygen into my lungs. I heard movement behind me and turned my head to see Heath, inching his way over to me. "You okay?" I asked.

He nodded. "Think so." He then patted himself tentatively to check for broken bones or other injuries. "Yeah, I'm good."

I crawled forward and felt his forehead. His body temp had gone back to normal. "That's weird," I said.

"Fever's gone," Heath told me. "I felt almost immediately better the moment you dropped the spike back there. It's as if I never felt sick at all."

In the next instant the door to the exit burst open and Gilley came dashing through, bearing about ten magnetic spikes and with crazy wide eyes. "I'm here!" he announced. "I'm here!"

He looked so comically serious that I couldn't help it—I started to giggle.

Heath also began to laugh and pretty soon the both of us were slapping each other and whooping it up. Gilley frowned. "All right, chuckleheads," he said as he bent down to reach under my arms and pick me up. "Let's get you both out of here."

Once I was standing and trying to collect myself, I reached a hand down to help Heath up, but his laughter abruptly stopped and instead of taking my hand, he made an odd noise and pointed behind us.

"What?" I asked him. But he just continued to point. Beside me I heard Gilley let out a little squeal and I slowly turned my head.

About twenty feet away was the clear outline of a prone man lying on the floor of the cavern. "Why do I think that's going to be *really* bad?" I whispered.

Heath stood up. "Hello?" he called to the person on the ground.

There was no response. Gilley shifted the metal spikes in one hand to under his arm and reached out for my hand. "Let's just go," he said softly.

Heath and I exchanged a look. "We can't just leave him here," Heath said. "I think he's hurt."

I squinted in the dim light of the close. My eyesight

wasn't as sharp as Heath's, because I couldn't tell if he was hurt or just sleeping. "Maybe one of us should go check on him?" I asked.

"Rock, paper, scissors," Heath called.

"You two cannot be serious!" Gilley said, the quiver returning to his voice. "The guy's probably just a drunk who wandered down here to sleep it off. I don't think we should get too close."

"Gil," I said as I shook out a rock and Heath formed scissors. "Heath's right. We can't just leave the guy down here with the kind of poltergeist activity we saw just a few minutes ago."

Heath sighed heavily, realizing that he was going to be the one to investigate the prone figure. "Wish me luck," he said, but I grabbed his arm and pulled him back.

"You're positive you feel okay?" I asked him.

He smiled. "I'm fine," he assured me.

"All right then," I said. "Take these." I took a few of Gilley's spikes from under his arm and thrust them into Heath's hands. "Just in case."

Heath nodded, then edged away from us. Gilley moved closer to me, and again he took my hand. "I don't like this place one bit, M. J."

"You say that about every bust we do, Gil."

"Yeah?"

"Yeah."

"Well then, I don't like this one the most."

"'Nough said," I told him with a smile, then fell silent as Heath reached the figure and squatted down. We watched as he tapped the guy on the shoulder, and shook him a little when he got no response. The prone man rolled onto his back and Heath stood up immediately, then came running back toward us.

"Out!" he shouted. "Get out!"

Gilley and I didn't waste time asking why—we simply bolted for the exit. Once we were through the door, we took the stairs two at a time, winding our way up to the surface again.

At the top and back on the street, the three of us bent over and waited to catch our breath. "It's about time you guys came back!" I heard Gopher say. I glanced sideways to see him standing next to the van looking nervous. "I was getting really scared there."

I stood tall again and narrowed my eyes at him. "Yeah, we saw you get really scared there, Gopher. Twice."

Gopher blushed uncomfortably. "About that . . . ," he tried, but Heath cut him off.

"Forget about that, you guys! We've got bigger issues."

"What did you see?" Gilley asked.

"That guy down there?" Heath reminded us, motioning with his head toward the entrance to the close. "He was dead."

I sucked in a breath. "No!"

"Yes."

"You're sure?"

"Positive," he said grimly. "He was stone cold, totally blue, and his eyes were all buggy."

Gilley looked around at us and asked, "What do we do?"

"Call the police, I guess," I said.

Gopher already had his phone out. "Does nine-one-one work in Scotland?"

The local police arrived very shortly after Gopher figured out how to call them (and for the record, 911 does *not* work in Scotland . . .), and after Heath, Gilley, and I had all been individually questioned and the body was brought up in a black bag on a gurney, we had a chance to regroup by the van.

"Did they say what killed him?" Gopher wanted to know.

Gilley looked over his shoulder as a couple of men pushing a stretcher were making their way down the street to an ambulance. "They think it was a heart attack," he said. "I overheard one of the techs tell the policeman who was talking to me that there were no obvious signs of trauma. They also found some ID and paperwork on him. He's a maintenance worker for the village, and his shift ended hours ago. They think he was down in the close replacing a lightbulb and that he had a heart attack and died."

Heath looked unsettled. "What's up?" I asked.

He shook his head. "You didn't see his expression, M. J. He had the most terrified look on his face."

"Well, yeah," I said. "I mean, if he knew he was having a heart attack down in an underground tunnel with no one around to help him, he'd probably be scared witless." I remembered the small radio Heath and I had trampled and wondered if it had belonged to the maintenance worker. I imagined him dropping it and stumbling down the close in a panic as his chest filled with pain.

"Or," said Heath, "something else scared him to death."

Gilley made another little squeaking sound and put his hand up to his mouth. "You think maybe the witches weren't just chasing you guys?"

Something cool and wet hit the top of my head and I glanced skyward as another raindrop landed on my nose. "It's starting to rain," I said. "Let's ask them if we're clear to leave and find someplace to eat so we can talk about what happened tonight."

"Sounds good," Heath said, and he was about to turn away when I caught him.

"Hey, are you feeling okay?"

"I'm fine."

"Can I see under your arm?"

Gilley laughed. "Why do you want to see under his arm?"

"He had a lump there earlier," I said. "A big lump."

Heath moved his shoulder in a shrugging motion. "It's gone," he said. "And so is my fever."

"Still," I insisted, "mind if I take a quick peek?"

Heath raised his sweater and T-shirt for me, and sure enough, there was no sign of the large black boil I had seen down in the close. "Okay," I told him. "You can lower your shirt. You're right. You are fine."

Both Gilley and Gopher were looking at me funny, but two policemen were walking past us so I discreetly held up a finger and mouthed, "Wait."

Once the men had passed us, Gopher asked, "Want to explain what that was all about?"

I sighed and motioned for us to all get in the van. Once we were settled, I explained, "Down in the close Heath began to take on all the symptoms of the bubonic plague. He was running a fever, his complexion was pale, and he had this huge black boil form right under his left armpit."

"No way!" Gopher said.

Gilley stared at me in horror. I knew he was about to freak out, because my partner is a gigantic germaphobe, so I quickly laid a hand on his shoulder and added, "Gil, he doesn't have the plague."

"How do you know?" Gilley asked, his voice high and squeaky again.

"Because I know," I said firmly. "Really, he's fine."

Heath nodded his head vigorously. "Phantom symptoms," he agreed. "Really, Gil. It was just my body's way of reacting to all that residual energy of those grounded spirits who died from the plague."

Gilley still looked unsure, and I saw him reach into his pocket and pull out a small bottle of hand sanitizer. "Did M. J. have symptoms?" he asked.

That caught me by surprise; then I remembered the ibuprofen I'd taken earlier. I knew that certain pain meds actually worked to lower my antennae a little. I told Gil about taking the pain reliever and said, "It had to have been the meds, Gil. It lowered my sixth sense just enough where the energy of the plague only affected Heath."

Gilley didn't look convinced and continued to squirt hand sanitizer all over his hands, arms, neck, and face. Heath merely chuckled, Gopher started the van, and we pulled away from the scene.

We found an all-night café a bit later and once we'd been seated and placed our order, we got back to the discussion of Heath's phantom illness. "I think M. J.'s right," Heath said. "I think that there were so many grounded spirits down there who died of the plague that their symptoms manifested physically on me."

"Can that actually happen?" Gopher asked.

"It can," I told him. "For example, when I'm reading for a private client, the way many of their loved ones identify themselves to me is by causing a physical reaction."

"Huh?" Gopher said, his brow furrowed.

I smiled, thinking about how to best explain it.

"Say I'm doing a reading for you," I said, mentally turning on my sixth sense and hoping the ibuprofen didn't get too much in the way, "and I'm trying to pick up on your deceased relatives. The first clue they'll give me about who they are is a physical sensation associated with their crossing. For example, I know that connected to you there was an older man, right above you, who is making my heart beat a little harder. At this very moment, I feel a slight acceleration of my heart, and I'm pretty sure this man is indicating he had an issue with his heart. There is also a younger female connected to this male who is making me feel a little off-kilter—like a sickness of some kind, and I think it's related to something like cancer. I get the names Bill or William and Ellen or Helen."

Gopher's jaw dropped. "Whoa!" he whispered.

I smiled. "I want to say that the heart-issue guy was a father figure. . . ." I paused for a second as I felt out the female and was surprised when I realized that she must be Gopher's sister. "Your sister died of cancer?"

Gopher nodded, his eyes wide and unblinking. "My older sister had leukemia. She died when I was seventeen. Within six months the strain of her death caused my dad to have a heart attack and he died on the operating table when they were doing the bypass surgery."

I reached across the table and squeezed his hand. "I'm so sorry, Gopher. I had no idea."

"It was a tough year for the family."

"Your dad is very proud of you," I told him as the older man I'd brought through began to pat me gently on the back. "He also wants to know when you're going to get around to making that movie."

Gopher laughed, but there was moisture in his eyes. "He does, does he?" I nodded. Gopher saw that we were all waiting for him to explain what his father meant, so he elaborated. "I wrote this screenplay in college and I always wanted to try and get it made, but over the years the timing never felt right or I was busy with other projects."

"Give it two years," I told him, continuing to pass on the message from his dad, "and the project will be given the green light."

Gopher beamed like I'd just told him he'd soon win the Lotto. "Thanks, M. J."

"Sure," I said, closing the connection and turning us back to the previous discussion. "So, Heath took on the physical attributes of the bubonic plague down in the close. That means that we're dealing with some seriously intense energy, guys."

"Do you think that if Heath had stayed down there longer that the symptoms could have physically caused him to die?" Gil asked.

I glanced at Heath and he shook his head. "I think that it went as far as it was going to," he said. "At the very worst it would have just made me miserable for a while until my energy started to push back."

Our food arrived and we all took a minute to dive into our breakfast, which was greasy and flavorful, just the way I liked it. "So let's talk about these ghostly witches," Gopher said after everyone had eaten a little.

"Scariest thing I've ever seen," Heath admitted with a meaningful look at me. "I think they beat the serpent hands down."

Several weeks prior, Heath and I had encountered an awful, demonic serpentlike spirit that had attacked us pretty regularly over the course of several days until we'd managed to contain it. Its portal exit—a dagger—was now bound by two pounds of magnets, and locked in an iron safe back at my office.

I didn't know if Rigella and her crew were worse than that, but I knew I wasn't exactly thrilled with the idea of finding out.

"I never got a good look at them," I said. "What'd they look like?"

Gilley shuddered. "They were like nothing I've ever seen, M. J. They were shadow spooks, no clear definition of features or anything detailed, but they sort of left a trail of black smoke when they were in motion."

"Ectoplasm?" I asked.

Gil shrugged. "Maybe," he said. "But it was more than that—they sort of moved in this really menacing way. The lead spook was clearly on the hunt and knew exactly what we were up to. I kept getting the feeling like when she was in front of the camera, she was peering through it at *me*. I swear the temperature in the van dipped below normal."

Gopher nodded vigorously. "You're right, dude!" he said. "I felt it too."

I took another bite of food and thought about what they were telling us. "Considering how creepy these things were, I really have to hand it to you, Gil, for coming to our rescue." In my heart I knew how much courage Gilley would have had to muster to make his way down to us.

He beamed at me and puffed out his bulky sweatshirt. "I couldn't very well leave you guys alone down there. You two were getting your asses kicked."

Heath looked at me with a curious glint in his eye. "Actually, about thirty seconds before you showed up, M. J. managed to get a spike out of the canister and that stopped the attack."

Heath mentioning that made me think back to that moment when I'd had the wind knocked out of me and I'd heard that voice coaxing me to breathe and get the lid off the grenade. "You know what, Heath?"

"What?"

"I believe your grandfather was the one who actually came to our rescue."

"Really?"

I nodded. "I heard a voice telling me to take a breath and get it together, and it was the same voice that I'd heard from your grandfather in my OBE earlier this afternoon."

"I still can't get over the fact that you got physically injured during a dream," Gopher told me. "I mean, that just freaks me out!"

When Gopher had taken one look at me at dinner, he'd demanded to know how I'd managed a split lip and a black eye, and I'd done my best to explain my out-of-body experience to him. He'd made me recite it all in front of the camera, of course, and he'd punctuated the story with plenty of breathy gasps and exclamations, which I assumed were solely to ratchet up the drama for the television-viewing audience.

"Speaking of freaked-out," Gil said, "what's the deal with Jake and Russ?"

Gopher swore and his face turned angry. "Those assholes," he said. "They quit and refused to consider coming back. As far as I know, they're booked on the first plane back to the States in the morning."

"Are you going to get us some replacements?"

"I've already sent my administrative assistant back

home a text. We've got to hire our crew from the union, so it may take a day or two to get some new guys out here."

"That'll give us time to find some added protection," Heath said.

"What kind of protection?" Gopher asked.

I polished off the last bite of eggs and potatoes before answering him. "We're thinking we may want to find some crystals or charms to wear while we're in the close."

Gopher looked skeptically at me. "You think wearing a piece of quartz will keep the evil spirits at bay?"

"It's all about finding the right charm or crystal," Heath told him. "You have to remember that, on the spiritual plane, thought drives everything. So if you can find the right crystal to absorb a powerful thought of protection, it can go a long way to protecting you from bad energies."

"Sounds like a bunch of voodoo black magic to me."

"It actually works on much the same principle," I told him seriously. "Only, in black magic, the thoughts that the charms are absorbing are negative which is what can potentially make them harmful."

Gilley gave me a quizzical look. "You believe in voodoo?"

I smiled. I had a reputation for being somewhat skeptical of outlandish claims of hexes and spells, so I could understand why he was calling me out. "To a degree," I conceded. "I mean, I don't think a charm exists that can take someone's life, but I do believe that the right charm can call forth a good spirit or a bad. I mean, we saw that ourselves with the knife we've got locked up in our safe back in Boston."

"Good point," Gil said with a yawn and a sleepy glance toward the window, where the first hint of dawn was beginning to turn the black of night a smoky lavender. "Man, I'm beat."

"Me too," Heath said.

"Me three," Gopher agreed.

"Okay, boys," I said. "Let's pay the check and get back to the inn for some shut-eye. We can go in search of charms and added protection later. I also want to do a little more research on Rigella and her backstory."

"That's mine," Gil said, raising his hand. "I'll do some digging later on today after I get some sleep."

On that note, we laid some money on the table, and headed back to the inn. When I got to my room, I noticed a new message on my cell phone. It was from Steven. "Hello, M. J.," he said, his voice a teensy bit terse. In the background I could hear someone paging a Dr. Williams. He must have been calling me from the hospital. "Can you call me, please? I have not heard from you since you landed in Scotland."

I clicked off the voice mail and stared at the phone. I was exhausted, and didn't really need the guilt trip. For the record I'd left him a message the minute I'd landed. So, technically, *I* hadn't heard from *him*.

With a sigh I hit the speed dial and he answered on the third ring. "Hi," he said warmly. "How's the busting?"

I sighed tiredly. I wasn't really in the mood to recap everything. "It's going," I said. "How're you?"

"Fine. Busy. You know. They have me on double shifts right now."

"Ah," I said, struggling for something to say, but only an awkward silence filled the airwaves.

"How's the weather over there?" he asked.

I closed my eyes and pinched the bridge of my nose with my fingers. Was this what our relationship had come down to? Talking about the weather? "Cold and damp. How about for you?"

"The same." In the background I heard a page for Dr. Sable. He must still be at the hospital.

"That's me," he said. "I have to go."

"Okay," I said, relieved to have an excuse to end the conversation. "I'll talk to you soon."

"Bye," he said, and hung up.

I sat on the edge of the bed for a long moment, just looking at my phone. He hadn't even said, "Love you." And I tried to think back to the last time either one of us had said that to the other, and I couldn't remember. It hadn't been recently, that's for sure.

With a sigh I got up and set the phone on the charger, vowing to think about it later. All I wanted to do for the next few hours was sleep.

Later that afternoon, Gil, Heath, and I all gathered down in the sitting room to meet up with Kim and John, whom Gil had texted about finding us a shop in town that might specialize in crystals or charms used to thwart evil spirits. I knew also that Gopher had filled Kim and John in on what had happened in the close, so I was fairly confident that they knew what to look for.

"We found the perfect shop!" Kim sang happily.

I shivered a little in the pervasive damp chill that seemed to invade every nook and cranny of the drizzly Scottish village, and asked, "Where?"

"Miss Lancaster's Crystal Emporium," Kim said. "It's located right here in the village, in fact. John and I have just come from there, and look!" Kim extended her hand and several very pretty varieties of quartz and agate sparkled in her hand. "Aren't they gorgeous?"

I laughed. She was just so enthusiastic that I found her delightful. "They're beautiful," I agreed. "Can you take us there?"

John held up a set of car keys. "Whenever you guys are ready."

It took less than five minutes to make our way to Miss Lancaster's, and when we arrived, I could see that the place had real appeal. The exterior was exactly like what you would picture a quaint European shop should look like: almost like a gingerbread house with plenty of white trim, cute wooden shutters, and a bright blue door with a lovely floral wreath. There was even a picket fence surrounding a small rose garden.

"I love it," I said as we walked through the gate and up the short walk.

"Wait until you see the inside," Kim told me. I stepped through the door after her and came up short.

As an intuitive I'm acutely sensitive to crystals. When I hold one, especially one that's large in size, I can feel it sort of vibrating or humming on the edges of my energy. It's an incredibly cool sensation, and sometimes I'll get near a particularly powerful crystal and feel like I'm floating up, up, and away. There are also crystals that pull me down, or ground me, and I might have the sensation of feeling heavy.

In an environment like the one we stepped through when we entered Miss Lancaster's, it was a mixture of all these sensations, but heightened to an intense degree. Mostly due to the quality and abundance of crystals gleaming from every surface, shelf, corner, and countertop.

The place was a feast for the eyes, a rainbow of color really. There were amethyst cathedrals five feet tall, rose quartz lamps, white selenite wands, blue agate beads, and on and on and on. Everywhere I looked, bright humming energy washed over me. I glanced at Heath, and he seemed equally spellbound.

"Cool!" he said when he caught my eye.

"Totally," I agreed, stepping forward to explore further. "We should definitely be able to find a few crystals in here to help mitigate some of the effects of the spooks. Remember, we're looking for stuff that's grounding, so if you hold it in your hand and you feel heavier or weighed down, that's going to be a good choice."

"Got it," he said, eyeing a cluster of fluorite crystals on the far side of the store. I myself moved immediately over to the collection of amethyst cathedrals that were arranged from smallest to largest. The smallest was about two feet tall, and intensely purple, and the biggest was large enough for me to sit in. I couldn't resist the urge to recharge my intuitive batteries, especially after getting beaten up in the spiritual realm the previous night, so I carefully squatted down and eased myself to a sitting position inside the cathedral.

I closed my eyes and just absorbed the energy. "Hummmmm . . . ," I sang softly.

"Having fun, are you?" asked a light voice with a distinct brogue.

My eyes snapped open. A plump-looking woman with rosy cheeks and straw-colored hair smiled happily down at me.

"I'm so sorry!" I said, moving quickly out of the cathedral. "I know I probably shouldn't have done that."

The woman waved her hand lightly. "Oh, puff that," she said with a grin. "Of course you're welcome to sit in the cathedral. That's what it's there for, after all. And as long as you're careful not to break it, I'll hardly mind."

I breathed a sigh of relief. "You have an amazing store."

"You like it?"

"Are you kidding?" I asked. "It's wonderful! The energy here is just . . . whoa, you know?"

She eyed me critically. "Are you sensitive, lass?"

I furrowed my brow. "Am I what?"

"Sensitive," she said. "You know, can you really *feel* the energy in here?"

I laughed, understanding what she meant. "Yes, actually. I am." I then got up and extended my hand to her. "I'm M. J., and I'm a psychic medium."

The woman nodded, taking my hand and giving it a firm shake. "Bonnie Lancaster. Nice to make your acquaintance."

"M. J.!" Heath called from across the shop. "Come here! You've got to feel these!"

Bonnie looked at Heath. "Don't tell me," she said with a wink. "He's also a medium?"

I grinned. "He is. We came here because we were down in the close last night, and met up with some nasty energy. We're trying to find some protective crystals or charms to take with us the next time we go down."

Bonnie looked alarmed. "What kind of nasty energy did you encounter, then?"

Out the corner of my eye I saw Heath pick his head up again, probably to see where I was, and spotting me, he began to walk over. "Well," I said, "I believe we encountered some spirit who thinks she's a witch. I suppose she didn't like the fact that Heath—my partner—and I were down there, so she chased after us."

Bonnie's expression turned from alarm to abject fear. "Witch, did you say?"

I nodded just as Heath came up next to me. "Hello," he said cordially. "Are you the owner?"

Bonnie's eyes swiveled to him. "Did you see her too?" she asked without answering his question.

"See who?"

"The spirit of the witch in the close last night," I explained.

"Oh!" Heath said. "Yeah. There were three altogether and they chased us clear to the opposite exit. I believe the main witch's name is Rigella. She's pretty intense!"

"Oh, my," said Bonnie. "Oh, my, oh, my!"

"You've heard about her?" I asked.

Bonnie fidgeted with a small crystal necklace about her neck. "Yes, of course," she said. "Everyone's heard of the Witch of Queen's Close. And we all know she'll return someday, but she's thirty-five years early!"

"What do you know about her?" Heath asked.

Bonnie's hand flew across her chest in the sign of the cross. "She's a wicked one, that witch," she said. "And if you really did encounter her, then I daresay none of my clan is safe round here."

I blinked. "I'm sorry, but why would your clan be in danger, exactly?"

"Well, because of the curse, of course."

Heath and I exchanged a look. "Curse?" we said together.

Bonnie nodded. "You've not heard of it?"

"No," Heath said.

Bonnie moved away from the cathedrals and over to a counter where Kim was peering intently at a group of earrings. We followed the shop owner, waiting for her to explain. "Can I see those?" Kim asked innocently.

Bonnie forced a smile and opened the case, pulling out the earrings and handing them to Kim. She then motioned us over to a second counter and began whispering. "Over three hundred and fifty years ago when the village of Queen's Close was being encroached upon by the ever-expanding city of Edinburgh, a terrible plague set itself against almost all the inhabitants of the city and the village. People were desperate, you see, because this particular plague spread so quickly and attacked everyone from the lowliest urchins to the wealthiest noblemen. No one was safe. No one, that is, except one particular family.

"A woman of significant influence named Rigella, who was both feared and revered, lived just a few streets away from here, in fact. She was purported to be a powerful witch with ties to the devil himself." Bonnie paused here and made another sign of the cross before continuing. "And when all about there was such terrible suffering, and only her family was left untouched by the plague, the village became suspicious and it wasn't long afore the terrified residents turned against Rigella and her family.

"It is said that a mob of the village's angriest residents came looking for her. Rigella and her family sought shelter in the close. They thought they'd be safe down there, as that's the place where the village used to send all the sick people who showed any sign of having the plague. Rigella didn't think the mob would chase her into the underground caverns, but she was wrong. The mob came after her and trapped the whole family there, murdering first the witch's lover, who was beaten and run to death. He simply collapsed and died, probably from a heart attack. Next they stoned the oldest, before the mob caught Rigella's middle sister and set her on fire, leaving only the witch and her youngest three sisters trapped in the close

"It's said that she and the two second-oldest begged the mob to spare the life of their littlest sister, who was all of fourteen, but the villagers were too crazed to listen to reason. In front of the witch and her sisters they ravaged the poor girl and left her for dead. Then, they took the remaining three and hanged them together.

"But before the witch and her remaining sisters died, it is said that Rigella set a curse upon the mob. She swore that she would have her revenge and that every one hundred years she would return to claim a life for each of her clan members killed by the mob. She would seek the death of seven souls to atone for the horror that befell her family."

I felt a chill go down my spine. Like I said, I don't normally believe in things like curses and spells, but something about what Bonnie was telling us was really hitting home. "You say that every hundred years she comes looking for revenge?"

Bonnie nodded, her eyes large and fearful. "Aye," she said. "It began within a month of her death. Seven members of the mob that attacked the witch were killed—and not by the plague but through other mysterious circumstances. And then, over the centuries in the years seventeen forty-five, eighteen forty-five, and nineteen forty-five here in this village seven lives have been claimed within a week's time and all the deaths were mysterious in nature and were never resolved."

"But why are *you* so worried?" Heath wondered. And I remembered the remark Bonnie had made about no one in her clan being safe. "I mean, this village must have a few thousand in population at least, right?"

"My great-great-great-great-grandfather was a member of that mob," Bonnie said, her voice no louder than a whisper. "And since that terrible day, several members of the Lancaster family have fallen victim to the curse, including me own uncle who was found hanging right after returning home from the war."

My jaw fell open a little. "Your *own* family has been a target?"

Bonnie nodded gravely. "Aye. And not just me uncle was taken. One of me second cousins and his oldest brother died in a lorry accident the same week as poor Uncle Curtis." Bonnie shivered. "Me grandfather used to tell us stories, in fact, of that terrible week when I was just a wee girl. He told me with a tear in his eye how frightened of the witch's curse he was, but the war was particularly hard on our clan, and we had no money to move away and nowhere really to go even if we did. So we'd stayed here and tried to get through it, and it still cost us three of our kith."

"Why so many victims from your family?" I asked as another chill went through me.

Bonnie grimaced. "There were four main clans that chased the witch's family into the close. The Lancasters, the McLarens, the Hills, and the Gillespies."

I did a double take. "The *who*?"

"The Lancasters, McLarens, Hills, and Gillespies,"

she repeated. "In fact, Thomas Gillespie and his daughter Donaline were burned alive in a fire that destroyed their home. After that terrible day, the remaining Gillespies packed up everything they owned and moved to America, but the Lancasters and the McLarens and the Hills still have living members of the original families here in the village."

"Hey, guys!" Gilley said, sidling up next to me, which caused me to jump almost a foot. "Cool place, right?"

Heath and I stood mute for a full three seconds before I finally managed to reply, "Um, yeah. It's terrific."

Gilley was too busy taking in all the sparkling crystals in the shop to really notice our alarm, but he seemed to realize that he'd walked in on a conversation, so he extended his hand out to Bonnie and said, "Gilley Gillespie, nice to meet you."

Bonnie shrieked and pulled her hand out of Gilley's grasp like she'd been stung. She then made another sign of the cross and shuffled several feet back. Gilley stood there looking shocked. "What just happened?" he asked me.

I took him by the hand and hurried away from Bonnie before she could say something about what we'd been discussing. Heath followed me and we made it outside, where Gilley pulled his hand out of mine and demanded some answers. "What's going on?"

I looked at Heath, he looked at me, and neither of us spoke for several seconds. "It's probably just a coincidence," I began.

"And it may not even matter," Heath added.

"We're positive you're not going to be affected in any way," I assured, and then, I didn't know what else to say. Gil was going to freak, no matter how hard we tried to sugarcoat it.

"Will you just *tell* me?" he growled impatiently.

Again, Heath and I shared a look, and at that moment Kim came out carrying a little bag. "I have a gift for you!" she sang.

All our eyes swiveled to her as she tipped the bag upside down and out fell the green peridot earrings she'd been eyeing right before Bonnie told us about the legend of the witch. "Oops, not those, hold on, it's in this bag," she said, and tipped out the contents of a second bag into her palm. In her hand I eyed the *very* charm that Samuel Whitefeather had placed around my neck in my out-of-body experience.

"Whoa!" I exclaimed, momentarily forgetting about Gilley and reaching for the charm.

"It's awesome, right?" Kim asked.

I held it up to the light. "Kim," I began in a deadly serious tone.

"Yeah?"

"How did you find this?"

"M. J.!" Gilley squealed. "Will you stop it? Tell me why that woman inside reacted like that!"

"Hold on, Gil," I said, putting him off for a minute. I had to know how Kim found the very charm from my dream.

"Bonnie gave it to me to give to you. She said an American Indian dealer from Santa Fe, New Mexico, had come over here and sold her a bunch of charms and jewelry, and she remembered him telling her that this particular charm had the power to thwart evil spirits. She wants you to have it. She seems to think that if you're investigating the witch's ghost, you'll need it."

"Free of charge?" I asked, astounded by Bonnie's generosity.

Kim nodded. "Yes. But between you and me I saw the price tag before she took it off. It was tagged at seventy-five pounds."

I opened my purse and pulled out all the cash I had on me. "Can you please take this inside and give it to Bonnie with my profound thanks?"

Kim smiled. "Absolutely. That'll give me an excuse to buy that turquoise bracelet I was eyeing. I was really looking for a reason to go back in there!" With that, she dashed off.

After she'd gone, I turned to Gil, who had his arms crossed and was impatiently tapping his foot. "Out with it."

I secured the charm around my neck and took a deep breath. "It turns out that the witch that attacked us the other night may be looking to exact some revenge."

Gilley's brow furrowed. "What kind of revenge?"

"She and her family were killed about three hundred and fifty years ago when an angry mob blamed them for the plague."

"Uh-huh," Gil said with narrowed eyes, as if he was looking for some hidden meaning in what I was saying.

"Supposedly the witch cursed the mob and their descendants. She said that she would return every hundred years to claim the lives of seven members of the mob's families."

"Okay," Gil said. "I'm following."

"And about sixty-five years ago she took the lives of seven village residents who were descendants of the group that killed her and her family."

Gilley gave me a level look. "What aren't you telling me?" he demanded.

"The family name of some of the victims was Gillespie."

Gilley turned starkly pale and he just stared at me as if I'd told him he had two weeks to live. "Say what, now?" he whispered.

"The witch has been attacking members of the Lancasters, McLarens, Hills, and the Gillespies. The last few members of the original Gillespie family fled Scotland fearing the curse—and relocated to America."

Gilley audibly gulped. "Uh-oh," he said.

"Maybe it's just a coincidence," Heath repeated. "Seriously, dude. I mean, there must be tens of thousands of Gillespies all over the world. Just because you have the same last name doesn't mean *your* family came from this part of Scotland."

Gilley whipped out his cell phone and began punching numbers on the screen. Holding it up to his ear, he waited a beat, then said, "Mom? Hi, it's Gilley." There was a pause, then, "Yes, I know it's early, and I'm sorry, but I just have to ask you one question: What part of Scotland did Grandpa and Grandma Gillespie come from?"

I stared at Gilley's face, waiting to see the relief I was sure would come, but instead he went a shade paler and made this little squeaking sound before saying, "Some little village on the outskirts of Edinburgh named Queen's something? Uh, okay, thanks, Ma, call you later." He hung up and stared at me in horror. "Why is it *always* me?!"

We headed right back to the inn after the crystal shop. On the drive back I held Gilley's hand and tried to prevent him from hyperventilating. "I have to leave town!" he said. "She's coming after me!"

"She's not coming after you," I reassured him, really hoping that was true. "I mean, before we go fleeing the country, let's try and figure out if this legend is true or if it's one giant fable the locals cooked up to attract tourists."

"Bonnie didn't seem to think it was a fable," Heath said. "She looked genuinely scared."

I glared at him and whispered, "Ixnay on the On-niebay, please!"

But Heath wasn't backing off. "I think we need to take this seriously, M. J.," he said. "I mean, we can't just discount what we saw in the caverns last night. And what about the images Gilley captured on tape? It's pretty clear that some spook is haunting those caverns and believes she's a witch."

"But you heard what Bonnie said," I told him. "The very first thing she said to us was that the witch's appearance is a full *thirty-five* years early. Maybe she isn't coming after anyone right now. Maybe she was just irritated that we were in her territory, and that sparked her into action."

"But what about that maintenance worker?" Gilley insisted. "I mean, that man looked scared to death. *Literally!*"

I sighed heavily as we pulled into the inn's parking lot. "Of course he was scared!" I yelled a bit louder than I'd intended, and I saw John's eyes glance at me in the rearview mirror. "The man was having a major heart attack down in some dark cavern where no one could help him, Gil. He was probably terrified that his worst fear was coming true!"

"Or his worst fear was coming right at him," Gil mumbled.

"Didn't Bonnie say that the witch's lover was run down by the mob? That he was chased until he collapsed and died?" Heath said.

"Just like the maintenance worker!" Gil exclaimed, pointing at Heath like he was Sherlock Holmes.

I rolled my eyes. "Well, there's an easy way to put an end to the mystery," I said. "All we need to do is find out the last name of the maintenance worker. If it's something other than Lancaster, Hill, McLaren, or Gillespie, we know it was just a coincidence."

"It was McLaren," John called from the front seat as he put the van into park. "While you guys were in the crystal shop, I went for coffee, and the locals are all talking about it. Jack McLaren was the name of the maintenance worker who collapsed and died down in the close."

Gilley made another squeaking sound and thrust his fist into his mouth. "Terrific," I sighed. "Juuuust terrific."

# Chapter 5

"Why is he packing?" Gopher asked as we all huddled in Gilley's room while my partner ran around like a frightened hen, frantically stuffing articles of clothing into his suitcase.

"There's been a development," I said, then went on to explain everything we'd learned from Bonnie at the Crystal Emporium. Gilley hadn't even heard the whole story and I noticed him pausing at times as I retold it for Gopher. Still, by the time I'd finished, Gil was zipping up his suitcase, ready to head for the airport.

"I still don't get why Gilley's packing," Gopher said, scratching his head.

"Weren't you listening?" Gilley screeched.

Gopher winced. "Yes, Gil, I was listening. But that doesn't mean your family is from the exact same part of Edinburgh, does it? I mean, it's a big city. They could have come from any village on the edge of it."

But Gil was shaking his head. "It's the same place," he said. "I've already looked up my grandfather's name on Ancestry.com. Both he and my grandmother were born just a few streets away, within one block of each other!"

Gopher sat down in a chair near the window. "Okay, okay, but, Gilley, *you're* not from here! You're from America. And maybe this witch will just assume once she hears you talk that you're just another American tourist."

But Gilley was shaking his head. "Nope," he said, heaving his suitcase off the bed. "I'm not taking any chances. I'll rendezvous with you guys at the next location. Good luck."

As Gil tried to walk out the door, Gopher called him back. "You realize you'll be in breach of contract, right?"

Gilley halted in the doorway and turned to look back at Gopher. "Say what?"

Gopher stuffed his hands into his pockets, clearly uncomfortable. "The network likes you, buddy. They think you're one of the more-colorful members of the team. I sent them the footage from yesterday and they ate it up when you went running to M. J. and Heath's rescue. I'd hate to think what they'd do if they found out you'd left the shoot."

I narrowed my eyes at Gopher. "You *wouldn't*!"

Gopher pulled his hands out of his pockets and held them up in surrender. "Hey, don't blame me," he said. "It's out of my control. Gilley signed a contract and if he walks, then he's in breach, and the network won't look favorably on that. I'm convinced they'll sue."

"How vigorously?" I asked. I'd read that contract backward and forward. All the chips were in the network's favor. Essentially, for the next eight to ten weeks they totally controlled almost every move we made.

"The last reality-TV star to dis them will never be solvent. Never."

"But she'll *kill* me!" Gilley wailed.

Gopher gave Gil a look like he understood fully. But I wasn't buying it. "Maybe not," Heath said into the heavy silence that followed.

All eyes swiveled to Heath, and he, in turn, leveled his gaze at me. "We're ghostbusters, M. J. Shutting down these evil poltergeists is what we *do*. And I think that this job is exactly what we're about. If this witch's ghost has risen again, then it really should be up to us to send her to hell—permanently."

"You mean you want to take her on?" I asked incredulously. It'd been all I could do to muster the courage to simply investigate the caverns. I hadn't planned on any actual ghostbusting, especially with someone so powerful as the ghost of the Witch of Queen's Close.

But Heath was nodding his head as if his mind was made up. "I think we have to bust her. If the legend is true, then six more lives could be at stake. We can't just sit back and gather footage of spooky stuff while people are dying."

I thought on that for a minute while Gilley continued to grip the door handle to his room like he was holding on for dear life. "What are you thinking?" I asked him.

"I don't want to be poor," he said honestly. "But I don't want to be dead either."

I smiled, and made up my mind then and there. "Okay, people, new plan: We're going after Rigella's ghost. But our first priority is to make sure that Gilley is safe at all times. I don't want him anywhere near the caverns, and I want him protected by extra magnets and backup twenty-four/seven."

"He should wear a meter," Heath said. "If it starts

to spike and one of us isn't around, he'll have a heads-up that he needs to call one of us."

"Oh, he'll wear a meter all right," I said. "And he'll have me playing watchdog at all times except when we're down in the close." Turning to Gopher, I said, "Can you please move Gil and me into one room with two beds?"

"Absolutely," Gopher promised. "Anything else you'll need to make sure he's safe?"

I looked at Heath. He shrugged. "I can't think of anything."

"As many magnets as we can find," I said after thinking on it. "I want him so surrounded by disruptive electromagnetic frequency that no ghost within ten miles could possibly get to him."

"Where am I going to be when you guys are in the close?" Gil wanted to know.

"In the van," I said. "And I want the entire interior padded with magnets."

"On it," Gopher said, making a note in his iPhone.

"How soon before the camera and sound guys get here?" Heath asked.

Gopher glanced up and said, "Their plane gets in tonight around ten. We could start filming by midnight if you want."

My heart skipped a beat. I didn't want to go back down to the close, but I also knew that putting it off was going to make my anxiety worse. "Great. Most of our cameras and meters are still in place, right, Gil?"

He nodded. "I checked on them this morning. They're all still sending data."

"Good. We'll consider the baseline complete, and we'll start this bust tonight. Heath, you and I need to come up with a plan to deal with some of that overpowering plague energy that tackled you in the close last night."

"Good idea," he said. "But at least now we know why it was so intense."

"Why?" Gopher asked.

"The close was where the town sent anyone who was showing symptoms of the plague. I figure those caverns were where hundreds, if not thousands, of people perished from the disease. And all that fear and suffering has left an imprint. If Heath and I are going to take on the witch, we'll need to be completely present and clear of any residual energy."

"How are you going to manage that?" Gilley asked me.

"We'll have to strike a delicate balance," I told him. "We'll need to be really grounded, and we'll have to tone down our radars."

Gopher looked curiously at me. "You guys can tweak the intensity of your radar?"

"I can," I said, and eyed Heath to see if he agreed.

To my relief he nodded. "I think it's a survival technique," he said. "If I didn't dial back my antennae there'd be no way I'd be able to walk through a crowd or get to sleep at night."

Gilley finally let go of the door and came back over to sit down on his bed. He still looked upset. "Won't that be a dangerous thing for you to do, M. J.?"

I knew what Gilley was hinting at. If I went into the close on anything but high alert, the ghost of Rigella could move in on me before I had the time to feel her coming. "It's a risk we'll have to take, Gil."

Gilley frowned. "I really don't like this at all."

"None of us do," Heath said. "But I don't see how we have any real choice."

I glanced at my watch and said, "I've got to check on Wendell. Gopher, let me know when you've arranged to put Gil and me together; in the meantime, Heath, if you could babysit him until we move, that'd be awesome."

"On it," Heath said.

Later that evening most of the crew was gathered around the van, which was parked a full block east of the entrance to the close. I had wanted it—and Gilley—to be farther away, but anything beyond one block messed with the reception, which was already challenged due to the signals coming from underground.

Gil was seated inside the van and was surrounded by magnets. He had on his trusty sweatshirt, and there were refrigerator magnets stuck to every conceivable surface. And I had to admit, I felt pretty good about his being surrounded by so much protection.

Heath and I had spent a few hours in deep meditation, gathering protective shields to our energy, and then we'd done an exercise to ground ourselves, which involved a visualization where we imagined our bodies as tree trunks with thick roots planted deep into the ground.

I'd also brought along the charm Bonnie had given me, explaining to Heath that it was an identical match to the one his grandfather had placed around my neck in my OBE. "Where's my charm?" he'd asked playfully when I'd told him the story.

"Oh, I think you come with plenty of charm already," I said with a laugh. Heath liked to flirt with me and I wasn't about to let up teasing him about it.

The new cameraman and sound guy weren't much in the way of personality. Both men were middle-aged, overweight, quiet, and seemingly very skeptical about what we were doing here. They didn't say anything, of course—they were professionals after all, and I was pretty sure they'd seen all kinds of weird behavior over the years. But it showed in their eyes when we talked through our game plan and how we would try to provoke Rigella's ghost into appearing, then follow her to her portal. "If we can find that portal, we can shut her down before she has a chance to hurt anyone else."

"And if she gets violent, we'll pull out the grenades," Heath said, demonstrating to the new crew members what he meant by pulling off the cap to the metal casing housing the magnetized spike.

"Did you want me aboveground or below?" Gopher asked when we'd gone over the plan.

"Aboveground," I told him, and hid a smile when I saw the relief in his eyes. "You stay with Gil and make sure he's okay."

"I'll be fine," Gil said, pointing to the array of magnets all over the interior of the van. "This place is reinforced like Fort Knox."

"Yeah, well, I don't want to take any chances. You keep in constant radio communication with me, you hear?"

Gilley saluted. "Yes, sir!"

I narrowed my eyes at him. "I mean it, Gil. I'm nervous enough about having you this close to the caverns. That witch is the most powerful thing we've ever encountered, and I don't think she'll be stymied for long."

"I'll be fine!" Gil insisted. "Now go along and get to busting her ass, would you?"

I smiled ruefully and motioned to Heath and the

camera and sound guys—whose names I'd already forgotten.

We made our way to the entrance of the close and I did a sound check. "Gil, you copy? Over."

"Copy that, M. J. Over."

Heath gave me a thumbs-up to indicate that his headset was working fine, and we opened the door and descended the stairs to the caverns. There was a thick door at the bottom of the staircase, which was very hard to open, and Heath had to help me, but we made it inside without further incident. "We've entered the close," I said to Gil. "We're making our way over to camera one. Over."

"Copy that," he said. Then more quietly I heard him tell Gopher how hot he was. "It's friggin' stifling in this van."

"Then take off your sweatshirt," Gopher said.

"No way," Gil said. "Uh-uh."

"Oh for cripes' sake, Gil," Gopher snapped. "You've been complaining about the heat ever since we got in here. Just take off the sweatshirt and set it on your lap. You'll still have the magnets on you and besides that, we're surrounded by magnets. As long as you stay in the van, you're covered."

There was a muffled sound in my ear and I knew that Gilley was taking Gopher's suggestion. I also breathed a sigh of relief, because Gil does tend to whine a lot when he's uncomfortable, and I saw nothing wrong with Gilley keeping the shirt on his lap instead of wearing it.

As we walked, I glanced sideways at Heath to make sure he wasn't suffering any early effects of the plague. He looked totally fine, so I kept moving. A short time later we came to a stop in front of camera one and I waved up at Gil. "How's the reception?" I asked him.

"Great."

I turned to Heath and said, "Might as well test the waters."

Heath put his hand on the canister secured to his belt and nodded. "Ready when you are."

I looked up and down the close. Even though my radar was dialed way down, I could still sense a bombardment of souls knocking on my energy. I opened my mouth, ready to call out to Rigella, when we all heard a terrified shriek. It was female and it came from about one hundred yards ahead. "What was that?" the soundman demanded.

"Don't know," I said honestly. "Gil? Can you tell me what you see on camera two?"

There was a pause, then, "It's clear, M. J. There's nothing there."

"And what about the meters? What're they registering?"

Another pause then, "A small spike," he said. "But not at camera two. I'm getting increased electromagnetic frequencies coming from where you guys are by camera one."

Heath and I locked eyes and then I pulled out the meter around my belt. The needle was bouncing back and forth between normal and high. I pointed the meter around in a circle. It continued to bounce; then it went to high and stayed there. Near my left shoulder I heard a moan and the camera guy jumped. "What the . . . !" he gasped.

"Hold still!" I commanded, just as a loud knock rattled the cavern.

"Uh-oh," Heath whispered, and I felt the first hint of mounting danger beginning to form all around us.

"Everyone hold still!" I ordered just as another series of knocks sounded right behind us.

"What's happening?" Soundman asked in a squeaky whisper.

"M. J.!" Gilley yelled in my ear. "I'm getting crazy-high meter readings from camera five . . . now four . . . now three . . . !"

I looked at Heath. "Brace yourself!"

From down the cavern we all heard it coming, a progression of thunderous thwacks that sounded like a thousand baseballs dropping on a tin roof all at once. It came like a wave, pounding its way toward us, building and building, until even the sound of Gilley shouting right in my ear was drowned out.

I ducked low and covered my head with my hands when something crashed into me and took me down to the ground. As a terrible racket sounded all around, I realized that Heath had thrown himself on top of me and was attempting to shield me with his body. I struggled to breathe with his added weight, and he held on to my arm and my shoulder so hard that it hurt. I squeezed my eyes closed and in my mind's eye a crystal clear image appeared of Samuel Whitefeather hovering over Heath and me protectively with his hands splayed, and a white dome of protection covered our bodies—as if he was producing an energetic force field. And at my neck the charm I was wearing became incredibly hot—almost searing against my skin.

Meanwhile all around us the thwacking sounds continued, until I thought they would never stop.

But abruptly—they did.

And all that was left was Gilley's frantic pleas. *"M. J.?! Heath?! Come in! COME IN!"*

I'm not sure who moved first. It might have been Heath, or it could have been me, but eventually we both sat up and looked around in a daze. Dust swirled in the air, which was foggy and thick. "We're here, Gil," I said, my voice cracking slightly before I coughed.

"Ohmigod!" he said. "I was scared to death! Are you okay?"

"Yeah," I said. "I mean, I think so."

"What about Heath?"

I squinted at my fellow medium. He nodded to indicate he was fine. "He's okay."

"And the crew?" Gopher's voice asked.

I coughed again and waved my hand at the air, trying to clear it. I couldn't figure out what had caused so much dust, but the other thing I noticed was that it appeared to be noticeably darker here in the cavern.

"They got the bulbs," Heath said as if reading my mind. He pointed to the edges of the ceiling where the industrial lightbulbs were lined up one every ten feet or so. I could see that several lights along the cavern's cieling had been broken, but one just down from us cast an eerie glow to the floor, which looked uncharacteristically bumpy.

"M. J.?" I heard Gopher say. "Are you there?"

"I'm here," I said, trying to get to my feet. "I'm here."

"What's the status of my crew?"

I realized as I stood up that the ground was littered with stones and rocks and even pebbles of all sizes. There were thousands of them strewn all about, and I sucked in a breath of surprise when I realized that none of them had hit me. I glanced at Heath again in alarm, wondering if he might be covered in bruises, but he looked all right.

"M. J.!" Gopher shouted, clearly impatient now. "What is the status of my crew?!"

"Um . . . ," I said, turning in a half circle, looking for Cameraman and Sound Guy. Coughing again, I said, "I don't see them."

There was a pause before Gilley asked, "What do you mean, you don't see them?"

"They're not here," Heath replied.

There was another pause as Gilley and our producer took that in. "Exactly *what* happened down there?" Gopher asked.

"Can't you see it?" I asked, right before my eye fell on the broken glass and pieces of black plastic littering the floor underneath where we'd secured camera one.

"We have no eyes on the ground," Gilley said. "All the cameras are feeding us snow."

"Well, it's a mess down here," Heath said. "It's like a tornado whipped through here or something."

"Yeah, we're definitely not in Kansas anymore," I concurred.

"Guys!" Gopher snapped impatiently. "*Where* is my crew?!"

I waved the dusty air with my hand, coughed, and squinted into the gloom. "Gopher, they're not here. My thinking is they've either run deeper into the cavern or headed up top."

"That's it," I heard Gopher snap. "I'm going down there."

I was about to tell Gopher to stay with Gilley and we'd look for the crew when Heath stepped awkwardly on a rock and fell down.

"Careful!" I said, hurrying to him. "You okay?"

He tried to laugh it off as he got up quickly and said, "I'm fine." He then kicked aside several stones. "How the hell did we dodge all of these?"

I shook my head and almost smiled. "I believe your grandfather might have granted us a little protection."

"Yeah?" Heath asked curiously.

I nodded and then remembered how hot my charm had gotten during the onslaught and I reached up to my neck and pulled out the charm I'd been wearing.

"Whoa," Heath said, pointing to the necklace. "It's cracked in half!"

I took it off carefully to inspect it more clearly in the dim light. Sure enough the charm had a huge fracture running through the middle of it. I tapped it, and the whole thing just broke apart.

"Crap," I said as several pieces of the charm fell on the floor. "There goes our added protection."

"The energy that came at us was so strong that it must have absorbed right into the charm," Heath said. "And when he was alive, my grandfather used to tell me about charms that could do that, but I've never actually seen it."

"Until now," I said, wiping my hands on my pants and coughing again in the dirty air. "You ready to get outta here?"

"More than ready."

We moved over toward the nearest exit and as we got close, we could clearly see something fuzzy lying on the floor. We hustled over to investigate and found the furry-covered microphone still attached to its boom, which had snapped in half.

"Our brave crew must have made it out," I whispered.

"Let's hope so," Heath said.

"Gil?" I said more loudly into the microphone.

"Yeah?"

"We think Cameraman and Sound Guy made it out of the cavern."

There was a small chuckle in my ear. "They have names, you know," he said.

"Oh yeah?" I asked him. "What are they?"

"Heck if I can remember," Gil said, giving in to another laugh. "And you guys still haven't told me what happened."

"Rocks," I said.

"Rocks?"

I stared around the close, littered with debris. "Yep. The whole cavern was pelted with them."

"Are you sure you two are all right?"

"Yep," I assured him, eyeing a shard of the charm on the floor. "At least for now we are."

Just then the door to the cavern burst open and Gopher stood there looking sweaty and out of breath. "Hey!" he said when he saw us. "I got here as soon as I could."

His appearance made me angry. "I told you to stay with Gilley," I snapped.

"I was worried about my crew," he replied defensively.

"Yeah, well as far as we can tell, your crew made it out of here okay, and my guess is that they're already on their way to the airport. I'll also bet you dollars to doughnuts that they're not coming back for round two."

In my ear I heard a faint knocking sound and Gilley ask, "Is that you, Gopher?"

"He's here with us," I said.

"Then who's knocking on the van?"

"Probably Camera Guy and Soundman."

Gilley chuckled again. "I thought it was Cameraman and Sound Guy."

Heath smiled. "They all look alike. Or at least, they all look alike when they're running away."

There were shuffling noises and I knew Gil was making his way over to the door of the van, and in the second before I imagined he opened the door, I got a terrible prophetic feeling. "Gil!" I shouted. *"Don't open the door!"*

But it was too late. No sooner had I finished shouting out my warning than I heard the door to the van slide open, and a frightful shriek sounded in my ear loud enough for me to yank off my headset. It came to rest around my neck as muffled cries of terror erupted from the earpiece.

*"Gilley!"* I yelled, and bolted to the door. "Hang on! We're coming!"

Heath was next to me in an instant and together we pulled the heavy door open and flew up the stairs. *"Get off me! Get off me!"* I heard Gilley scream. I knew intuitively that something had pulled him out of the van, and I also knew that without his sweatshirt he was a sitting duck.

My heart was thundering in my chest as I charged up the steps, shouting, *"Gilley! Get back into the van!"*

I had the headset back on my head and was listening to Gilley struggle and fight with some unknown assailant. Then, a small ray of hope when I heard him bang hard on something metallic, and the door of the van slid either open or closed again.

"We're . . . coming!" I panted as I struggled to hurry up the steps.

Heath was faster than I and he made it to the top door first. But when he pulled on the handle, it wouldn't move.

I reached him just seconds later. "Open it!" I shouted impatiently.

"It's locked!" Heath exclaimed. "It won't budge!"

I was so afraid for Gil that I rudely bumped Heath out of the way, grabbed the handle, and pulled with all my might. But he was right. The door was shut tight.

"What's happening?" Gopher called up from the bottom of the staircase.

I didn't answer him. Instead I yanked the microphone up close to my mouth and shouted, "Gil! What's going on?"

Gilley was crying and blubbering incoherently, but I did manage to catch, "M. J., I'm back in the van, but something's still outside! Help me!"

I slammed my fist against the door and shouted for anyone who might be passing by to help. But through the dirty window I could see only darkness outside.

"The other exit!" Heath shouted, and without waiting for me, he bolted back down the stairs.

I took off after him and cried, "Gilley! Hang on! We're coming!"

To make matters worse, Gilley's terrified cries reached a new level of fear and volume. *"Go away!"* he shouted. *"Get away from here!"*

Heath grabbed the railing and swung up and over the last flight of stairs, landing at the bottom with a loud thud. I took his cue and launched myself after him. We passed a confused and frightened Gopher without pausing to explain, and tore back down the cavern as if our lives depended on it, tripping and stumbling over the rocks as we went.

I knew the other exit was nearly a half mile down the close, and that meant we were also a half mile away from the van. I didn't know what was attacking Gilley, but whatever it was, it was super scary and apparently powerful enough to get to him despite all the magnets. I was panting heavily as Heath and I ran, but pressed the microphone up to my lips and called out, "Gil! Tell me what you see!"

Gilley was sobbing so hard it was tough to make out what he was saying. But after several tries he managed, "There's something outside the van! I can see it through the windows! I think it's the witch!"

A tiny ripple of relief ran through me. If Rigella's ghost was outside the van, then that meant she couldn't make it past the huge magnetic field we'd set up inside. "Is the door closed?"

"Uh . . . yeah . . . ," Gil said. "I slammed it shut right after I made it back inside."

"Are you hurt?"

Gilley sniffled and his voice quivered. "No, just a little bruised and my new shirt's torn."

"Where are you in the van?"

Something pounded loudly in the background and Gilley shrieked. "I'm in the middle!" he said. "But something just hit the door hard!" Another tremendous thud echoed through the earpiece, followed by another shriek from Gilley. *"M. J., where are you?"*

"We're coming, honey!" I shouted. "Hang on!" I didn't want to let Gil know that we were taking the long way. I knew that would just add to his fear.

By this time Heath was about twenty yards ahead of me, and from behind I could hear Gopher's footfalls pounding after us. "Wait up!" he called, but there was no way I was slowing down. Especially when I heard another loud boom making its way through my headset, followed closely by yet another screech from Gil.

It occurred to me that maybe the witch was attempting to frighten Gilley out of the van, and I knew that he was so terrified that he could well dissolve into panic and attempt to flee. "Gil!" I shouted while I fought for more air. "Whatever . . . you do . . . don't get out . . . of the van!"

I had no idea if Gil heard me because immediately after I'd said that, another thunderous crash sounded in my ear. I saw Heath glance at me over his shoulder. He'd heard it too. "She's trying to get him out of the van!" he shouted back.

I nodded and dug deep to put on a little more speed. "M. J.!" Gilley squealed. "Please! Help me!"

Tears of frustration stung my eyes and I fought to get a grip on my emotions. My best friend was being attacked by a murderous spirit—and by now I was convinced that the ghost of the witch was powerful enough to kill Gilley if she could get at him—and I was still about a hundred yards away from making it out of the cavern. "Hang . . . on . . . buddy!"

For the longest ten seconds of my life I said nothing as I heard the witch pounding on the side of the van and Gilley screaming with each new assault. The things I imagined were happening to Gil were enough to drive me to the brink. The only thing that kept me going was to see Heath reach the exit door and tug hard on it. He disappeared through it and five beats later I was through it too.

I could hear him out of my other ear as he rushed

up the steps, and his own labored breathing echoed down to me. I was fighting hard myself to suck in enough air, but there was no way I was going to stop and rest now.

Meanwhile it sounded as if Gil had simply dissolved into a puddle of blubbering incoherency. I imagined him sitting in a little ball in the center of the van with his hands over his head while the witch threw everything she had at the side of the van. "Stay . . . inside . . . Gil!" I gasped as I crested the first landing and willed my wobbly legs to keep climbing.

Above me, Heath got to the top and pulled at the door. I heard it open almost immediately. "M. J.!" he called down. "It's open!"

"*Goooooooooooo!*" I shouted. "Get to Gil!"

Heath disappeared through the door and I pumped my legs up the last few steps. I realized as I got to the door and yanked it open myself that I hadn't heard any crashing sounds through the earpiece in several seconds. But Gilley's sobs continued.

I paused for just a moment outside the door to gulp in air. I was in really good shape from the daily jog I always took at home, but I'd run at almost a full sprint for a half mile, then up two flights of stairs, and I was winded.

I could see Heath still racing down the street, but even his pace had slowed. I bent over and grabbed my knees, my sides heaving. "Gil . . . ," I finally managed.

There was no response.

"Gil!" I said more forcefully, standing up again and stepping forward to hurry down the street.

"I'm here," he answered with a sniffle. "I think she's gone."

But I wasn't so sure. "Stay . . . put . . . ," I ordered.

I could hear Gilley moving around. "Seriously, M. J.," he whispered. "I really think she's gone."

"We're almost to you," I lied. Even Heath was at least a quarter mile away.

Gil sniffled again. "I'm gonna look out the window."

I was panting too hard to reply, but I *knew* the witch had not given up. Still, I listened to the muffled sound of what I thought was Gilley putting his sweatshirt back on, then shuffling over to a window.

"I don't see her," he said softly. And then, "Hold on. . . ." Every nerve in my body tensed. ". . . What's that noise?"

"Don't move!" I heard Heath's ragged voice command. "Gil! Get to the middle of the van and stay there!"

"Someone's under the van!" Gilley shouted. "Ohmigod! I'm moving!"

"Do you have the keys?!" I yelled. "Gilley, start the van!"

"Gopher has them!" Gil screamed. Then there was more shuffling and he yelled, "The steering wheel is locked up and the brake isn't working!"

"Shit!" I swore, and cranked up my pace again. I could just see Heath two hundred yards ahead of me also find a second wind and pour on the speed.

"I'm moving backward!" Gilley shouted. "I think I should jump for it!"

*"NO!"* Heath and I both roared together.

I remembered where the van had been parked. It was at the top of a small hill. If the van really was moving, it was heading downhill toward a row of brownstones.

*"I'm going to crash!"* Gil screamed.

"Brace yourself!" I pleaded, rounding a corner and seeing the van for the first time still a hundred yards away, moving backward down the hill.

"*Ahhhhhhhhhhhh!*" Gilley cried just as a dark shadow dived after the van.

"*Heath!*" I shouted when I saw him closing in on the van. "Get to him!"

I took maybe three more strides, running as fast as I could go, when I heard a terrible scream that didn't come from my headset and then a horrible crash that seemed to go on far too long. "*Gilllllllllley!*" I cried, as tears trailed down my cheeks and my heart felt like it was going to burst out of my chest.

I couldn't see the van anymore. It had rolled out of sight. But I could still see Heath, who faltered, nearly stopped, then raced forward again.

My limbs were like rubber as I dashed after him, and when I crested the hill, I took in the nightmarish scene at the bottom. Debris littered the street, and parts of the van were spread out over a wide area.

I came to a stop at the top of the hill, too shocked to move the rest of the way. My eyes took in a demolished brick wall, a light post that'd bent nearly in half, broken glass, crumpled pieces of metal . . . and one obviously dead body covered in blood lying in the middle of the street.

# Chapter 6

Already the street was filling with people. Residents of the quiet neighborhood raced out of their homes wearing robes and nightgowns and shocked expressions.

A couple knelt by the body, their hands covering their mouths in horror. Others raced toward the van, which had come to rest on its side. Heath was already there, pulling with all his might on the handle to the crumpled door.

My chest was heaving so hard that my ribs hurt, and panic raced through my veins. I stumbled a few steps forward, nearly tripping over some debris under my feet. I looked down, tears blurring my vision as I vaguely noticed some wires and broken black plastic at my feet. Then I hurried forward another few steps, staring hard at the crumpled form in the middle of the street. I couldn't tell if it was Gilley. I stopped again and until I knew one way or the other, I didn't think I could move another foot.

Someone came up alongside me. "Holy Christ!" he exclaimed. Absently I realized it was Gopher.

"Gil?" I said meekly, and pointed down to the prone figure in the street. "Is that . . . is that Gilley?"

Gopher gripped my hand tightly. "No," he said, his voice hoarse. "At least, I don't think so."

My eyes swiveled to Heath again. He and two other men had managed to yank open the door. In the distance I heard the urgent sound of a siren. It occurred to me absently that it was a different noise than the sirens back home made.

Heath disappeared inside the van, and I let out a sob. "Please . . . ," I whispered. "God, *please* let him be okay!"

"Come on," Gopher said, and he tugged me forward down the hill.

I stumbled along on stiff legs. I couldn't face it if Gilley was hurt—or worse. He'd been my best friend since I was a little kid and he was more my family than my own relatives. "There!" Gopher exclaimed, pointing ahead of us. "See?"

I blinked, but I was crying too hard to see what he was indicating. I wiped my eyes just as a police car and an ambulance whizzed past, pulling up next to the van and obscuring our view. "Did you see him?" I asked Gopher desperately.

"I think so!"

I willed my limbs to move again and loped the rest of the way down the hill, trying hard not to stare at the beaten and partially squashed figure nearby.

We reached the ambulance and just when I didn't think I could take not knowing one more second, Gilley appeared, wobbly and bruised but otherwise okay from around the side of the police car.

"*Gilley!*" I cried, and threw myself at him, hugging him fiercely and sobbing into his neck.

"Ow," he complained, and I quickly backed away.

"I'm so sorry!" I told him, running my hands gently along his cut and battered face. "I'm so sorry!"

Gilley eyed me grumpily. "What took you guys so long?"

"The door to the exit was locked," Heath said as he joined us. I noticed he was soaked through with perspiration and he looked terribly winded.

"Are you all right?" I asked Gil.

Gilley rubbed the back of his head. "I think so," he said. "Just a little banged up."

"Are you the driver responsible?" someone to my right asked. I turned and saw a wide-eyed constable asking Gilley the question.

"I wasn't driving," Gil explained.

"Had anything to drink this evening?" the constable pressed as if he hadn't heard Gil's answer.

"Constable," Gopher said to the policeman. "My associate here was merely in the van when it rolled down the street."

The constable had a small notepad and a pen out and was taking notes. One of the paramedics came over to him and whispered something, but I managed to catch the words. ". . . no signs of life and massive head trauma . . ."

The constable nodded gravely and eyed Gilley with obvious contempt. "Looks like you've just won a visit to the station."

"But I didn't do anything!" Gilley protested. "M. J.! Tell him I didn't do anything!"

I stepped in front of Gil and attempted to talk to the constable. "My friend was in the van, which was parked at the top of the hill. The van's brakes must have given out and it rolled down the hill and into that poor pedestrian. Gilley wasn't driving at the time. He didn't even have the keys."

"That's correct," Gopher said, and for emphasis he took out the van's keys from his pocket. "I had them with me the whole time."

"And where was you," the constable said to Gopher, "while this bloke was in the van?"

"Running back to the van," Gopher replied.

The constable eyed Gopher curiously. "Why was you running back to the van, then?"

"Because my associate was under attack."

"Under attack?" the constable asked.

Gilley was pumping his head up and down. "Yes!" he said in that tone that was extra high and squeaky. "The ghost of the Witch of Queen's Close was attacking the van, and I think she vandalized it enough to make it roll down the hill!"

I tried to make a subtle slicing motion across my neck. Gilley was sounding crazy to anyone but those of us aware of Rigella, and I knew he and Gopher were about to get us all into trouble.

The constable looked at Gilley with disdain. "Oh, so you've heard about our village spook, have you?" he asked, but I had the feeling it was a rhetorical question.

Still, Gil answered him. "I have, and I've seen her firsthand! She jumped me, you know. It's a miracle I'm still alive actually."

The expression on the constable's face changed, and it was clear he was completely out of patience with Gilley and he didn't for a second believe anything we'd said to him. Before we could say anything more, the constable had Gilley twisted around and was placing handcuffs on him. "I'm arresting you," he said, and motioned with his head at Gopher. "You too."

Gilley's face drained of color and he looked at me with buggy eyes. "M. J.!" he pleaded. "Do something!"

"Sir," I said, "this is all just a simple misunderstanding!"

The man finished handcuffing Gilley and regarded the body in the street. "Tell that to the man's family," he said gruffly before reaching for Gopher, who looked ready to bolt.

Heath laid a firm hand on his shoulder and said, "Easy, guy. Just go along with them for now and we'll work all this out in time."

Gopher's jaw clenched, but he turned cooperatively around so that the constable could cuff him.

Gilley, however, was still crying and staring at me with pleading eyes. "But, M. J.!" he said again. "I'm too pretty to go to jail!"

"Gil," I told him softly, "just go along for now and we'll figure this whole thing out as soon as possible, okay?"

My partner didn't have a chance to answer as he was pushed roughly toward a police vehicle and placed inside. A minute later, Gopher joined him.

It took much longer than expected to get Gil and Gopher out on the British equivalent of bond. First, we had to locate a barrister willing to help us, and that took several calls to the United States embassy as loads of red tape and diplomatic channels had to be navigated.

But eventually, after meeting with our barrister, we understood that both Gilley and Gopher were being charged with the equivalent of vehicular homicide.

We were also told that our friends would need to remain in jail for a day or two until they had an opportunity to go before the court and be let out on bond—and at that preliminary hearing, both men had to surrender their passports and were ordered not to leave the area.

This was a major setback for us, as after the incident with the van I fully realized that the only safe place for Gilley was anywhere but Scotland. The ghost of the Witch of Queen's Close and her coven were hell-bent on doing him in—of that I was certain. So when I greeted him with a warm hug the moment he emerged from the police station, looking a little thinner and depressed, I wondered if I'd be able to keep him out of harm's way long enough to figure this whole thing out.

"Get me out of here," he whispered desperately in my ear as he gripped me tightly.

I pulled away from him and stared him straight in the eye. "Soon, honey," I promised.

Gilley's head hung and a tear leaked down his cheek. "She's going to kill me, isn't she, M. J.?"

I was saved from answering when Heath came up next to us and handed Gilley a bag. "Your new sweatshirt, buddy," he said, indicating the one we'd put together after the old one had been shredded in the accident. "I'd put it on and leave it on no matter how hot you get."

Gilley ripped open the bag and immediately donned the shirt. While he was shrugging into it, Gopher came down the steps of the police station with a thick file in his hand and his cell phone to his ear. "I know it's bullshit, Mike!" he was saying, and after a pause he added, "Sure, we can beat it. No sweat. The barrister we hired is one of the best in Scotland. We'll have this whole thing cleared up in no time."

"Who's Mike?" I asked Heath.

But it was Gilley who answered. "One of the network dudes. Gopher had to call him and let him know we'd been charged and that our shooting schedule's been delayed."

"What do you mean, 'delayed'?" I asked, and then it dawned on me. "You mean to tell me Gopher still wants us to continue the ghost hunt?!"

Gilley nodded. "Yep."

I waited impatiently while Gopher wrapped up his call. "*What* are you thinking?" I shrieked the moment he clicked the End button.

"Hey, M. J.," he replied with an unfazed smile. "Yes, it is nice to breathe fresh air again after my incarceration. Thank you so much for asking about how I'm doing!"

"Cut the crap," I snapped. "How can you even *think* about having us finish this bust after what's happened? Gilley was almost killed and both of you are now facing criminal charges!"

Gopher's eyes swiveled to Heath, but if he was looking for loyalty there, he came up short. My fellow medium merely folded his arms across his chest and raised a judgmental eyebrow.

Gopher frowned. "You have to finish it," he told me bluntly. I opened my mouth to tell him where he could stuff it, but he cut me off quickly by saying, "And the reason you have to finish it, M. J., is because Gilley's freedom and possibly his very life depend on it."

I shut my mouth but continued to glare at Gopher, hoping that he'd just offer more information without my needing to ask. But he played the game well, because he waited me out and I finally grumbled, "*How* exactly do you figure *that*?"

Gopher continued down the last few steps to the sidewalk and raised his arm to hail a cab. "I figure," he said over his shoulder, "that unless you can prove that a ghost was responsible for pushing that van down the hill, we're going to spend a long time in a Scottish jail. We've *got* to get evidence on tape that not only does the spirit of Rigella actually exist, but that she's powerful enough to cause some serious damage." When I looked at him skeptically, he added, "You saw the way our own barrister responded to the idea that a ghost moved the van down the street. He laughed in our face and he's on *our* side, M. J.!"

Gopher had a point. Still, I wasn't fully convinced by his logic. "It's too dangerous," I told him just as a cab pulled to a stop in front of us.

"Yes," Gopher said, holding open the door and waving us inside. "But the alternative isn't much better."

I stewed on that the whole way back to the inn. When we got out of the taxi and headed inside to the sitting area, I made sure to put Gilley in a chair close to the fire and rub his shoulders supportively.

"Gopher's right," Heath said, taking up the seat across from us.

"I know," I groused.

"We're all doomed," Gilley moaned, burying his head in his hands.

Just then Meg came in with Wendell, and the puppy must have sensed Gilley's distress because he went right over to him and nudged his shin. Gil looked down forlornly and picked Wendell up, cradling him in his lap like a talisman.

"You guys okay?" Megan asked, noticing the glum mood.

"No," I said softly. "Not really."

"Anything I can do?"

I smiled at her. "You can watch Wendell for me for the next couple of days. I won't be around much."

"Where're you going?"

"On a bust," I said firmly, then addressed my team. "Gil, Heath, we need a plan."

Several hours later Gilley was looking a little more like his old self as he suggested for the tenth time, "Guys, I'm telling you, information is power! We've got to do some more homework on this Rigella chick and her coven."

"But what will that gain us?" I asked. My suggestion had been to skip the history lesson and go straight into the close with a truckload of magnet grenades, pound them into the walls every five feet, and hope that we got lucky and shoved one square into her portal—the gate she used to travel from the lower, nastier realms to our plane. Barring that, I knew that if we went in the close and started to agitate her by pounding in the magnets and disrupting the electromagnetic frequencies, she'd show herself by emerging from her portal and then we'd get her on film. Once we'd documented her, we could chase her back into her portal, shove a spike into the gateway, and the ghost of the Witch of Queen's Close would be locked in the lower realms forever, unable to interact with the living and cause any more havoc. "I say we attack her underground and we don't let up until we've got her cornered and on film. Then we'll shut her down for good."

"But, M. J., we don't know that her portal is even *in* the close!" Gilley said. "And we know that she's just as comfortable aboveground as below and she can attack in both places. The close appears to be only where she died—"

"Which is the most typical location for a ghost's portal," I argued, cutting him off. "And why my idea is the most sound."

But this time, Heath wasn't on my side. "I think it's too risky to assume that, M. J.," he said gently. "Gilley's right. We have to find out more about her and isolate each and every possible location for her portal. I think we then have to hit all those suspected locations at once, and hit them hard."

"That would involve more people than just you and me," I reminded him, and why I was so against the proposal, which Heath had mentioned earlier on in the discussion. "And that would also mean sending unqualified people into harm's way."

"Not necessarily," Heath said, his voice calm and reasonable. "I mean, we could give them all sweatshirts like Gilley's to protect them, and if we can pinpoint the two most likely locations and have a few others as options, then you and I can handle the hot spots and have our crew deal with the others for backup."

"I think it could work," Gil said. "In fact, I think it's our only choice, really."

"I agree," said a voice right behind me. I looked up to see Gopher coming in to join us.

"Surprise, surprise," I said woodenly, still irritated that our producer was mining our current predicament for ratings gold.

"We're in," said a female voice behind Gopher. I

craned my neck farther and saw that Kim and John had also just come into the room. "That is, if you need us," she added shyly.

"We'll need you," Heath assured her.

"If only to help get the witch on film," Gopher said. We all looked at him and he added, "The union rep called. A complaint's been filed. We'll have to do our own camera work for the rest of the shoot."

"Okay," Gil said, and for the first time in several days I saw his face take on a slightly hopeful cast. "We do our homework, find out everything we can about the witch and her coven, and shut the spooky bitches down."

That night I moved into a new room with Gilley. I was still worried about the ferocity of the witch and wanted to be close enough to protect him should she rear her ugly face again.

For all the trouble he'd been through recently, he had a much easier time of getting to sleep than I did. At least the sound of his soft snores brought me a little comfort. I tossed and turned and slept restlessly throughout most of the night, until about three a.m., when I finally fell into a nice deep slumber.

I don't think it was much after that when my dreams turned disturbing. A woman with sharp features and jet-black eyes interrupted the cozy chat I'd been having with my high school English teacher. With a firm clasp on my wrist the stranger yanked me out of class and pulled me into a long, dark cave. "He's marked," she told me, her voice cutting into my dream like an icy dagger.

I knew exactly whom she meant, and I knew exactly who she was. "You keep away from him!" I shouted at her, feeling a small surge of energy trickle through me as I stood up to her.

"He's one of them," she replied. "Therefore, he's cursed."

I could feel my hands ball into fists. "He's done nothing to you!" I shouted. "Nothing! What happened to you and your family took place hundreds of years ago with people long since dead! Leave their descendants in peace."

"I cannot," she said simply. "It would defy the curse."

I could feel myself growing frustrated, but I worked to lower my voice, thinking maybe I could reason with her. "But why?" I asked her. "What will you gain? The people from the village who came after you were panicked by their fear of the plague and their own superstitions. If they had been in their right minds, I'm sure they never would have caused you or your family harm."

The witch spat derisively on the floor. "Bah!" she snapped. "You know nothing! This is what they did to my family!" And with a wave of her hand the darkness of the cave behind her became illuminated by a soft glow punctuated by the flicker of torchlight as shadows bounced and undulated along the walls. I could hear something of a roar in the distance. Angry shouts echoed incoherently all the way down to where I stood with the witch. From around a corner dashed a group of five women. I squinted and saw that they struggled to carry a beaten and bloodied female whose limp body hung between them. As they dashed forward toward us, I gasped when I saw that one of the people struggling with the weight of their burden was the very image of the woman standing next to me.

Another girl—clearly related to the witch—shouted, "She's dead, Rigella! Our sister is dead!"

Rigella stopped abruptly, panting heavily under the labor of carrying her broken sister. Steeling a look behind her at the bouncing shadows, she gave one curt nod and lowered the body gently to the floor. She stroked her cheek, while her sisters all cried, then kissed her lightly on the forehead and stood. She then grabbed the hands of two of her other sisters. "Quickly!" she said. "To the back of the close!"

One of the women—more of a girl really—stopped next to the body and refused to move. "That's where they send the sick ones!" she protested. "Rigella, we can't go in there!"

"We've no choice, Sabina! We've already lost Daire! My love's been driven to his grave not half a mile from here! And now our sister Vacia, beaten to death by that murderous crowd! We've got to hide and the back of the close is our only hope! Now no more arguin'! Follow me and not another word out of you!" With that, Rigella dashed forward again and the other women followed—except Sabina, who continued to stand undecided by the body of her sister. She gave one last forlorn look to her fleeing family and squatted down and lifted Vacia's head into her lap, stroked back the tangle of hair from the bloodied face, and began singing a soft lullaby.

My heart felt panged because it was obvious that Rigella thought Sabina was still with her as she and the others raced by where we stood to disappear down the close. And all too soon the angry mob chasing the witch and her family came upon Sabina and the body of Vacia.

Sabina did nothing more than hug her sister when

the mob reached her, and they quickly surrounded her, blocking our view. What happened in the next instant was hard to see, but I could hear angry words and then a bloodcurdling scream. The mob backed away quickly, and to my horror I could see as they stepped aside that they'd set Sabina on fire!

I turned away, sickened by the scene, and shouted, "Stop!" to the cold stony face of Rigella in front of me. "I'm so sorry for your loss, Rigella, but please don't make me see any more of this!"

Her lip curled up distastefully and I knew I hadn't endeared myself one iota to her. "Gillespie was the man who set the torch to my sister," she said as the images behind her faded back to black. "And he and all his descendants will pay!"

"No!" I told her firmly. "You leave Gilley alone! I mean it, witch, because if you dare to hurt one hair on his head, know that I will stop at nothing to hunt you down and destroy you!"

Rigella smiled wickedly at me. "Oh, you may try," she said derisively. "But while you labor to find out where I am, I can accomplish my task by doing this." Rigella calmly held up her right hand and snapped her fingers.

It was odd, because the sound her fingers made wasn't the small snap I expected. Instead I heard a noise like an electric current being sparked—and it was loud. Loud enough to wake me.

I sat bolt upright in bed, my pajamas soaked with sweat, and shouted, "Gilley!"

He came instantly awake. "What?!"

My heart was pounding and I threw off the comforter, fumbling in the dark for my slippers. "Whatever you do, don't turn on the li—" and that was as far as I got before Gil snapped on the bedside lamp.

There was a loud ZZZZZT! and a blue flame surged from the cord connected to the light all the way down to the outlet. Immediately after that, a small explosion of electric current, sparks, smoke, and heat shot out of the wall.

Gilley screamed and flew out of bed as the area behind his headboard erupted in flame. "*Fire!*" he screeched, and I reached for his hand and pulled him toward the door.

"Get out of here!" I shouted, opening the door and throwing him out into the hallway. "Warn the others!" I commanded, then ran back inside, picked up my pillow, and began smacking it against the flames.

I pounded in earnest against the wall, but my pillow quickly caught fire and the smoke became intense. Out in the hallway an alarm sounded that was high-pitched and painful to the ears. I ducked low and coughed some more, thinking now was a really good time to leave. I put my shirt up to my mouth, closed my eyes, stuck my hand out, and felt for the door.

But I couldn't find it. I was completely blinded by the smoke stinging my eyes. I kept hitting hangers, and luggage. I knew that the exit was close by, but the more I turned this way or that, the more disoriented I became.

I tried not to panic, but the heat was growing intense. Where was the door? Was it to my right or behind me? I coughed again, and again, as the fumes filled my lungs and my eyes were stinging so much that I could no longer keep them open even a slit. I wanted to scream for help, but I could only cough, and I sank to my knees thinking that maybe I could crawl out of the room. I made it about three feet before the intensity of the smoke and heat wouldn't allow me to move another inch. *Ohmigod!* I thought. *I'm going to die here!*

*No, you're not,* a voice inside my mind said, and I immediately thought of Samuel Whitefeather. *I've brought you some help.*

That's when I felt a strong arm snake around my middle and lift me off the ground. I was barely aware that I was moving, and it wasn't long before the thick black smoke seemed to wane down to a gray misty haze and as I fought for breath, it became just a bit easier.

There were other people brushing against me and my rescuer, everyone moving urgently in the same direction, while the sound of the alarm continued to drown out all other noise. And then the warmth of our surroundings vanished and I was hit hard by a cold breeze.

"Bring her over here!" someone shouted above the noise of people and sirens and alarms. "Heath! Over here!"

In the back of my mind I now knew that it was Heath who had rescued me, and that made sense in a way, but I was really too busy trying to suck in air without coughing it back out again to focus.

Before long I realized I was on the ground and someone was throwing a blanket over my shoulders while I shivered. I wiped my eyes and was able to open them a crack, but they still leaked tears and stung fiercely. "How are you?" Heath's gentle voice asked.

I coughed twice more before answering, "I think I'm okay," I told him. "How are you?"

Through my watery eyes I could see Heath smile. "I'm fine," he said. "I always could hold my breath longer than any of my friends."

"Jesus, M. J.!" Gilley squealed. "What the hell were you thinking?"

"Is everyone all right?" I heard Gopher ask. I didn't even try to open my eyes again. I just let the tears do their work and wash out all the soot.

"I'm fine," I said, my voice a little ragged.

"Our lamp exploded!" Gilley exclaimed. "And M. J. shoved me out of the room first, and I ran down the hallway to the alarm thinking that she's right behind me but she's not! She stayed in there to fight the stupid fire!"

"Seemed like a good idea at the time," I said, trying to make light of it.

"This is not funny!" he yelled at me. "You could have died in there and then where would I be?" His voice cracked as he said that last bit and he started to cry.

That tugged at my heart a little. I'd known Gilley so long that I could barely remember a time when he hadn't been my best friend. I knew from a few nights ago what it felt like to fear for the life of the other. "Aw, Gil," I said, wiping my eyes and trying to peer out at him. "Don't be like that."

Firefighters and rescue workers appeared on scene and we were told we had to move farther away from the building. I realized why when I caught a glimpse of the inn. The entire second story was now completely engulfed in flames. I got to my feet and my knees buckled. Heath caught me again and pulled me close to him for support. Even though most of my senses were fuzzy, I was aware that he was quite warm and it felt good to have him next to me. "Did everyone make it out okay?" I asked, suddenly feeling hot and a little bothered.

Gopher answered. "All our crew made it," he said. "But I'm not sure about the other guests. They'll do a head count here in a little while, I think."

I nodded, then gasped. "Wendell?"

"He's here," Meg said, and she placed the puppy in my arms. "We heard the alarm and got out right away."

I hugged the little guy and smiled when he licked my face, which had to be covered in ash. "She all right?" someone with a brogue asked our group. Belatedly I realized he was talking about me.

"Fine," I said, but at that moment I had another coughing fit.

"Why don't you come with me," the paramedic said gently. "I've got some oxygen to help you breathe right over here." I tried to refuse, but Heath was still holding me by the waist, and he rather unceremoniously picked me up again and trailed behind the paramedic to a white ambulance, where I was covered in yet more blankets before my vitals were taken and an oxygen mask was secured to my face.

I tried to take deep calming breaths, but my lungs burned and my head started to ache. I closed my eyes and leaned against the side of the cab, barely aware of the conversations around me.

Still, I managed to catch the gist of what was being said. "The lamp just exploded!" Gilley repeated. "If M. J. hadn't shoved me out of the room, I'd have been toast!"

"It's an old inn," Gopher was saying. "They're bound to have electrical issues now and again. Still, I'm surprised that turning on a light caused *that*!"

At this point I pulled down the mask and said, "It was Rigella."

Heath laid a hand on my knee. "The witch?" he asked.

I felt a little tickle in my lower plexus and squinted down at his strong hand resting right on my kneecap. *Uh-oh,* I thought. "Yes," I said after taking a few more deep pulls from the oxygen mask. "While I was sleeping, she showed up in my dream and pulled me into another OBE. One of her sisters was literally torched by one of Gilley's ancestors. Which is why she's targeting him specifically."

There was a squeaking sound that I recognized came from Gil. "She tried to set me on fire?!" he shouted. "Ohmigod!"

"Yes, but she didn't succeed," I reminded him. "And she won't."

"How do you know that?" he demanded, his eyes close to panic.

I took another deep inhalation before answering. "Because she'll have to come through me."

"And me," said Heath.

"Yep, me too," Gopher added.

"All of us," said Kim, and I could see she was also speaking for John and Meg, who were both nodding.

"We'll keep you safe," I tried to reassure him while keeping the thought *Or die trying* to myself.

# Chapter 7

I spent much of that early morning hooked up to an oxygen tank and refusing to go to the hospital. I really wasn't being stubborn as much as I knew intuitively that I'd be okay, but I also knew that I had to take it easy until my lungs had a little time to rest and recover.

Gopher quickly found us another place to stay—choosing a much less quaint but far more fireproof chain hotel in town, and Meg got right on the job of getting all of us some new warm clothes, as most of our stuff had been either scorched or waterlogged in the fire.

John had been quick-thinking enough to save all the camera equipment at the inn, while Gilley's laptop and monitors and all our ghostbusting gadgetry that had survived the van crash had been confiscated by the police as evidence—so that at least was safe, but inaccessible.

While everyone else was tending to the supplies and equipment, I had a chance to get some sleep, but I agreed to that only after Heath promised to keep a close eye on Gilley.

Around one o'clock in the afternoon I woke up from my nap and took a long, luxurious shower. While I was drying my hair, a knock sounded on the door and I opened it to find Meg and Wendell. "We were worried," she said when I invited her in and helped her with the several additional bags of clothing and toiletries she'd brought me.

"I'm fine," I assured her with a smile before bending down to pick up my wriggling puppy. "How's he doing?"

"He's great. We were on the first floor right next to the exit when the fire alarm sounded. I think we were the first two out of the building, in fact."

I nuzzled Wendell's soft fur and sighed contentedly. It had been a last-minute decision to have Meg puppysit Wendell the previous night, and now I knew that was a good decision.

"What's everyone up to?" I asked, handing Wendell back over to her while I carried on with drying my hair.

Meg raised her voice to answer me over the sound of the dryer. "Gilley and Heath headed into Edinburgh to work on getting us resupplied with monitors, two new laptops, and night-vision cameras, while Gopher's been working the phone to get us more money."

I clicked off the dryer. "More money?"

Meg nodded. "We've already blown through our budget on this shoot, so Gopher has to convince the network that we're worth a little more investment."

"Do you think he can get it?"

Meg smiled. "I do," she said. "I heard him on the phone with one of the executive producers, and it really sounded like he was having some success. Especially when Gopher brought him up to speed on the fire."

"You'd think that those guys would consider this whole thing a little too dangerous and pull the plug."

Meg laughed like I'd made a joke. "Are you kidding?" she asked. "With all this built-in drama, M. J., we're ratings gold!"

I clicked off the dryer and shook my head ruefully. I'd never understand the Hollywood mind-set.

Once I'd finished putting myself together, Meg, Wendell, and I headed to the elevators in search of the rest of our team. On the way down, Meg reached into her pocket and pulled out a brand-new iPhone for me. "It's already programmed with everyone else's number," she assured me. "I didn't have a list of your other contacts, but at least you can reach any one of us."

As she said that, I felt a small jolt of alarm. My cell phone had burned up in the fire, and it had all my contact names and addresses—including Steven's. I realized suddenly that I had no idea what my boyfriend's number was. I'd plugged it into my old phone months ago, and I'd never had to look at it again. "Oh, crap," I said.

"What?"

"Nothing," I said quickly, not wanting her to think I didn't appreciate all the new stuff. "I just realized that I don't know any of my contacts' information."

"Do you have a backup on a computer somewhere?"

I brightened. "Yes!" I said. "Back at my office in Boston . . ." and then my shoulders slumped again. It would be weeks before I could get back home to reinstall the names and addresses.

The doors opened then and we stepped out into the lobby. "Gopher said that he was going to have a meeting with everyone at three thirty," she said.

"Where?"

Meg pointed to the hotel pub next to the front desk. "There."

We were a few minutes early but found Gilley and Heath already seated at the bar.

When I sat down next to Gil, my foot hit something that made a hollow sound. "What *is* that?" I asked, looking down.

"Fire extinguisher," Heath said, and I could tell that he was working hard to hide a smile, while Gil was looking at me as if he double-dog-dared me to say something snarky.

I knew he'd been through an awful lot in the past couple of days, so I went easy on him. "I think it's a great idea."

Gilley's eyes widened in surprise. "You do?"

I ordered a bottled beer from the bartender, then said, "Yep. Rigella is hell-bent on carrying out her threat. And she'll work pretty hard to see it through, so having that handy might be a real lifesaver. I also think that when you're in our room, you should avoid flipping any switches or using anything electrical. No TV or turning on the lights, okay?"

Heath ducked his chin again and said, "Look in his vest pocket."

It was then that I noticed Gilley was wearing one of those sports vests with lots of pockets. Many of them looked quite bulky. "Whatcha got there, partner?" I asked.

Gil was only too happy to show me and he enthusiastically began to pull out several small flashlights, some additional magnets, two electrostatic meters, and a squirt bottle filled with a clear liquid.

"What's in the squirt bottle?"

"Fire retardant," he said.

"Ahh," I said, choosing to take a long swig of beer before I too had to duck my chin to hide a smile.

John and Kim joined us shortly thereafter and Gopher came in about ten minutes later. "Hey," he said with a rather smug smile.

"Good news?" I asked.

Gopher nodded. "We're getting moved up to a better time slot. The network is busting at the seams to get this out on prime time!"

"So they're going to up our budget?" Heath said, but it came out less of a question and more of a statement.

"Yes!" Gopher beamed, and motioned to the bartender. We waited while he ordered a glass of the bar's best scotch, then filled us in on the details. "They loved the footage the camera crew took back."

"What footage?" I asked.

"Cameraman and Sound Guy sent in all the footage they took the night of the accident," Gilley said drolly.

I blinked hard. "Wait a second," I said, forming a time-out gesture with my hands. "When did they send in this footage and where are they?"

"They flew back to the States that same night," Gopher said. He'd obviously told this part to Gil earlier. "I haven't seen the tape yet, but I guess they captured more stuff than we thought and they also got some footage of the van being attacked."

My jaw fell open. "They got footage of the van being attacked?"

"That's what I hear," Gopher said, knocking back the rest of his scotch and ordering another by tapping the empty glass with his finger. "Can you imagine the ratings once *that* airs?"

I looked at Heath to see if I was the only one getting this, and luckily, he seemed to be right there with me. "Gopher," he said with a hint of impatience. "Why the hell haven't you asked for the footage? If it does show the van being attacked, then it might also be enough for the charges against you and Gilley to be dropped!"

Gopher's hand that held his new drink paused midway to his mouth and he smiled at Heath. "I'm all over it, buddy. I'm just waiting on the film tech to come in for his shift, download a digital copy to a secure server, and send it to me. Don't want that footage to end up on YouTube early and spoil our first episode."

"We need to see that tape," I said firmly. "How long before the tech comes into the office?"

Gopher glanced at his watch. "Any minute now," he said, upending the glass before banging it loudly on the bar and heading quickly away.

"How are we on replacing the ghostbusting equipment?" I asked Gil after Gopher had gone.

"We're good," he assured me. "Except I could only get two of these," and he held up one of the meters.

"Oh, crap, Gil. We're definitely going to need more than two. Can we recover any from the close?"

Gilley took another sip of his appletini. "If you're brave enough to go down there and retrieve them, then yeah. Probably."

Heath eyed me nervously. "You really think we'll need them?"

"I do. And I think that we need to do a little more exploring of the close itself. We've got to try and identify where the witch's portal is. She keeps pulling me there and I think I might recognize the section where she and her sisters died."

"Portals are usually close to the point of death," Gilley said. "It's worth a try at least."

"When did you want to go down?"

I glanced at my watch; it was four fifteen. "No time like the present," I said, though there was little enthusiasm for the task at hand.

But Gilley was shaking his head. "No way," he said. "We're not ready, M. J. I haven't had a chance to set up the new equipment and I can't track you guys until that's in place. There's no way I'm letting you go down there without some backup."

I sighed and leaned back against the bar. "How long will it take you to set everything up?"

Gilley pulled out a pen and began scribbling a short priority list on a cocktail napkin. Next to each task he assigned a time. "At least five hours," he said once he'd tallied the list.

I glanced at my watch again. "Do we really want to head back down there at night?" I asked Heath.

"I don't know that it would make much of a difference. The close is dark and damp, making conditions perfect for the spooks to come and go as they please. Time of day is pretty immaterial down there."

He had a point. "You're right. Okay, Gil. You've got five hours to get your equipment up and running." Turning to John and Kim, I said, "Can you guys stick close to Gil? He'll be working with stuff that requires electricity and I worry about any power surges."

John picked up a shopping bag that he carried and

pulled out several brand-new surge protectors. "We've got his back, M. J."

"Meg, can you watch Wendell again?"

She smiled and I could tell she was relieved to have such a safe assignment. "Absolutely."

"Great, thank you." I then turned to Heath and shrugged my shoulders. "Guess that means you and I don't have much to do until around nine tonight, guy."

Heath stared thoughtfully down at his beer while his fingers gently tugged the label away from the bottle. "Actually," he said softly, "I was hoping that you might grant me an indulgence."

I arched an eyebrow and my mind immediately went to more carnal thoughts. "Um . . . ," I gulped. "Indulgence?"

Gilley stared at me and arched his own eyebrow. He knew me too well.

"Yes," Heath said, his eyes lifting to mine. I suddenly found myself unable to look away. "If you're up for it, I'd like you to give me a reading."

I didn't answer him immediately, and when Gilley nudged me with his elbow and whispered, "Exhale, honey," I was able to collect myself and reply.

"A reading?"

I don't think Heath noticed what must have been my very flushed appearance, because he merely nodded and said, "My grandfather keeps coming to you, not me. I think that's significant. I think he may have a stronger link to you right now, and I was hoping you could connect with him while you were awake by doing a reading for me. Hopefully we can get some direct answers from him that way. He's obviously trying to help us. Maybe we can use him to help us locate the witch's portal."

My eyes widened. "Heath!" I exclaimed. "That's a friggin' *brilliant* idea!"

He looked relieved and gave me a warm smile. "I thought of it this morning, and wasn't going to ask because I know how tired you must be after all you went through last night."

"No," I said quickly to reassure him. "I'll be just fine. Come on, let's find a quiet corner and see if I can connect with him."

As it happened, there were no quiet corners in the bar, or in the lobby for that matter, and it was Heath who finally suggested that we try one of our rooms to hold the session.

I immediately broke out into a nervous sweat, cursing this very sudden and unwanted attraction that I was feeling for Heath.

This time he seemed to notice because he looked at me and asked, "You feeling okay?"

"Sure!" I said, my voice a little too high and squeaky to be believed. I cleared my throat and tried again. "I'm fine," I insisted. When he still looked at me doubtfully, I added an extra, "Really."

He let it go and we headed to my room, which I remembered had a nice large table and two chairs by the window that would be perfect for us. Five minutes later I was seated across from Heath, attempting to center and focus my energy.

I could feel an internal switch flick on, and my already-congested lungs felt a little more clogged. I also swore I could smell the scent of cigarettes. "The first energy I'm picking up on is an older male," I said, sensing the "heavier" energy that is so typically male. "He's hovering right above your head—on the same level as your father," I said slowly, but I knew that this man who was displaying himself to me was not Heath's actual father. "He's showing me the initial G," I added. "And he's telling me he's your uncle, but not your uncle."

Heath laughed. "That's Uncle Gus," he said, the obvious affection he held for this man displayed in his wide smile. "He was my mom's best friend on the reservation. They even dated in high school, but found that they were better off as friends."

"He smoked, right?"

Heath's expression turned sober. "Like a chimney. He died of lung cancer about three years ago."

"He went very quickly, too," I said, delighted to be receiving such strong information from Gus. "He keeps showing me a valentine, so I'm guessing he crossed over close to February fourteenth, right?"

Heath's smile returned. "You're really good, M. J.," he said, and I felt the heat flush my cheeks again. "Gus was diagnosed on the first of February, caught pneumonia a week later, and his lungs were already so weak that he died on the fifteenth."

"He's showing me a Scrabble board," I said next.

Heath laughed again. "He was the county Scrabble champion three years running."

I nodded while I sorted through the feelings and images that Gus was sending me. But in the back of my mind I remembered that although it was nice to be able to pull such a warm and engaging energy like Gus's into the reading, it was not the point of this exercise. So I gently asked Gus if I could communicate with Heath's grandfather Samuel, and he graciously moved aside and allowed another spirit to come through. "I've got Sam," I said softly, closing my eyes to concentrate. I could feel his familiar energy, but it wasn't like my experience in the dream where his actual persona had stepped forward. His interaction with me now was typical for my sessions; I could feel his essence and his personality, but I had no real image of him. Still, he was familiar enough to me to be able to identify him as Heath's grandfather. "He's happy we're doing this," I said.

"Can you ask him about Rigella?"

"He says we need to be really cautious with her."

I heard Heath chuckle. "Can he tell us something we don't know?"

I opened one eye to squint at him. *"Right?"* But Sam was in my head, calling me back to focus on his message. "He says we need to get serious," I muttered.

Heath sighed. "Okay," he said. "I'm serious. Ask him how we deal with her."

I sorted through the sensations, thoughts, and impressions Sam was giving me for a minute before I spoke again. "He says we're focused on the wrong thing. He says that we need to look in another direction."

"Is he talking about her portal?"

I asked Sam that and felt a mental nod in my head. "Yeah," I said. "He doesn't want us down in the close again until we investigate something else. He says it's too dangerous and that it's a dead end anyway."

"Is he being punny?" Heath asked, and for a minute I didn't get it and then I laughed.

"Oh, dead end, yeah, I don't think he was intentionally being funny. He's telling me that he's pretty sure Rigella's portal isn't down there and that's not what we need to focus on anyway. . . ." My voice trailed off as I worked out what he meant.

In the silence that followed, Heath asked, "What?"

"He says the bigger issue we need to figure out is why the spirit of the witch is here so early."

I opened my eyes and looked at Heath, who seemed to register that as quickly as I did. "Bonnie said Rigella showed up every one hundred years like clockwork."

"But this time she's thirty-five years early," I added.

"Which means there's a reason," Heath said, his eyebrows furrowing. "So what's different about her appearance now?"

And I knew the answer almost immediately and it sent an icy chill up my spine. "Gilley's here," I whispered.

Heath stared at me for a long minute before he spoke again. "How did the witch know that Gilley would be in Scotland, M. J.?"

Sam spoke actual words then, loud and clear in my head. *She was called forward,* he said. *Coaxed out of her portal by someone who wanted to use her.*

I looked at Heath in shock. "Someone living must have pulled her out of her portal, Heath." The moment I said that, I felt Sam's spirit nod vigorously.

"Who would *do* that?" he gasped.

I rubbed my temples. "Someone powerful," I replied. "Someone dangerous. And someone with a grudge."

"A grudge against Gilley?" Heath pressed. "He wouldn't hurt a fly! Who would want to harm him?"

"I don't know," I said honestly. "But your grandfather is insisting that we find out."

"And then what?"

"Then we focus back on finding her portal, I guess."

"Does my grandfather know where it is?"

I asked Sam that question, but his energy was already fading, which is the one big bummer about connecting with the dead—they can't sustain the contact for long before all their energy is drained. "He's pulling back," I told Heath, "but I think he'll come around again to help us tackle that bridge when we cross it." And then I felt the energy sever completely and I was alone again in the room with Heath.

"I think I might know where we should start," Heath said.

"Where?"

"We need to go back to the Crystal Emporium and ask Bonnie about anyone local who might be powerful enough to call up the witch."

I pointed a finger at him. "Good thinking. She seemed to know a lot about the legend."

Heath cocked his head slightly as if he was listening to something very faint. "And I also think we should check out the footage from Cameraman."

"Why?"

Heath shrugged. "Just a feeling," he said. "My gut says we need to view it."

We left the room and went in search of Gopher. While we were walking, Heath sent him a text and Gopher replied that he was just finishing downloading the footage to his computer. He suggested that we meet in his room to view it together.

Gopher's suite was on the second floor—one level down from Gilley's and mine—and Heath and I arrived just a minute or two later to find his door partly ajar. "Come on in, guys," he called when we knocked.

We entered and found him hovering over his computer, set on a table identical to the one in my room. Heath indicated that I should take the only other available chair, and I sat down next to Gopher, leaning my body to one side to make sure Heath could see over my shoulder. "I haven't looked at this yet," Gopher said, his fingers moving over the mousepad to the folder where he'd stored the footage. "And play," he said, tapping the Enter key.

I squinted at the small rectangle on the screen as it came to life, and at first I didn't know what I was seeing, but then the focus was adjusted and I could see that Cameraman was following right along behind Heath and me as we traversed into the close before all the rocks started flying.

The footage was nearly a replica of what I'd witnessed down in the caves, but I could see where Heath's posture had suddenly shifted, and knew that was roughly the moment we began to hear the knocks.

The rest of the scenes down in the close were again very similar to what I remembered right up until small rocks and stones began to pelt the walls as the wave came toward us. The camera moved to capture Sound Guy's terrified face before he ran to the nearest exit and threw aside his fluffy microphone and boom.

The ensuing footage was a little nauseating for me to watch because Cameraman was also running and the scene jostled and bounced along to the top of the stairs. There was no sound on the footage, but you could tell the men were still running scared as they reached the street and continued fleeing away.

At one point they came to a stop, and the camera swiveled side to side. I imagined the pair were trying to decide which way to go. Sound Guy pointed toward an alley and then the footage was in motion again showing the crew running down a side street that I thought might have been parallel to the van.

It turned out I was right, because at the end of the alley both men stopped again and tried to determine where to go next, finally choosing to head up the street they were on, which would have put them very close to where the van was parked.

My sense of direction was right on target, because a moment later the unmistakable image of our rented vehicle came into view. "The van!" I gasped, pointing to the screen. Gopher nodded, but stopped when he saw the camera capture his own mad dash out of the van to race up the street. I knew that was the moment Gopher decided to leave Gil and come to our rescue.

Sure enough, as he bolted out of sight, the crew must have determined that they should get to the van, because they began to head straight for it. But as they drew near, a shadowy, smoky figure appeared. Clearly a spook. It hovered above the ground, and it approached the van menacingly, like a predator stalking its prey. Something else flickered just off to the side, but I was too caught up by the image of the ghost making its way to the van to pay it much attention.

As it got very close, the camera dipped, and nothing but the cobbled pavement was visible. I waited tensely with my heart pounding, hoping the camera would swing back up to the van again.

I got my wish just a moment later when the van came back into view, and what I saw caused me to cover my mouth in horror. The black smoky shadow appeared to be struggling with Gilley next to the open door of the van. My partner was flailing his arms and legs and obviously screaming his head off, but he managed to squirm his way back into the van, where he slammed the door, shutting out the ghost.

The spook appeared angry and it zipped all about

the van looking for a way in. When it found no weak
spot, it began to slam into the van. We could tell that
the ghost was making an impact, because the vehicle
visibly shook every time it was hit.

It was awful to watch, because I could remember
the sound of Gilley screaming for help in my ear, and
I could only imagine how terrified he must have been.

I also realized that Cameraman and Sound Guy
appeared to be rooted to the spot, watching it all un-
fold, because the view through the lens was still and
focused correctly. I also knew that what they were seeing must have scared the crap out of them.

In the next set of frames Cameraman zoomed in on
the eerie shadow still zipping all about the van, slamming into it. It was the ghost of Rigella—of that I was
certain—and horrified as I was by what she'd done
to Gilley, I was also fascinated by her strength and
ferocity.

Her ghost had no real shape to it, just a large black
glob of smoke darting all over the van. It was obvious
that she had significant power, because the van was
now rocking slightly from side to side and then the
passenger-side window shattered and glass splayed
out in a thousand directions.

"Whoa!" I heard Heath whisper.

"Holy shit!" Gopher remarked.

"Good God!" I added, and then the three of us collectively sucked in a breath when the van began to
roll down the hill and out of view. Cameraman dashed
forward to the corner and pointed the lens at the van,
which hit something in the street, causing it to bounce,
veer sharply left, then tumble end over end out of
view again.

For the longest, most horrific minute the camera

simply continued to record the image of the street, and I could clearly see now that there was a body lying smack-dab in the middle of the path that the van had taken . . . and something else glistened under the lamplights as well.

"Hold on," I whispered as the camera swiveled back up to where the van had originally been parked, then down to where it had disappeared, and then was abruptly shut off. "Go back a little, Gopher," I said, moving my chair closer to the screen.

Gopher rewound the tape about ten seconds and I pointed at the screen. "There!" I shouted.

"Where?" Gopher and Heath said together.

"See that?" I asked, moving my finger along the monitor.

Gopher squinted. "What am I looking at?"

"That puddle there," I said. "That's where the van was parked, right?"

"I think so," Gopher said. Then he slowly wound the tape forward frame by frame. "Yes," he said. "I remember I parked under that streetlamp to give Gil as much light as possible."

"What does *that* look like?" I asked.

"A puddle," Heath replied.

I nodded. "But look at the rest of the street, guys. There aren't any other puddles around. Remember? It hadn't rained all day."

"What's your point?"

"Where'd that puddle come from?" When both men looked at me with confused expressions, I said, "The van!"

"Condensation?" Heath offered. I knew he wasn't catching on to what I was getting at.

"Brake fluid," I said. "I bet it was brake fluid."

I saw Gopher's eyebrows shoot up high on his forehead. "You think the van's brake lines were cut by the witch's ghost?"

I shook my head slowly and looked meaningfully at Heath. "No, I think they were cut by the person who called the witch up thirty-five years early."

Gopher sat back in his chair and looked at me as if he was missing something. "Thirty-five years early?" he said. "What're you talking about?"

Heath explained to Gopher how the woman who owned the Crystal Emporium had told us that the spirit of the witch arose every one hundred years, but this time around she was three-and-a-half decades early.

"Maybe the witch got her dates wrong," Gopher said reasonably. "You know how these ghosts can get confused. Maybe she thinks she's right on time."

But I was shaking my head. Intuitively, I *knew* I was right. "Roll the tape back again," I suggested. "Right to the point where the spook first appeared."

Gopher rewound the footage and sure enough, in slow motion we could clearly see the witch's shadowy image arrive as a big black blob, but that flicker of something I'd seen for only a second was also apparent. Something just out of view edged toward the van from the rear, then slipped down near the ground. It then bobbed back up, then down, then up again, until it disappeared altogether near the front of the van.

"What *is* that?" Heath said.

I got up from my chair and moved to the narrow strip of carpet between the beds and the dresser. I squatted down into a crouch and duckwalked forward a few steps—like someone trying to keep out of view of a window.

Both men stared at me in stunned silence. Gopher was the first to speak. "I need to take this footage over to the police station pronto, and I need to insist that their crime lab check the brake lines."

I stood and pointed at Heath. "And you and I need to go ask Bonnie if she knows of anyone who might have wanted to call up the witch."

# Chapter 8

We found yet another shocking surprise when we arrived at the Crystal Emporium. The store was closed. A sign was posted on the door that read CLOSED DUE TO A DEATH IN THE FAMILY.

"Uh-oh," I said to Heath. "That can't be good."

"I wonder if Rigella's already struck down someone in Bonnie's family."

"Let's hope not," I said, but I had a sinking feeling all the same.

The sign did not suggest when the store might reopen, but as we walked away, a woman standing in the doorway of the shop next door said, "It's a cryin' shame, isn't it?"

I stopped. "Who died?"

The woman shook her head sadly. "Bonnie's brother, Cameron," she said. "He was run down just the other night comin' home from the pub. Was crossin' the street, mindin' his own business, when out of nowhere a van just ran over him, the poor soul!"

I felt the blood rush out of my face. "Oh, no," I whispered, turning to Heath and grabbing the sleeve of his coat to steady myself. Our van had killed Bonnie's brother!

"Do you know when the funeral services will be?" he asked the woman carefully. "We've met Bonnie and liked her very much. We'd like to pay our respects to her if we could."

"Why, they're goin' on today, lad," she said to him. "In an hour or so. I was just about to find my way there, in fact. Would you like to join me?"

"We would," I said, working to get control over my shock. "But we'll need to pick up some flowers."

The woman smiled and crooked her finger at us. "Then come inside," she suggested. "You can be my final sale of the day."

Belatedly I realized the shop she was standing in front of was a florist's.

Heath followed behind the woman from the flower shop; her name was Mary McCartney and she arranged a beautiful bouquet for us to give to Bonnie and her family.

When we arrived at the church, there was already a throng of people there, and Heath and I held back a little, as we were clearly not dressed for the occasion. But I still felt attending was the right thing to do.

We placed our flowers near all the others and I looked around for Bonnie. I caught sight of her in a section of the church right near the casket, seated next to a younger woman in her early twenties who was obviously pregnant. I assumed that must be either Bonnie's sister or Cameron's wife, and either way it enhanced the tragedy of Cameron's loss, especially since both women looked so stricken. Another wave of guilt washed over me. "I feel like it's my fault," I whispered to Heath when we took our seats near the back of the church.

"How could it be?" he asked. "Did *you* call up the witch? Did *you* cut the brake lines to the van?"

I looked up at him and our eyes met and I felt another tickle of attraction, which only added to my guilt. I had a boyfriend, after all. And Heath was several years my junior. What the heck was wrong with me lately? I averted my eyes and stared down at my hands. "I was the one who made the decision to come to Edinburgh," I admitted. "Gopher was really okay with our first pick, but when I saw Wendell being abused by that bastard ghost-tour guide, I couldn't stay away."

And just as I said that, I felt the hair on the back of my neck stand on end. Someone was watching me. I glanced up again and discreetly looked about. It was a total shock to see the very man I'd just been talking about staring pointedly at Heath and me.

"Speak of the devil," Heath said, and I saw he'd also caught sight of Fergus Ericson.

"What is that awful man doing here?"

"It seems to be a fairly tight-knit community," Heath observed, his eyes straying around the room at the people moving about to comfort Bonnie and the woman beside her. "I guess even jackasses can do the right thing now and again."

I sighed and went back to staring at my hands. This whole trip sucked and at the moment I didn't care if we'd soon be ratings gold—I just wanted to take Gilley home where I could keep him safe. "Maybe Gopher will have some luck at the police station and they'll look at that footage and then discover that the brake lines really were cut and drop the charges."

Heath grimaced. "The brake lines being cut might be a little hard to prove," he cautioned.

"Why?"

"Remember what the van looked like once it had finished rolling down that hill? It was knocked up pretty bad, M. J. I bet they'll theorize that the lines were severed during the crash."

That had me worried. I couldn't even entertain the thought of Gilley spending time in a foreign jail. My best friend was like a pampered Pomeranian. He tended to yap loudly when he wasn't getting enough attention, and I doubted the thugs in prison would put up with that for long. I knew he'd never survive the experience.

I sighed in frustration and thought about how I could best help him, but nothing came to mind. I was going to have to hope that Gopher could show the police the video and they'd see enough freaky stuff to be convinced that not only were Gilley and Gopher not responsible, but that at least Gil had actually been a victim right along with Cameron.

Beside me Heath's posture stiffened and I glanced his way. "What's the matter?"

"He's here," he whispered.

"Who's here?"

"The guest of honor," Heath whispered. "Cameron."

"Bonnie's dead brother is *here*?!" I exclaimed a little too loudly. Several heads swiveled round to stare at me with reproachful glares.

"We're at a funeral," an old man snapped. "Try to have some respect for the dead!"

I held up my hands in surrender. "Sorry!" I whispered. And when he seemed satisfied that I wasn't about to commit another faux pas, he turned back around. I leaned in close to Heath and asked, "Is Cameron grounded?"

Heath dipped his chin. "Yes."

"Oh, no," I muttered. That was the worst possible news. If Cameron was stuck in the land of ghosts, I didn't think I could ever forgive myself for insisting on coming here and causing this unfortunate chain of events. "Can you get him to cross over?"

Heath closed his eyes and mouthed, "I'm trying" just as the priest began to call for quiet and for everyone to take their seats because the service was about to begin. My knee bounced and my impatient attention went from Heath to the priest conducting the ceremony. I couldn't sense Cameron at all, and I was stuck waiting for Heath to fill me in.

My fellow medium took his time. Heath's brow furrowed while he concentrated, but finally he relaxed his posture and leaned over to whisper in my ear, "I can't get him across."

"Damn it!" I swore under my breath, completely forgetting I was in church. "Is he giving you a reason?"

"He's worried about the baby," he said, pointing to the pregnant woman sitting next to Bonnie. "He's saying this is all wrong, and he's very anxious about the child."

"So he knows he's dead?" I asked, careful to keep my voice very low while the priest read some scripture.

"He seems to," Heath confirmed.

"Which makes it harder for us to convince him to cross."

"It does," he agreed.

Not all ghosts are confused about their demise. And while it is true that the majority of grounded spirits haunting our world do not fully comprehend that they have actually died, a strong minority in their ranks fully comprehend that their bodies have stopped living, but their souls refuse to cross over because something is keeping them stuck in the middle. Many of these spirits are worried about a loved one who they think is still alive, or they're afraid of crossing over and being judged because they didn't live a virtuous life.

And then, of course, there are energies like Rigella, who refuse to cross because they are so evil that they continue to get a kick out of scaring, messing with, or harming the living. These energies are by far the most dangerous, because they're not content with merely making scary noises or moving the occasional chair. No, they actually create a portal to the lower realms—a place where nothing good roams—and they gather power and knowledge down there to use against poor unsuspecting types. Or those against whom they hold a grudge.

Those spirits who fall into Cameron's category of being aware of their death but still refusing to move on are tough customers when it comes to convincing them that they would be better off letting go of this world and moving to the next. Still, I couldn't very well leave Cameron in a constant state of worry over his unborn child, because I knew that his connection to real events in the present and future might be obscured by the fog of the ghost world.

Ghosties aren't always conscious that time is passing, and I believed that it was highly possible that Cameron's child could be born, grow up, and live a completely full life and Cameron would never be the wiser. He might always believe that his wife was still pregnant.

"Are you still connected to him?" I asked.

"Barely," Heath whispered.

"What's he doing?"

"He's over there, trying to talk to the pregnant woman."

I had a jolt of clarity at that moment and reached out to squeeze Heath's hand. "The baby!" I mouthed.

"What?" he mouthed back.

"Cameron's child could be in danger from Rigella!"

Heath's eyes darted to the pregnant girl sitting forlornly next to Bonnie. "Shit," he whispered. "I hadn't thought of that."

He squeezed my hand back, and I felt a jolt of electricity shoot up my arm so I pulled my hand abruptly away. Heath seemed startled by the move, but he didn't comment, which was a relief.

We waited until long after the service had ended and almost everyone else had filed up to pay their respects to Bonnie and Cameron's wife. We were the last to approach them and I hoped they didn't notice that we'd come in jeans. "We're so sorry for your loss," I said when we reached the pair.

Bonnie didn't seem to recognize me at first, but she took my hand and said, "Thank you."

There was a little awkward pause after that, so I added, "We were in your shop the other day."

Recognition blossomed in her eyes. "Oh, yes! The mediums from America. How lovely of you to come by and pay our Camey your respects," she said kindly.

"Of course," I said, completely relieved that she didn't seem to be aware that it was our van that had run her brother over. I wanted to ask her about the charm she'd given me, and maybe ask her if I could purchase another one, but this didn't feel like the time or the place. Instead, my eyes swiveled to the woman next to Bonnie. "I'm so sorry you lost your husband," I said, wishing there was something else I could say to take that awful, sad expression from her face.

Her eyes snapped to mine and there was a flash of anger there. "He wasn't my husband, you rude cow!" she barked.

I took a step back, utterly shocked by her reaction. Bonnie quickly placed a protective arm around the woman's shoulders. "There, there, now, Rose," she said, a tinge of red hitting her cheeks as she looked apologetically at me. "She didn't mean any offense." Rose ducked her chin and tears leaked out of her eyes. I felt terrible for having mentioned something to cause her additional pain.

"I'm so sorry," I said hoarsely.

Bonnie attempted a smile. "Rose has had a terrible time of it. My brother never got around to asking for her hand and so this is a terrible thing to have happened to a poor pregnant lass."

"I completely understand," I said. "And again, I'm very sorry for your loss and to have spoken out of turn."

Bonnie gave me a sympathetic pat on the arm and said, "Not to worry, miss, and thank you again for showing such kindness to us by coming by." She then turned back to Rose and said, "Let's get you home, deary, and into a nice hot bath, shall we?"

Rose's chin hadn't lifted after she'd snapped at me, and she continued to weep miserably and stare at the ground. Heath and I moved out of the way, allowing the pair to pass, and we waited until they were out of earshot to say anything. "That stung," I admitted.

Heath wrapped his own arm around my shoulders and squeezed. "She didn't mean it," he said gently.

"She's just hurting right now and wants everyone else to hurt too."

"Oh, I really do understand," I told him, trying not to feel the heat of his body pressed against mine. "I just wasn't expecting it and would rather not have encountered her, to be perfectly honest."

"Yeah, well, then I'm not sure you're going to like my next suggestion."

"You want to follow them?"

He looked at me in surprise. "How'd you know?"

I pointed down the aisle to the departing women and to the little orb traveling along right behind them. "I figured you'd want to chase after Cameron and work some more on convincing him to cross."

Heath smiled. "Come on," he said. "But let's try not to make it too obvious."

It was a fairly quick trip to Bonnie's. She lived two blocks away from the church, and Heath and I didn't even have to get in our car. We just followed about fifty yards behind and halted the moment we saw Bonnie and Rose walk up to a lovely cottage with a clay-tiled roof and cute yellow shutters.

It tugged at my heartstrings to watch how caring Bonnie was with Rose. The pregnant woman waddled slowly, and Bonnie offered her an arm and a gentle word now and again to coax her along.

Once they'd gone inside, I lost sight of the gray little orb. "He went in," I said.

Heath nodded. "I'm trying to get him to come back out," he said, and just like that, I saw the orb reappear.

"Wow," I said with a smile. "You're good."

"I didn't do it," he confessed.

"Then who did?"

At that moment a clicking noise called our attention and we turned to see a man with an umbrella which he used like a cane to walk down a street just opposite the one Bonnie lived on. I thought I recognized him, even though we were a bit too far away to make out his features. "That's Fergus," Heath whispered.

I glanced back in the direction of the orb. It was crossing the street and moving rapidly toward the ghost-tour guide. "Maybe they were friends," I said, remembering that Fergus had come to the funeral.

"Maybe," Heath said, his eyes far away. "But maybe not."

I was about to ask him what he meant by that, but I didn't have a chance because in the next moment Heath was grabbing my hand and tugging me across the street. We followed behind Fergus and the orb, keeping back far enough not to alert Fergus to our presence.

By now the sun was starting to set and there was a chill in the air. I wasn't cold, thanks to Meg's most recent shopping trip, but I still wished for some gloves. Well, at least one glove. My free hand was cold. The one Heath was holding had grown all warm and tingly.

Abruptly, Fergus turned a corner, disappearing from view behind a huge hedgerow. Heath and I trotted forward to the edge of the foliage and peeked around the corner.

The Scotsman was approaching a dead end with one lone house in sore need of some upkeep. "He must live there," Heath said.

But the older gentleman showed no signs of going up the walk to the front door. Instead, he kept well to the side of the house and entered a cluster of woods. "Where the heck is he going?" I wondered.

"Do you think he saw us and is trying to ditch us?"

"Only one way to find out," I said, tugging on his hand and trotting after Fergus again.

We approached the woods cautiously. The sun was setting rather quickly now, which gave the woods a particularly creepy cast. Heath and I continued to edge deeper into the trees, and I no longer felt a tingle as I gripped his hand tightly—I felt nervous.

"I don't think I like it in here," I said. "Something doesn't feel right."

Heath nodded. "I know what you mean," he agreed. "Do you by any chance have any magnetic grenades on you?"

I groaned. "No," I said. "I'm completely unarmed."

Heath stopped. "Maybe we should head back."

The hairs on the back of my neck stood on end again and I sensed something terrible lurking in these woods. "I think that's a great idea," I whispered. "And I also think we should hurry."

Heath and I turned as one, took a single step, and came up short. We were both too stunned to move, because not ten feet in front of us was a big black broom.

It was lying on the ground looking particularly creepy, and for a moment I had to struggle to breathe. "Where'd that come from?" I whispered, taken aback by its sudden appearance.

"It wasn't there a minute ago," Heath said. "See? That's the path we've been following, and it's lying right in the middle of it."

I moved forward to inspect it and attempted a laugh. "*Harry Potter* fans would love it!" I joked, trying to shrug off the memory of the broom from my dream. The one on the ground was a perfect duplicate. "I mean, it looks like something right out of the movie, right?"

Heath didn't respond, so I added, "Heath, some-one's *got* to be messing with us, right?" I glanced back at him, but his eyes were locked on the broom. I continued to try to rationalize it. "Seriously, dude, it's a little cliché, don't you think? The witch rises again and we come across a creepy-looking broom on the ground? If it weren't so dopey, maybe I'd buy it," I added in an extra-loud mocking voice.

Heath's eyes finally pulled away from the black stick on the ground. "You think?"

I forced myself to laugh again. "Sure!" I said. "It's an obvious joke, and a lame one at that. Someone's just trying to screw with us."

I looked back down at the broom and swallowed hard, trying to push down my own nerves. I wouldn't admit it, but the similarity to the one from my dream was really unsettling me. "Oh, this is ridiculous!" I said, and bent to pick it up to prove that it was just a harmless piece of wood. But without warning, the broom snapped up to stand erect just a foot away from me. My heart began to slam against my chest. "Wires," I whispered, backing up just in case to stand next to Heath. "It must be on wires or something, right?"

But just as I finished that sentence, something emerged slowly from the ground. It was a black shadow, vaguely in the shape of a person, and I watched in horror as it reached out an arm to grab hold of the broom. In the next instant the broom was off the ground, and the shadowy figure appeared to be riding it. It then sailed through the air with tremendous speed. Heath and I barely had time to drop to the ground and I could feel it whiz over my head and hit a tree with a loud crack. "Holy shit!" I yelled, scrambling to my feet. "What the—" My voice cut off as three loud thwacks sounded all around us. Heath and I pressed our backs against each other and turned in a circle. Two more identical brooms with black shadows astride them were clacking loudly against nearby trees, joining the first one as they taunted and teased us.

"Are you thinking what I'm thinking?" I gasped.

"If you're thinking we should get the freak out of here, then yeah!" Heath said, and without another second's hesitation we took off running as fast as we could.

Behind us we heard what can only be described as a series of cackles—high-pitched and terrifying like a pack of hyenas mocking our flight.

Heath was faster than I, and he began to inch away, which sent an added shiver up my spine because if he gained too much ground, I knew the spooks riding those brooms would focus on attacking only me. At least with Heath beside me they'd have to split up and we might have a chance to make it out of the woods.

"Wait up!" I tried to shout, but I was so terrified that the sound was barely above a whisper. Something long and slender whizzed by me and cracked me on the head and I nearly tumbled to the ground.

When I'd regained my footing, I saw that Heath had slowed enough to grab me under the arm and pull me forward. I risked looking over my shoulder and saw that the brooms and their shadows were still chasing us, weaving in and out among the trees, but just then one of the brooms caught a branch and it skidded to the ground.

"Heath!" I said as I pulled him to one side to avoid getting hit by an oncoming broom. "We've got to zig-zag! If you go right and I go left, and we move in and out of the trees, I think we can lose them!"

He looked at me with large, frightened eyes, but he

didn't question me. Instead he let go of my arm and took off to the right. I headed left, ducking under limbs and looking for trees that were smaller with branches a little lower to the ground. I figured if I could cut a path through the smaller trees, it might slow the witches down. The tactic worked brilliantly as was evidenced by the series of thwacks that sounded behind me when the brooms encountered the foliage and got tangled in the branches.

The only problem was I'd lost complete sight of Heath, but I knew if I stopped to see where he'd gone, the spooks would only gain ground on me. I wanted to call out to him, but it was all I could do on this mad sprint to keep focused as I wove through the trees and tried to keep my footing. I knew I had to make it out of the woods as fast as I could. I doubted the witches would chase me through the streets of Queen's Close. At least, I hoped they wouldn't. I also hoped that Heath had the same plan and that we'd find each other once we cleared the woods.

And I'd almost made it out when I darted around a tree and nearly ran right into one of those brooms. Somehow the spook riding it had managed to get ahead of me and double back. A loud crack behind me told me that at least one more of the ghosts was still chasing after me from behind, which meant that I was now trapped between them.

I stopped dead in my tracks, my chest heaving and my back up against a tree. The first shadow and her broom hovered about four feet off the ground as if she was waiting for me to make a move. Very quickly she was joined by a second spook, who'd cleared the trees and come around to hover about three feet away from her sister.

My mind raced through options. The last threads of dusk did nothing to help me and only made the surrounding woods murkier. In mounting panic, I shouted out Heath's name. There was no response. The ghosts seemed to notice my desperation and took that as a sign to frighten me a little more.

They began to spin their brooms in place, side by side, slowly at first, then building in speed like horizontal tops until the black spiky tails were just a blur. They were twirling so fast that they started to hum, then buzz, like two enormous wasps, quivering menacingly on the edge of the wood, ready to attack.

My heart was hammering hard inside my chest, and my cheeks and hands stung where my bare skin had been scraped by foliage. Tears sprang to my eyes and blurred my vision as a well of fear and panic bubbled up from inside. I blinked rapidly and willed myself to think of a way out. I thought my best chance might lie in darting to my right, as the brooms were crowding my left side, but just before I was going to take that option, there were several loud thwacks and the violent rustle of leaves, and out of nowhere, the third witch riding a broom with a long crack down its middle appeared.

Immediately, I wondered what had happened to Heath, and my pounding heart skipped a beat as I thought about how the fracture had gotten into the wooden broomstick. I thought maybe it could have happened if it'd struck something—or someone—very, very hard.

And that made the unbidden tears stream down my cheeks with earnest, but another emotion surfaced almost as quickly. I got mad. And by mad, I don't mean just a little pissed. I mean *royally* ticked off. My eyes darted to the ground and right away I spotted a long thick stick. Without thinking it through clearly, I dived for the stick, snatching it tightly as I rolled to one side just in time to avoid being speared by one of the brooms.

Another came at me and I managed to block it by gripping the stick firmly in both hands across my chest and knocking the attacking witch and her broom out of the way. I then sprang to my feet and used my weapon like a sword to knock the third witch-riding broom down to the ground. The smoky spook riding it tumbled away, and in the meantime I stomped on her broom with both feet, holding it pressed against the earth.

The other two witches attacked again and I had a hell of a time beating off their brooms while keeping my balance on top of the third broom, but I managed to land a really good blow to the cracked broomstick that sent it spiraling into a tree, where it hit hard enough to break the broom right in half, and the smoky spook riding it vanished into thin air. I was stunned to see both halves of the broom then fall to the ground, lifeless and still. But I didn't have very long to dwell on it, because the remaining broom ratcheted up the attack, coming at me with a fury and bombarding me with pokes and prods until I finally lost my balance and fell forward off the trapped broom.

The witch who'd been riding it sprang from the ground to reclaim it and she and the broom both rose up quickly and she got her revenge by swinging hard against the backs of my knees. I cried out in pain and sank to the earth, barely getting my stick up in time to block the first broom, which was aiming right for my head.

By now I was exhausted and the muscles in my arms ached from swinging my weapon and using it to block the brooms' blows. I knew I couldn't keep this up much longer. I had little doubt the brooms were being controlled by Rigella and two of her sisters, and I also believed she would kill me if she could.

And if I couldn't fight, then I might as well run for it. Turning around to face the witches, I raised my stick and feigned a forward attack. The ploy worked; both brooms backed away, which allowed me just enough time to turn and bolt out of there.

I still held tightly to my stick, just in case I should become trapped again, but pretty much all my remaining energy went into zigzagging wildly through the trees. I could hear the spooks give chase as branches split and broke behind me. It was hard to see now—there was very little light left from the setting sun—but I still managed well enough to avoid slamming directly into a tree. One of the brooms was not so lucky.

I heard a tremendous crash, followed by two more thwacks and then the sound of splintering wood. Chancing a glance over my shoulder, I clearly saw one of the brooms crash to the ground in three pieces, and I silently thanked God that two were down and only one more broom threatened me.

By this time I'd lost all sense of direction and wondered if I was running in circles, but abruptly the woods ended and I found myself dashing straight out into the open.

It was a little lighter here, and I quickly assessed that I had stumbled onto a huge well-tended lawn . . . with no cover.

I thought about darting back into the thicker forest, but then my eye caught a mammoth-looking tree on the far side of the lawn, and tucked just behind it—a house with the lights on. I knew instantly that if I could make it to the tree before the broom cleared the woods, I could use it as cover to race for the house. And if I made it to the house, I might be safe.

Tossing aside the stick that would only slow me down, I gritted my teeth and called up every ounce of reserve energy I had. I tore as fast as I could across the open grass, using my breath and pumping my arms to help get me there in time.

I also pricked my ears, listening as the witch and her broom struggled to get through the remaining foliage, but very quickly my own breathing and the distance I was creating obscured the sound.

I couldn't very well glance back—that would only slow me down. So I focused on the trunk of the tree, closing the distance as fast as I could. And then, I was there and I hurtled around to the other side, using the tree to hide from the approaching spook. I dropped to the ground and crawled to sit in between two massive roots. I pulled my knees up, making myself as small as possible, and just focused on breathing quietly. It was really hard because my chest was heaving while I took great gulps of air.

I was also sweating profusely, and my hands were slick from both nerves and exertion. I kept waiting for the witch and her broom to round the tree and find me, but the seconds ticked by and nothing happened. I wanted to take a peek on the other side of the tree, but quickly dismissed that idea, reasoning that it would be difficult in this dim light to pick the broom out and I'd have to expose part of my head in order to take a look. Too risky.

Once my breathing had calmed a bit, I switched my

focus to the house. It was maybe thirty yards away and several of the lights were on. As I looked at it, I saw a figure move across the window, and I knew someone was home.

Gathering a little more courage, I eased myself to my feet, but remained low. I'd have to be careful to keep the tree directly at my back until I made it to the house. I was just about to go for it when something right over my head made an eerie creaking sound. I froze. And waited.

A gust of wind pushed across the lawn, rattling the leaves and bringing that creepy creak again. The sound was right above me, making a long unsettling noise, like rope rubbing against wood. Slowly I tilted my chin up and stole a glance. Right over my head was a pair of shoes. I leaned slightly to my right and saw the shoes were attached to feet and legs and a torso . . . and then another gust of wind caused the object above me to swing back and forth.

And then it hit me. Literally. Out of nowhere a broom struck my shoulder and sent me crashing sideways. I cried out as I hit the ground and put my arms up defensively, my eyes swiveling wildly between the dead person hanging from the tree and the broom coming in for another attack. "Stop!" I screamed right before closing my eyes and turning my head away.

I braced for the impact as a loud *THWACK* resounded in my ears, and something large and heavy fell right next to my head. I lay there shivering for a few beats until someone gripped my shoulder hard and asked, "Miss! Are you all right?"

# Chapter 9

"M. J.!" a familiar voice spoke next. "Jesus! Are you okay?"

I opened my eyes and saw Heath hovering over me, looking terrible. His face was a crisscross of angry scratches, his nose looked bruised, and one of his eyes was completely swollen shut. He also appeared to be gripping his left arm tightly. I sat up quickly and glanced around. Two halves of the remaining broom lay on either side of me, and a man holding a large ax hovered near my feet.

"I'm okay," I said, trying to get my bearings. The man at my feet looked really familiar, but before I could place him, he turned and walked around the tree to the side to retrieve a ladder. I watched him for a moment as he placed it against the side of the tree and climbed quickly up to the lowest branch.

"I found him about five minutes ago," Heath said. I looked at him and saw him staring up at the terrible sight of a middle-aged man with a blue face, a protruding swollen tongue, and bugged-out eyes. His body swayed grotesquely from side to side as the wind hit it.

I turned away from the awful scene as a wave of nausea threatened to make me lose my lunch, and focused on taking deep breaths. When I could talk again, I asked Heath, "What happened?"

"One of the spooks got me. I ran all the way to the edge of this lawn and I thought I'd lost her and started to double back to find you when one of the witches bashed me pretty good with her broom. She swung at my face first, which is how I got the shiner, and when I put an arm up to defend myself, she whacked me hard enough to break the bone."

I gasped, looking up at him. "She *broke* your arm?"

Heath nodded. "I heard it crack," he said with a painful grimace. "And that got me on my knees. That's when she hit me on the back of the head hard enough to knock me out for a few minutes. When I came to, I managed to make it here and saw the lights on in the house, so I was on my way there when . . ." His voice trailed off and he didn't finish his story.

"And that's when you saw the dead guy?"

Heath nodded, his eyes darting up to the swaying figure, then quickly away. "I came around the tree and was leaning against it to catch my breath when I saw him. I felt his ankle and it was stone cold and stiff, so I knew there was nothing I could do for him. That's when I went up to the house and got help."

There was a loud thump, like someone dropping a sack of potatoes, and reflexively I glanced over to see the hanging victim crumpled into a ghastly heap. "I think I'm gonna be sick," I groaned, closing my eyes tightly again and taking deep breaths.

"The police will be here shortly," said the man from the ladder. And as he spoke, I realized who he was and my eyes snapped open again to stare at Fergus

Ericson while he carefully descended the ladder with the ax he'd used to cut through the thick rope. "I called them right before we came out to cut poor Joseph down."

"You knew him?" I asked.

"Aye," Fergus said, making the sign of the cross as he stared grimly down at the crumpled remains. "That's Joseph Hill, my neighbor."

The police arrived about two minutes later. An ambulance was also routed to the scene, and once the paramedics determined that Hill was quite beyond their help, they focused on Heath.

His cuts and bruises were tended to, and they wanted to take him to the hospital for his broken arm, but he assured them that he would head there on his own later. They compromised by wrapping a makeshift splint around his arm, and setting that in a sling strapped around his neck.

A baby-faced inspector with a brogue so thick I could barely understand it took Fergus's statement first. He tried to move Fergus out of earshot, but the pervasive wind carried the sound of their conversation down to me. And even though I could understand only one side of the conversation—Fergus's—I listened intently to his rather uninformative account of what had transpired.

Fergus said that he'd heard someone knocking urgently on his door and found a young man in distress. He recounted how the stranger at his door was injured, and had leaves and twigs in his hair, so Fergus just assumed the young man must have fallen down a ravine in the woods and had come to his door for aid.

The young man, he said, pointing to Heath, wasn't so frantic about his own injuries as he was about poor Joseph Hill, hanging from Fergus's own tree! And Fergus suspected that after years of living with a terrible illness, Joseph finally succumbed to his depression and took his own life.

The constable asked Fergus about Joseph's illness and Fergus said, "I know he's been battling cancer for years. And I know that the poor man was running out of time."

The constable then asked what signs of depression Joseph had exhibited. Fergus replied that Joseph wasn't a man to show much emotion, but in the past two years he'd become more and more reclusive and hardly ever came out of his house anymore.

Fergus next told the constable that once he was told about a man hanging in his tree, he'd gotten his ladder and ax and hurried down to the tree as fast as he could to get poor Joseph down, but the man was clearly dead and there was nothing more for it.

The constable noted that Joseph must have been dead for hours, as rigor had already begun to set in, and he asked Fergus why he hadn't seen Joseph for himself from his own house.

In answer, Fergus crooked a finger and led the constable up the hill toward the house; then he turned around and pointed down. It was obvious that the bough of the tree had actually hidden the body from Fergus's view and quite unremarkable that the ghost-tour guide hadn't seen Hill dangling from the tree.

I wondered why Fergus hadn't mentioned anything about the witch, and as the inspector turned to me to get my statement, I caught the very subtle head-shake from Ericson, standing behind the constable, and then he placed a finger to his lips. His message was clear—I shouldn't mention her either.

I almost ignored that advice, but when I looked around for the evidence of the broken broom to prove that Heath and I had been chased through the woods by an unnatural entity, I couldn't find any trace of the broomstick that had been so neatly severed. And I would have found *that* very odd if I hadn't known the spirit world so well; material objects often disappear when there's a ghost on the loose, especially one as powerful as the witch. I suspected that while we'd managed to destroy the three brooms she and her sisters used to clobber us, we hadn't even dented the power of the spirits behind the attacks.

So I decided to trust my own instincts and tell the inspector that Heath and I had been taking a leisurely walk through the woods when we became separated, which was sort of true—he and I *had* taken a walk for at least a little ways into the woods, and then later we *were* separated.

Additionally, I told the inspector that I'd searched and searched for Heath, only to discover him injured but still attempting to help Fergus get Joseph down from the tree.

Meanwhile, I could see Fergus amble casually over to where Heath was just finishing up with the paramedics and whisper something in his ear. Heath didn't look happy, but he nodded.

Once all our statements had been given, and Joseph had been placed inside a body bag and set on a gurney bound for the morgue, Fergus offered to drive Heath and me to our car so that I could take Heath to the hospital.

On the way there I asked Ericson why he'd subtly advised us against telling the police about the witch. "They'd never believe you, now, would they?" he said simply. I had to agree; not many people on earth would've believed what'd happened to us. I fell silent and saw that Fergus was eyeing me in the rearview mirror like he had something else to say to me. I waited him out and he finally spoke. "Sarah tells me you've adopted the pug."

I tried to keep the anger out of my voice when he broached the sensitive topic. "Yes," I said, and left it at that.

"She also suggested I look elsewhere should I need a dog to demonstrate the effects of Briar Road." I pretended to be very interested in the passing scenery. "She says that her conscience won't be allowing her to rent me any more dogs."

I wanted to bite my tongue and not take the bait, but I couldn't. "And what I don't understand, Mr. Ericson, is how *your* conscience could allow you to subject those defenseless animals to such torture."

Ericson surprised me by chuckling merrily. "Oh, it's only a little unpleasant for them, Miss Holliday. And they all recover quite nicely after all."

"But *how* can you do that?" I insisted. "I mean, you're terrorizing them!"

Fergus sighed. "You have to keep in mind that I'm competing with some of the best ghost tours in the world," he explained. "The city of Edinburgh is one of the most haunted places on earth, dear, and tourists are far more likely to visit one of my competitors in the city. I need some theatrics to pull the patrons in, I'm afraid."

"So you're going to continue to torture these defenseless animals?" I asked.

Fergus's eyes met mine in the rearview mirror. "No," he said. "No other shelter will allow me to borrow the strays."

The car was silent for a bit while I wrestled with the fact that Fergus had probably saved my life with his ax, and I'd gone and wrecked his business. Even if it was justifiable, I still felt bad.

"I'm sure you can find another way to pull in the tourists," I said to him, although I didn't quite know how.

Fergus smiled kindly at me. "I'm sure I will," he said, stopping in front of our newly rented van.

We got out of his car, thanked him, and hopped into our rental, where I had to take a turn at the wheel. This was something I'd been hoping to avoid, as driving on the opposite side of the road looked mighty tricky. Looking at the little map Fergus had drawn for us, Heath said, "We take this straight for about two kilometers, then turn right onto Hedgeforth and it should be on our left."

I helped Heath with his buckle and got settled, checked all my mirrors, and prayed that I didn't get into an accident for the next two kilometers. Once we were under way, Heath said, "Pretty crazy afternoon, huh?"

"There aren't even words," I told him with a sideways glance. "And I'm not buying that Joseph Hill committed suicide," I added.

Heath pulled his head back to look at me in surprise. "Why not?"

"I think the witch was responsible."

I could tell by Heath's expression that he wasn't

getting it and so I reminded him, "Joseph *Hill*," I said, emphasizing the last name. "Remember how Bonnie named the Gillespies, McLarens, Lancasters, and *Hills*?"

"Holy shit!" Heath exclaimed. "I'd totally forgotten about that!"

"Yeah, well, on this bust it sort of pays to remember the details."

"But how did she hang him?" Heath asked me. "I mean, that's a pretty mean feat for a ghost. Even one that can ride a real broom."

"I think Joseph did all the heavy lifting," I said, trying to stay over to my left and feeling like opposing traffic was coming right at me.

"Huh?"

I waited for two cars to pass before I explained. "I once saw a videotape made by a buddy of mine who's a parapsychologist up in New Hampshire. He was on a ghost hunt at this house with this supposedly really crazy spook up in the attic. The house is now abandoned—no one will live there because the last four residents all had someone in their family hang themselves from the rafters. Not one of the people who died had any history of mental illness or depression, and almost all of them died exactly six months after moving in.

"The other similarity, of course, was that all four victims reported hearing strange noises in the attic and showed a curiosity about investigating the source prior to their deaths. Finally, in nineteen ninety-six after the last victim was discovered, the owner of the house—a woman who'd just lost her eldest son, whom she found hanging in the attic—hired a paranormal investigative team to look into the rash of hangings.

"My buddy was part of that team, and they spent

the night at the house, and two guys took cameras up into the attic. No one heard anything from them, or anything unusual, for a solid three hours, but then around three in the morning the remaining crew overheard some shouts for help. When they ran up the ladder to the attic, they found one crew member dazed and confused, walking around with an electrical cord wrapped around his neck, while the other had a noose over his head and was sitting precariously on a beam while attempting to secure the other end of the noose to a nail on the rafter."

"Whoa!"

I nodded. "'Whoa' is right. If the guy on the beam had fallen, he would have snapped his neck. I saw the actual footage; they were talking to him while they tried to get him to come down. He seemed to know exactly what he was doing—I mean, in the video, you can see him methodically going through the motions of trying to hang himself. It took the crew nearly ten minutes to convince him he was doing something dangerous and to remove the noose from around his neck."

"Okay, now I want to see the tape," Heath said, and I knew I'd really piqued his morbid curiosity.

But I shuddered as I remembered watching the footage. It was incredibly unsettling because it was so clear that the paranormal investigator had been completely taken over by a murderous ghost. "Gilley has it stored somewhere on his computer. It's one of the most disturbing things I've ever seen."

"So the ghost took over his mind? Hypnotized him somehow?" Heath asked.

"Yes," I said simply. "I think that's exactly what happened."

"And you believe the witch did that with Joseph Hill?"

I shrugged as we arrived at the hospital. "I think it's entirely possible that anything that could command a three-broom attack and give us a few whacks hard enough to break your arm is powerful enough to creep into the mind of a poor unsuspecting individual and convince him to hang himself."

"But why in that tree?" Heath asked. "I mean, wouldn't the witch have been able to convince Hill to kill himself anywhere, like in his house, where it would have taken less effort? Why push him to walk over to Fergus's property, climb that tree, and kill himself there?"

"Made a hell of a statement, didn't it?" I said in reply, pulling into a parking slot and relaxing my white-knuckle grip on the wheel.

Heath eased himself out of the car and eyed me over the hood with a forlorn look in his eyes. "We're way out of our league here, aren't we, M. J.?"

I regarded him soberly. "Yeah, but that doesn't mean we can't go down fighting, my friend. Now, let's get you in there and fixed up, okay?"

We were lucky in that there wasn't much going on in the emergency room of the hospital. Heath was taken right into X-ray and a fracture of his right ulna showed up quickly, but the bone was still in place, so he wouldn't need surgery. He'd have to wear a cast for the next six weeks, but otherwise he was fine.

It took about an hour for the hospital staff to plaster over his arm, and during that time a kindly nurse took pity on me and cleaned up the scratches on my face and hands. I then called Gilley, who was worried sick about us, and Gopher, who had no idea we'd even left the hotel, and told both of them that we'd be back before midnight.

Heath was released with a prescription for pain-killers, and we filled that first at the hospital's twenty-four-hour pharmacy, then made our way back to the hotel.

Once we were inside the hotel, Gilley met us at the bar again for another drink. He took one look at me and sucked in a breath, but it was nothing to how he reacted when he saw Heath. *"Ohmigod!"* he shrieked. "Your face! What happened to your face?"

I had a funny moment where I wondered if Gil was more concerned that Heath was actually injured, or that his handsome face risked being made slightly less attractive now that he was cut and bruised from brow to chin.

The side of Heath's face that was the least swollen smiled. "It only hurts when I laugh," he said, but I knew differently. I also knew that even though Heath carried the bottle of prescription painkillers in his back pocket, he'd refused to take one because he was concerned it would affect his sixth sense.

"How about a drink?" Gilley offered as he pulled up a chair and helped ease Heath into it.

"A draft would be great," he said, and Gilley hurried over to the bar to place the order. I noticed with amusement that he'd failed to ask me what I wanted. "You drinking?" Heath said, probably catching on to that too.

"Yeah," I said. "As soon as Gil comes back with your drink, I'll send him back to the bar to get me one."

"So what do we tell them?" Heath asked, pointing to John, Meg, and Kim, just now entering the lounge.

I sighed tiredly. "The truth. They've agreed to help us with this bust, and they need to know how powerful this spook and her sisters are. If they can get a man to hang himself and chase us through the woods using real brooms for clubs—then they're powerful enough to do them some harm too."

"Yeah, but I'm not sure how much more Gilley can take," Heath said, motioning with his head to my partner, who was bringing back Heath's foam-topped beer and trying hard not to spill it.

"You're probably right," I agreed. "Let's keep the details to a minimum for now and talk with John, Meg, and Kim privately."

"And Gopher," Heath added, just as our producer joined us from the opposite entrance.

"What the *hell* happened to you?" he demanded by way of hello.

"Nice to see you too, Gopher," Heath said drily before taking a long sip of beer.

"Heath," Gopher pressed, clearly not amused, "I can't put you on camera looking like that!"

I saw Heath's one good eye narrow. I knew the poor guy had been through a hell of a lot in the past few days, and that on top of being chased and beaten by a very large stick, he didn't need to add a cranky producer to his list of troubles.

"Gopher," I said loudly, clearing my throat.

Gopher's eyes turned to me, and his eyes widened even more. "Jesus Christ!" he gasped, his gaze shifting between Heath and me. "Did you two get into fight with a grizzly bear or something?"

Belatedly, I remembered that my own face was pretty scratched up. "It wasn't our fault," I told him. "The witch nailed us both pretty good."

Gopher's expression immediately changed; he now looked interested. "The *witch* did that to you?"

I nodded, then looked around at all the fascinated faces from our crew and landed on one in particular. "Gil?"

"Yeah?"

"I've had a really bad day. Could you maybe get me a drink from the bar?"

Now, knowing my best friend as I did, I was certain that under normal circumstances he would have told me to just flag down a server, but in light of my appearance and because there were several other people at the table, Gil could hardly refuse. He hesitated only a moment before he said, "Sure, honey. You want your usual?"

"That'd be awesome," I said, trying hard to look really grateful.

The moment Gil hurried off, I filled everyone else in as quickly as possible, beginning with the discovery that Bonnie's brother had been the man killed by our van.

Gopher held up his finger at that point and said, "Let me tell you about what I learned at the police station after M. J. finishes."

I smiled at him, grateful that he seemed to understand that I didn't want Gilley to overhear certain parts of our tale. And even talking fast, I only got halfway through the story when Gil showed up with a tall pint of beer. I changed the topic as he came into earshot, and the moment he set the frothy brew down on the table, I asked, "Um . . . is that warm?"

Gil frowned, staring down at the pint. "That's how they serve it here, M. J. All drafts are room temperature."

I sighed dramatically. "Oh, okay."

Gil looked around at the other faces, which were practically demanding with their cross expressions that he offer me an alternative. "Can I get you something else?" he said tightly.

I smiled. "I'd love anything cold." Gilley turned to leave. "But I don't think I want a beer." Gil turned back to me and arched one eyebrow. "I think I need a mixed drink."

The brow lowered dangerously. "Like what?"

I shrugged. "I dunno. Vodka and cranberry, maybe? With a lemon instead of lime."

Gilley turned with raised shoulders and stiff arms. I knew he was fighting the urge to tell me to get my own damn drink and I had a moment where I really felt sorry for him.

The moment he huffed away, I got back to my story and hurried to finish. I was just at the part where Fergus whacked the broom with his ax after I'd discovered the body of Joseph Hill swinging in the tree above me when Gilley returned with a vodka and cranberry and a green garnish. "Is that lime?" I asked immediately, trying to appear disgusted.

Gil eyed the little wedge floating in my drink. It was common knowledge between us that I preferred lemons to limes. "The bartender must have forgotten and put in the lime," he growled.

I held the drink to my lips and took a tiny sip, then pretended to cough and sputter. "It's way too strong! Jeez, how much alcohol did they put in here?"

Gilley snatched the drink out of my hand with enough force to spill some of the contents on the table and stormed off with big angry clomps back to the bar. I held in a giggle and hurriedly finished my story, ending it with, "And I don't want to frighten Gilley, so when he asks me to fill him in and I lie—just go along with it, okay?"

Everyone nodded just as Gil came back with a small tray loaded with a shot of vodka, a rocks glass filled with ice, a small bottle of cranberry juice, and a soup cup overflowing with lemons. He said nothing as he took them one by one off the tray and set them on the table, then stood back and glared hard at me, silently daring me to express anything other than profound gratitude.

"Thank you," I said happily.

At that moment, the waitress arrived, apologizing for the delay in getting to our table, and offered to take any remaining orders. After she'd gone, I promised to fill an impatient-looking Gilley in just as soon as Gopher told us what he'd found at the police station.

"The brake lines were cut intentionally," he said. Everyone at the table looked shocked, then relieved. "The crime lab came back with conclusive evidence of a straight-edge knife cut right through the lines. They know it wasn't done during the crash, because none of the metal surrounding the lines was damaged."

"That means that you and Gil are off the hook, then, right?" Heath said.

Gopher ran his finger in a circle on the tabletop. "No, that doesn't get us off the hook."

"What?" Gilley barked. "Why not? I mean, what do they think? We cut our *own* brake lines and stayed in the van hoping it would hit a guy crossing the street?"

Gopher laughed softly, as if he was holding on to an inside joke. "No, Gil, what I meant was that the vandalism to our van doesn't get us off the hook as much as what was in the coroner's report."

"What did the coroner find?" I asked.

"Cameron Lancaster was already dead when the van ran him over."

I gasped. "No way!"

"Way," Gopher said, swigging the shot of tequila he'd ordered and chasing that with a great gulp of draft beer. "Blach," he said, wiping his mouth. "Stuff's awful when it's warm."

"But if he was already dead," I said, "then why dump his body in the street and cut our brake lines?"

"To cover up the murder," Gopher said simply. "And the cover-up was very clever indeed, because the coroner also found something quite interesting."

"What?" we all asked at once.

"Cameron's heart, liver, brain, and kidneys were frozen."

Gil scrunched up his face. "I don't get it."

"Cameron was murdered, then thrown in a freezer somewhere, and either partially defrosted or only partially frozen when he was laid in the street where our van ran him over. The inspector on the case revealed to our barrister that the coroner couldn't determine how long Cameron had been dead, but his girlfriend reported that he'd gone up the coast to look at a boat for sale a week and a half ago and she was expecting him back the very night he was run over."

"So Rigella didn't kill him?" I said, amazed to hear what the coroner had discovered.

"Doesn't look like it."

"But Rigella was there the night the van slid down the street," I insisted. "We all saw her ghost on video."

"Yep," Gopher said, rubbing his face tiredly. "And we also saw someone that looked quite human squatting down to cut the brake lines."

Heath and I exchanged a look. "Someone's working directly with the witch," we said together.

Gopher made the sign of a gun with his hand and pointed it at us. "Bingo."

"It would explain a lot," I reasoned.

John, who'd been listening to us intently, asked, "What exactly does that explain, again?"

"Well," I reasoned, "it explains first why the witch is thirty-five years early. Someone who knows her and her history was able to call her up and use her to wreak some havoc."

"It also suggests that someone with that kind of power knew we were coming and took advantage of the opportunity," Heath reasoned.

My eyes swiveled to Gilley. "I agree. I don't think it's a coincidence that someone from the Gillespie family arrived in the village the moment the witch was awakened."

"So someone planned this whole thing in advance?" John asked, and his voice suggested that he found the theory rather incredible.

"That, or it's one freaky coincidence," I told him.

"But what about the others?" Meg said. "What about Jack McLaren, and Joseph Hill?"

"Who's Joseph Hill?" Gil wanted to know.

"Later," I replied softly before answering Meg's question. "I think they're both a smoke screen and legitimately on the list of targets for the witch."

"But there's something we're missing," Kim said. "If the person that killed Cameron really was using the witch to cover up the murder—why murder him at all? Why not just call up the witch and let her do the work?"

"Because Cameron was killed before the witch was

called up," Heath said, and looked around the table to see if we were with him. "I mean, it makes sense, right? If the murderer killed Cameron prior to the witch becoming active, they could have stuffed him in a freezer long enough to call up the witch and have her create the smoke screen."

"Which suggests that his murder wasn't necessarily premeditated. And that hints to a possible crime of passion," I said.

"Rose?" Heath asked me. "Crimes of passion are usually committed by a significant other."

"Who's Rose?"

"Cameron's pregnant girlfriend," I said, answering Gilley before thinking through my response to Heath. "I don't think it was her," I told him. "I mean, the girl looks like she's ready to go into labor at any second. I can't imagine she'd be able to kill Cameron, heave his body into a freezer, then out to let it defrost, then over to the crime scene, place him in the middle of the street, then rush up to alert the witch, rush back in time to cut the brake lines on the van, and hope that the van would then run over Cameron. It's just a little too much for someone in her condition, don't you think?"

Heath nodded. "She also did look genuinely distraught at the funeral."

"She did," I agreed, remembering the forlorn look Rose had worn all through the service. "And she's short. I mean, how tall would you say she was, like five foot two?"

"Yeah, something like that," Heath said. "She was definitely a couple of inches shorter than you. And you're right, there'd be no way someone in her condition and small stature could do all that heavy lifting."

"Then who?" Gil asked.

I shrugged. "Now that I think about it, Gil, with all that preplanning, maybe it wasn't a crime of passion. Maybe it was premeditated after all, and Cameron was killed before the witch was called up because it was convenient. Gopher, you said that Rose had stated that Cameron was supposed to be gone on a trip up the coast for a week, so maybe someone who knew that he wouldn't be missed took the only opportunity they had right before he left town to kill him, then wait a few days for us to arrive and set us up for his death."

"That makes a lot of sense," Gopher said. "And if we focus on who murdered Cameron Lancaster, we'll probably be able to identify who called up the witch."

Heath rubbed the back of his head and winced. "And if we can find the person who called forth the witch, we might also be able to get them to send her packing, right before we turn them in to the police."

I nodded in agreement. "Let's hope so. And barring that, let's hope we can at least find the location where she was first called up, 'cause that's going to be her portal."

"Are you still thinking it's down in the close?" Gilley asked me.

I shook my head. "No. Sam Whitefeather came through to me in Heath's reading, and he said it wasn't there."

"Then where is it?"

I shrugged. "I've no idea, buddy. But we'll definitely need to keep looking for it."

"I'll be happy to watch you guys shove a few spikes into that gateway, let me tell you," Gil said. Then he looked excitedly at our producer. "Say, Gopher, if we're really off the hook for Cameron's death, did you get our passports back?"

Gopher scowled. "Naw," he said. "Idiot foreign-police procedure. They said they're going to revisit all the evidence to ensure they can eliminate us as suspects and that may take a little while."

"You gave them a copy of the footage, though, didn't you?" I asked.

"I did. And that might have caused us the delay. They're a little suspicious of Hollywood outsiders supplying them with footage of a crime. They didn't come right out and say it, but it was obvious they suspected I'd added some special effects."

"So how long will it take to clear you guys?" I pressed.

Gopher shrugged. "A few more days, or a week at the most."

Gilley picked up his fire extinguisher and hugged it. "Stupid Scotland," he grumbled.

I stifled a yawn and looked at my watch. It was well after eleven p.m. and I was still feeling jet-lagged. Turning to Gilley, I said, "I think I'll turn in, which means you're with me, toots."

Gil looked at his watch and frowned. "You're a kill-joy," he said. "It's not even midnight!"

"Okay," I said lightly, getting up from my chair. "Stay here and keep your fire extinguisher close."

When Gilley turned hopeful eyes on Heath, he was disappointed because Heath got up as well and shook his head. "Sorry, buddy. My arm's killing me. I'm going to take one of these pain pills and hope it knocks me out."

"Okay, okay," Gilley griped. "I'm coming."

Before we left the group, we settled on a plan for the next day. Gilley, Heath, and I would go back to Bonnie's and see if we could coax her into telling us a little more about the witch's history and who might be powerful enough to call Rigella up from the lower realms. We also made the decision to scout the perimeter of the woods armed with several pounds of magnets and electrostatic meters to see if we could home in on her portal, which I hoped was somewhere within the woods. I figured it was as good a place as any to search, due to the fact that she'd chased Heath and me through the forest. Maybe the angry mob from the sixteen-hundreds had flushed Rigella and her three sisters up from the close and chased them into the woods, where they'd killed them. It was worth taking a look at the very least. Gopher offered to join our search so that he could record it all on camera.

I agreed—grudgingly—and headed off to my room with Gilley walking sourly behind.

The next morning Gil and I were eating breakfast when Heath ambled in, looking better rested but his face was still swollen. "How you doin'?" I asked.

He gingerly felt the puffy area around his eye. "Better, but still sore. You?"

"I'm okay." I'd slept well the night before, which was something of a surprise because I'd fully expected Rigella to enter my dreams again and haunt me, especially after our narrow escape in the woods.

"Did my grandfather come to you?" Heath inquired.

I looked at him quizzically. "No."

"He came to me," he said. "It might have been the

painkillers and beer, but I swear I dreamt about him last night."

"What'd he say?" Gil asked.

Heath took a sip of the coffee our waitress had just poured for him. "He kept telling me to look for the ruins. That we'd find what we needed to know in the ruins."

I paused the spreading of more marmalade on my toast. "Was he talking about the close?"

Heath shook his head. "No. It definitely felt like he was talking about something aboveground."

"In the woods, maybe?"

Heath shrugged. "I'm not sure. I just know that it felt really important and that once we find whatever ruins he was referring to, we'll discover something important to this bust."

"The portal?" Gil asked.

"Again, I don't know," Heath conceded. "But maybe."

I chewed my toast for a minute and the table remained silent, everyone thinking about what that could mean. "We have another thread to follow here," I said, suddenly thinking of something.

Gilley looked curiously at me. "What?"

"Cameron Lancaster."

"Um . . . what?" Gil said.

"He's grounded," I explained. "Which means he might remember what happened to him and who murdered him."

"Can you talk to him?" Gilley asked, a bit of excitement in his voice.

"If I can find him," I said. "And I think the best place to look for him is at Bonnie's."

"Then let's hurry up and get over there," Heath suggested, rising from the table.

I was about to get up too when Gil whined, "But I'm not finished! Jeez, you guys, can't a guy eat a meal without running off all over hill and dale?"

As if in answer there was a loud ZZZZZT! just off to our left, and the plug where the coffeemaker was resting fried out and began to smoke. Gilley jumped to his feet and reached for the small red extinguisher he carried everywhere, but one of the managers was quicker and he moved in with a much-larger version that sent a spray of white foam all over the outlet.

There were collective gasps from the patrons and a mad dash of staff to pull out the plugs from the coffee machine and the small icebox next to it. The moment things appeared to be under control, Gil said, "On second thought, maybe I can skip breakfast today. Let's boogie."

# Chapter 10

Gopher came with us to Bonnie's. We needed him to drive because Heath's cast put him out of playing chauffeur, and I just couldn't face another excursion with me behind the wheel on the wrong side of the road, and Gilley was far too rattled by the electrical surge at the restaurant to be able to focus on anything more than chewing his nails while hugging the fire extinguisher.

I eyed my partner skeptically on the drive over. He looked more than stressed. He'd lost some more weight and his complexion seemed pale with big blue bags under his buggy-looking eyes. He seemed exhausted and anxious at the same time, and I suddenly wondered if he'd managed more than a few hours' sleep in the last several days.

We'd been very careful about unplugging anything electric in our hotel room, but still, it had to be a little disconcerting to be so close to an outlet that could at any moment explode into a shower of sparks and set your room on fire again.

I knew that the witch would not give up until either we shut her down or she killed Gilley, and with his passport still in the custody of the Scottish authorities, there wasn't much we could do to get him away from her by sending Gil far from here, preferably back home.

And if I knew anything about spooks—which I did—I knew that once they set their sights on haunting someone, they didn't let a pesky little thing like distance interfere. The more determined ones had no problem crossing oceans and continents to follow someone they were after.

We arrived at Bonnie's just in time to see the inspector who was working the case of Cameron's death step through her front door and come down the steps to his unmarked car in the drive. Gopher parked just down the street and we all silently understood that it would be better if the inspector didn't know we were paying Bonnie a visit.

"Wonder what that's about," I muttered as I watched the man get into his car.

"He's probably just filling her in on the findings so far," Gopher assured me.

"Yeah, well, in that case, maybe you should stay here in the car with Gil while Heath and I go talk to Bonnie."

Gopher swiveled in his seat to look at me. "You think she might blame us even in light of the new details?"

"I don't know," I said honestly. "But I'd rather not find out by having her slam the door in my face when we ask if we can talk to her."

"Good point," Gopher conceded. "Okay, we'll stay put."

Heath and I waited until the inspector was well on his way before we exited the car and approached

Bonnie's house. We hadn't even climbed the two steps when the door opened and out came Cameron's pregnant girlfriend. She stopped abruptly when she saw us. "What do you lot want?" she snapped. I was beginning to think that her lack of civility had less to do with her grieving Cameron's loss or her hormones and more to do with her just being a bitch.

"We're here to see Bonnie," I said. "Is she in?"

Rose shook her head. "Naw. She's out."

I willed myself to smile politely. "Do you know when she'll be back?"

Rose shuffled down the other stairs and moved to walk past us. "I don't, and if I did, I wouldn't tell you, now, would I?"

Her remark gave me pause and I turned as she brushed past me roughly to say, "Do you have some kind of problem with me or something?"

The girl took two more paces, then stopped. She stood without moving for maybe five heartbeats; then she slowly turned. "Yeah, I've got a problem," she practically growled. "You and your fancy cameras came here to film yourselves a ghost story and now my Cameron is dead. And now my babe will never know her father. All because of you!"

I took a step forward, wanting to both comfort her and assure her that we had nothing to do with his death, but the hard glare that she gave me stopped me in my tracks and all I could do at that moment was say, "I'm so sorry."

Her eyes narrowed and I thought she was going to say something else, but she didn't. Instead she turned and waddled off. Heath and I waited on the walk until she disappeared around the corner. "Now what?" he asked just as my phone rang.

"Hello?" I answered.

"Now what?" Gil asked. I assumed he'd guessed by the body language what kind of exchange the pregnant chick and I had had.

I smiled. "I think we should wait for Bonnie."

"Do you know where she is or when she'll be back?"

My smile widened. "Yes and yes," I said, lifting my other hand to wave at an approaching figure with several canvas bags walking down the street toward us.

Heath and I hurried to help Bonnie with her groceries. Heath insisted on carrying at least one bag and I juggled another two while Bonnie walked with the remaining small satchel of fruit. "That's very kind of you," she said. "We'll just get these into the kitchen and I can put on a spot of tea for our chat."

Heath and I exchanged glances. "How'd you know we wanted to talk to you?"

"You're part of the ghost-hunting team that ran over Cameron, aren't you?" she said.

I gulped. "I swear to God, Bonnie, that was an accident."

"Aye," she said, lifting her free hand, which held a set of keys to her door. "I know that, miss. I've heard from the inspector this morning and he told me you lot weren't responsible. It was the witch's doing. And where that devil woman's ghost is concerned, no one living is really to blame."

We followed Bonnie inside and I nearly tripped right over several suitcases parked in the hallway. "Don't mind those," she called over her shoulder, heading deeper into the house. "I'm off on holiday just as soon as I stock the icebox for Rose."

"She's not going with you?" I asked, thinking it

might be a good idea for the both of them to get some-place far, far away and deal with their loss.

Bonnie shook her head sadly as she set down her package on the kitchen table in the tiny but tidy kitch-en. "She won't come. I tried all last night to get her to listen to reason, but the girl's as stubborn as a mule. And I hate to leave her so close to her due date, but I've no choice, now, do I? If I stay, it's certain the witch will come along and kill me as well."

"Do you think Rose's baby is in danger?"

"You mean from the witch?" Bonnie asked, and I nodded. "No," she said. "Not even Rigella is that cruel. In all the years she's been sporting her revenge, she's never struck down anyone younger than fourteen. Still, that's terribly young to have your life taken by such an evil as that. And besides, Rose and Camey never married, so there's no name to pass on to the child but Rose's own."

Heath was quietly unloading the bags and setting the contents on the counter. He appeared troubled by something Bonnie had said, but he didn't interrupt us, so I continued.

"Bonnie," I began, "what can you tell us about the witch?"

Our hostess moved to fill a teakettle with water. "You mean what can I tell you that may help you stop her, don't you?" she asked, avoiding my question.

"Yes," I said honestly. "I've had a lot of experience shutting down nasty spooks like the witch."

Bonnie smiled, but her eyes held no mirth. She set the kettle on the burner and turned on the gas. "I'd wager you never encountered one quite so powerful, though, eh?"

"No, not really. Which is why I need to know anything you can tell me about her. The more I know, the better my chances are for putting her in her place before she kills someone else."

"I hear she's after one of your crew," Bonnie said, still avoiding my question. "That Gillespie character. The one in the van that ran over Cameron. The witch is working very hard to add him to her list, am I right?"

I hesitated before answering her. She seemed to know a lot about us and that was throwing me off, but when I caught Heath's eye, he gave me a small nod. "Yes," I told her. "I believe the witch is after my partner, Gilley. She keeps trying to burn him with fire, and she's using electrical outlets to send surges and get the sparks to fly."

"He'd best be careful, then," Bonnie said, crossing her arms and looking at me as if she could read my mind. "And you as well."

I felt a small chill travel up my spine and I was immediately uncomfortable. I didn't know what Bonnie meant by that, but I decided not to pursue it and attempted one last time to get some answers out of her.

"Thank you," I said, "and I will be careful. But if you could please tell us everything you know about the witch, that might give us an advantage here and we could work to keep everyone else safe too."

Bonnie turned away from me and reached for a plate from the cabinet, then began to arrange cookies on it. "I know a bit about the witch," she said. "But not nearly as much as someone else here in the village."

"Who's that?"

"The current Witch of Queen's Close," Bonnie said.

"She knows everything that can be told about Rigella and her coven."

My jaw fell open and when I glanced at Heath, I saw that he mirrored my expression. "There is a *current* Witch of Queen's Close?" I gasped.

Bonnie turned around and set the plate on the table. "Aye. And she's about as friendly as Rigella. Still, she might be worth paying a visit to."

"Bonnie," Heath said, "you told us at your shop that Rigella and her coven were thirty-five years early. Do you think this woman you're sending us to talk to could have called her up prematurely?"

Bonnie took a bite of cookie as the teakettle began to whistle. She waited until she'd poured the boiling water into a teapot before she answered. "Aye," she said, barely above a whisper. "And I also believe she was the one that killed Cameron."

"Why would you think that?" I asked carefully.

"She and my brother were once a couple," Bonnie said. "Things went sour about a year ago, when Camey took up with Rose."

Again I looked at Heath and our eyes locked. I felt a pulse of electricity coil up my spine. We'd already concluded that Cameron was likely killed by someone with a personal grudge against him. And who better to hold a grudge than your ex?

"Where can we find this woman?" I asked.

"Last I heard she was renting the small cottage on Joseph Hill's property."

I sucked in a breath. "The man that was found hanging yesterday?"

It was Bonnie's turn to gasp. "What?" she said, the hand holding the teapot over my cup hesitating. "Joseph's dead?"

I nodded solemnly. "Heath and I discovered him hanging in that huge oak tree out behind Fergus Ericson's house."

Bonnie's eyes darted to her luggage out in the hall. "Then the witch has claimed another victim," she said softly.

"So it seems," I agreed.

With a shaking hand, Bonnie picked up her steaming cup of tea and took a small sip. "Oh, my," she said. "Poor Joseph."

No one said anything for a long moment and Bonnie was the first to break the silence when she appeared to snap out of her thoughts and looked sharply at the clock. "I'll need to see you off," she announced, getting up and collecting our teacups and saucers. "Don't want to miss me train."

Heath and I got up and thanked her for the tea and the cookies. She ushered us out, giving her apologies for not being able to talk with us further, and suggested we find the living Witch of Queen's Close to get a better history and gave us very hurried directions on how to get to Joseph's house from her cottage.

We stepped out onto her front steps and she gave us one last farewell, before shutting the door in our faces.

Heath and I turned and walked down the steps. "That was . . . interesting," he said.

"I was leaning more toward odd."

Heath smiled and looked at me sideways. "I'll lean with you," he said, and physically leaned into me, bumping me with his good shoulder.

I started to laugh but caught myself when I looked up at him and found myself very attracted to that handsome face, even with the one swollen eye and scratched face. "What?" he asked, probably noticing how I'd caught myself.

"Huh? Um . . . nothing."

"You okay?"

"Sure!" I said a little too enthusiastically.

Heath laughed. "Well, you've been a little off the past couple of days."

I immediately became self-conscious. "Off? How have I been off?"

We were walking down toward the van, where Gil and Gopher were waiting for us with the engine idling. "I don't know," Heath said. "Every once in a while you look at me funny. And when I touch you or brush against you, you stiffen. If I didn't know better, I'd say you thought I was repulsive."

I attempted a laugh.

And failed miserably.

What came out was some sort of high-pitched impersonation of a hyena. "Don't be ridiculous!" I insisted, scrambling to turn the whole awful conversation into a joke. Waving my hand dramatically in a circle around his head and attempting a highbrow accent, I said, "You're gorgeous, dahling, simply marvelous-looking!"

"Especially with the shiner and the arm in a sling, right?" Heath said, turning his eyes to the ground.

And I realized that he must feel really self-conscious himself about his appearance, so I stopped and caught him by the shoulder. "Dude," I said seriously, "you really *are* hot, okay? Like . . . unfairly gorgeous. There are men who must hate you, and women I've seen firsthand practically swoon when you walk by."

Heath's mouth broke into a terrific grin. "And you'd totally be into me if it weren't for Steven, right?"

I couldn't help it; I blushed. I could feel the immediate searing heat hit my cheeks, and a cool sweat broke out across my brow. I darted my own eyes to the ground and hurried my pace. "Yeah," I said. "Right. Steven's my guy. My boyfriend. The man. My S.O. . . ."

Mercifully I reached the van at that point and had to stop talking. Gilley opened the door for me and I hustled into the backseat, forcing Heath to take the front. The moment I began to fasten my seat belt, however, my best friend blew any remaining cover by saying, "Jeez, M. J.! What's up with you? You're totally flushed. Are you all hot and bothered?"

I glared coldly at him and he immediately shut up, but his eyes also swiveled to Heath, who was also strapping himself in, and I saw a bit of understanding blossom in Gil's eyes. He opened his mouth wide and slapped a hand over his mouth and looked ready to squeal with delight.

I shook my head vigorously and mouthed, "NO!" at him, but his eyes were all big and his expression was absolutely giddy.

After a moment, he mouthed back, "You and Heath?"

"Shut up!" I mouthed back.

Gilley broke out into a fit of giggles.

"What's he laughing about?" Gopher asked.

"Nothing!" I said, punching Gil hard in the arm right before Gopher and Heath looked back at us. "I just hit his funny bone accidentally." Gilley continued to laugh and roll around in the backseat. I wanted to smack him. "Can we just go?" I snapped.

Gopher looked once more at Gil before he shrugged. "Sure, M. J. Where to?"

I recalled Bonnie's directions, discreetly hit Gil in the arm again, then pointed to a nearby intersection. "That way."

*     *     *

We arrived at Joseph's place about ten minutes and two wrong turns later. We could tell it was his house by the number of flowers on his front doorstep. It seemed that people in the neighborhood had heard the news and were stopping by to pay their respects through small bouquets laid on his welcome mat.

Gopher pulled to a stop at the front door and we all just stared at those flowers. Gilley had finally recovered himself, and he was the first to speak. "Well, that's just really, really sad."

I sighed. "It is."

"Are you sensing him, M. J.?" Heath asked me.

I looked away from the flowers and stared up at the house, opening up my sixth sense as wide as I could. "No," I said finally. "I'm not."

"Let's get out and take a look around the house before we go in search of the woman who rents his cottage," Heath suggested.

I knew what he was getting at. Suicides were tough cookies. They routinely refused to cross over, and they were also the hardest energies to get to communicate. I think it has to do with the amount of shame they feel for taking their own lives. It's as if they can't bear the thought of what they've done, so they shut down and try to hide from both worlds—the living and the dead. It can take years to convince them to cross over where they'll get some spiritual help and recover from the guilt.

And even though I believed that Rigella had somehow convinced Joseph to take his own life, I knew that the moment he realized he was dead, he'd be facing one huge guilt complex.

We all got out and unloaded several magnetic grenades from the trunk. I strapped mine into the tool belt Meg had purchased for me, as did Heath, Gilley, and Gopher. Gil also tugged on his magnetic sweatshirt, which he told us he'd spent the previous day "improving." The garment sagged weirdly on him, and I figured that might be due to the fact that he'd loaded on a few pounds' worth of extra magnets.

Heath unzipped a duffel bag and pulled out two electrostatic meters—the only two left after the fire besides the ones we'd left in the close. He handed one to Gil and the other to Gopher. "Wouldn't one of you need this?" Gopher asked him.

Heath tapped his temple and smiled. "We're good," he said. "I've got my internal meter turned up high."

I nodded. "Me too."

Once we were adequately armed, we set off. I was in the lead and kept us close to the house, which was a two-story gray stucco structure with a beautiful mahogany door and black shutters. A flower box near the window held the withered remains of some old blooms, and leaves had collected around the bushes, but otherwise the house was quite charming.

"Do you want to ring the bell?" Gilley asked.

"No one's home," Heath and I said together. I looked at him, surprised that we kept saying things in unison, and he added, "We've got to stop doing that."

I could feel the heat begin to creep back to my cheeks, so I hurried along and tried to distract myself. "Let's check the back," I suggested.

We rounded the corner of the house and came up short. From the road the house appeared to sit on a small parcel of property, as it was close to the street with only a small front yard.

The back was an utter surprise.

Huge trees lined an enormous yard that stretched down a low sloping hill for several hundred yards. Near a pond at the bottom of the hill was a small guesthouse, which mirrored the structure behind us except for being about one-quarter of the size. Far beyond the guesthouse and the pond, however, and up another sloping hill was the thing that really took my breath away.

"Whoa," said Gopher.

"Holy cow," said Gil.

"No way," said Heath.

"Way," I said. "And, on that note, Heath, your grandfather rules!"

We were all staring at the remnants of an ancient castle, weathered and crumbling but still with enormous appeal. It proudly perched itself at the far end of the lawn about a half mile away, and I knew it must be part of Joseph's parcel because the green pattern of the freshly mowed yard indicated that it was one contiguous piece of property. There was also little doubt that the castle represented the very ruins Samuel Whitefeather had suggested we should look for.

"Which one should we check out first?" Gil asked, completely forgetting about our first priority to find Joseph's ghost.

"Hold the phone," I said, and motioned to Heath to survey the rest of the back of the house, hoping for any sign of the man who'd died the day before. After ten minutes I shrugged. "He's not here."

"Nope," Heath agreed. "Let's hit the guesthouse." Heath spoke in a way that suggested he had a strong intuitive feeling.

Gopher and Gilley turned to me. "I'm with him," I said. "Let's go talk to the current Witch of Queen's Close and see if she's been playing with fire."

I immediately regretted my choice of words when Gilley blanched, and yelled, "My fire extinguisher!" He then dashed back to the van to retrieve it.

We waited for him to get back and my heart went out to him when I saw how firmly he was gripping it. Without another word, I led us down the path to the small house with a plume of smoke snaking its way from the chimney.

# Chapter 11

We got another surprise the moment we stepped onto the porch of the guesthouse. It made both Heath and me jump and immediately reach for our grenades. I uncapped one as fast as I could and threw the metal spike toward the offending object staring us in the face . . . and nothing happened.

Well, nothing except there was a delighted giggle from inside the house right before the door opened. "Now, what did that poor defenseless broom ever do to you? I wonder," said a tall woman with long silver hair and beautiful green eyes from the doorway.

My heart was hammering hard while my gaze swiveled from the woman in the doorway to the big black broom in the corner, which was identical to the three that had chased and beaten Heath and me the day before. "Where did *that* come from?" I barked, pointing to the broom. I wasn't trying to be rude, but in light of the circumstances, I felt I was owed a few answers.

"I made it with me own hands," said the woman as she placed those hands on her slender hips. "It's an exact replica of the sort the famous Witch of Queen's

Close used to carry through the village. It was a way
of embracing her title as the village witch," she said.
"It was also a way of showing off how powerful a
figure she was. To carry a broom about in those days
took true courage as accusations of heresy were quite
common. Many poor souls were hanged for much less
in fact. But the Witch of Queen's Close wasn't afraid.
She was a powerful lass, and no one dared challenge
her, that is, until the plague struck the village in six-
teen forty-five."

"She a friend of yours, this famous witch?" I practically growled, convinced that we'd just found the
very person who had in fact called up Rigella's ghost.

"Not especially," said the woman, evasively. "But I
hold her in the highest respect, and after seeing her
about these parts the last few nights, I thought it best
to place the broom on the porch out of reverence."

There was a long awkward silence that followed as
those green eyes just stared at me in challenge. I
didn't know what to say next, so I glared back, trying
hard not to blink.

Finally the woman said, "Sir, would you mind not
pointing that directly at me? You're rattling me nerves."

My eyes swiveled to Gilley, who was standing
right next to me holding his fire extinguisher chest-
high while aiming the nozzle at the woman. With his
wild eyes he looked like a frightened little kid, on the
verge of shouting, "Stranger-danger!"

I placed a hand on his shoulder and whispered,
"It's okay, Gil. Let's give her a chance before we jump
to conclusions."

Gilley lowered the extinguisher but kept his eyes
fully trained on the woman. She surprised all of us
when she stepped forward suddenly, causing all four

of us to leap back. Belatedly we noticed that she had her hand extended and a smile on her face. "I'm Katherine McKay," she said.

No one moved to take her hand. Instead we all just looked at it uncertainly. This made Katherine laugh, and she finally pulled her hand back to cross her arms over her chest. "For ghost hunters you're a bit squeamish, aren't you?"

"Are you a witch?" Gil asked.

"Aye," she said. "I am. But I'm not the sort that'll harm the likes of you, so why don't you come in for a bit of tea and talk?"

I looked uncertainly at Heath. He gave an almost imperceptible nod and said, "That would be very nice. Thank you."

We followed Katherine into her home and I was surprised by the spaciousness of its interior. From the outside it looked much smaller than it actually was. The door we walked through led into a beautifully furnished living room with two love seats and matching wing chairs upholstered in cool celery green and pale yellow with a bit of light pink for accent. There was a fire in the hearth that filled the room with cozy heat, and fresh flowers on two of the nearby tables. The whole house smelled of antiques, sandalwood, and fresh flowers. It was a lovely combination.

Katherine pointed to the seating area. "Make yourselves comfortable," she said, and only arched an eyebrow when Gopher held his camera up to get a good shot of the surroundings. "We're filming an episode of our television show," he explained.

"So it seems," she said with a chuckle. "I've already got the kettle on. Tea and bikkies will be just a moment."

"What's a bikkie?" Gilley whispered, sitting down uneasily on the edge of a wing chair and eyeing the fire in the hearth nervously.

"It's slang for biscuit. Or cookie," I said, my eyes and sixth sense roving the atmosphere for any sign of spooks. "You getting anything?" I asked Heath quietly.

"Nothing."

I made a head motion at Gilley. "Anything on the meter?"

He pulled it out of his back pocket and looked at the dial, then shook his head. "Weird, right?" he whispered. "I mean, we should be getting something, shouldn't we?"

I frowned. It was weird. I would have expected that this woman, if she was the person who called up the witch, would have one or two spooks lurking about. Katherine came back into the living room carrying a large tray with several beautifully decorated porcelain teacups. As she set the tray down, I noticed that no two were alike. "Choose your cup," she told us before heading back toward the kitchen again.

I was reminded with a pang of the coffee shop back home that I was a frequent visitor to. Patrons were encouraged to choose from a huge display of one-of-a-kind coffee mugs. Mine, of course, was a Halloween-inspired cup, with a black cat and ghost for the handle.

Thinking I should choose something a little lighter, I went for a peacock blue cup with gold trim. Gilley looked troubled and did not select a cup. "Don't like tea?" I asked him.

"What if she tries to poison us?"

The question was so unexpected that it actually made

me laugh. "Don't be ridiculous," I said, but immediately noticed that Heath and Gopher had set their chosen cups back on the tray.

I rolled my eyes. "I doubt she'd poison all four of us, guys. I mean, that could get a little messy, don't you think?"

We had no time to discuss it further because Katherine came back into the sitting room carrying a large steaming pot of tea and a plate of cookies. "I have a variety of bikkies today," she sang happily, setting the teapot in the center of the tray and handing the plate directly to Gilley.

He took it obediently and observed the arrangement. I knew it was really hard for him to pass up sweets. Gil loved his sugar. And sure enough, his hand wavered over one gooey chocolate and caramel creation while he licked his lips. "Go on, then," Katherine encouraged as she sat down. "It's not going to bite you, now, is it?"

Gil's cheeks tinged a slight red and he took the cookie, placing it directly onto his plate. Katherine then poured tea into all the cups, both those still on the tray and the one I still held.

"Cream?" she asked us politely. I declined, but Heath and Gopher and Gilley nodded as one.

"Sugar?" she asked next. That won her the same reaction. And it also won us a laugh as she saw through everyone's discomfort. "Now," she said at last when the refreshments had been seen to. "What brings you by my humble home?"

I decided that the best approach was a direct one. "We're looking for the person responsible for calling up the witch."

Katherine's eyebrows shot up. "The person responsible?" she said. "Why, the witch rises on her own, Miss . . ."

"Holliday," I said. "M. J. Holliday. And that's Heath Whitefeather, Peter Gophner, and Gilley Gillespie."

Katherine sucked in a breath and stared hard at Gilley. "Gillespie?" she whispered. "Oh, no, sir, you shouldn't be here on this side of Edinburgh at such a time as this!"

Gilley, who'd been ogling the still-uneaten cookie on his plate, looked up in surprise, and when he saw Katherine's expression, he seemed to shrink in his chair. "Tell me about it," he squeaked. "But I'm stuck here until I get my passport back."

"Who's got your passport?"

"The authorities."

"Why do they have it?"

"Because our van hit Cameron Lancaster, and they're not convinced yet that I didn't have anything to do with his death."

Understanding seemed to dawn on Katherine's face. "Oh, aye," she said, taking a bite of cookie. "But they'll clear all that up soon, now, won't they? As soon as they realize the witch is loose and where she flies, well, the dead bodies usually follow."

Gilley audibly gulped.

"Which brings me back to my original question, Katherine. Did you call up the witch?"

She looked at me oddly, as if I'd just asked her a question she couldn't really understand. "Now, why would I do that?"

I thought her choice of words was interesting. She didn't deny calling up the witch; she simply turned the question back on me. "We know Rigella and her coven are thirty-five years early," I said. "They always come in one-hundred-year intervals, and no one expected them to arrive here now, did they?"

Katherine appeared uncomfortable for the first time since we'd arrived. "I didn't call her up," she said, her eyes avoiding my own.

"But someone did," I insisted.

"Perhaps," she admitted, and seemed to want to say something more, but caught herself, and took a sip of tea instead.

I took a deep breath and pulled in my temper. "Who would be capable of calling her up, then?"

"I'm sure I wouldn't know," Katherine replied a bit too quickly.

I set down my teacup and fixed her with determined eyes. "Hypothetically speaking, then."

Katherine sighed. "Three decades ago when I was very young and stupid, I was the head witch in a small coven of women who were quite enchanted with the legend of Rigella. Though she has been immortalized as an evil witch who placed a terrible curse upon our village, before that, she was a master healer and a keeper of great wisdom and knowledge.

"Most of the villagers reviled her, and yes, some even feared her. So, when the plague struck and she tended to those most loyal to her first, many of them survived, while so many others did not.

"That incited fear and panic and eventually rage against the very woman who was trying so desperately to save the village. She and her entire family were killed unjustly and by a terrible cruelty. So back when I was young and silly, I sympathized with Mistress Rigella and did not fault her for wanting to exact her revenge."

"What changed?" I asked, seeing the regret in her eyes.

"I met Cameron," she said simply. "I never thought I'd fall in love with a Lancaster, but I did. And although we never married—Cameron was against it because of the curse—we were certainly as close as any husband and wife could be. After I fell in love with him, I disbanded the coven and vowed to keep him and any of our children safe should the witch arise again. But Cameron and I were never blessed with little ones. No matter how much care I took, I was never able to carry a babe to term. It put a terrible strain on our relationship, and soon we drifted apart and our discussions became one terrible row after another, until we couldn't stand the sight of one another. I left him for good eight months ago when I learned that the lass he'd been seeing behind me back became pregnant.

"I'll admit, I cursed him then, but I had nothing to do with calling Rigella up early, and as much as I was hurt by Cameron carrying on behind me back, I would never use the witch to hurt him."

"But the witch wasn't used to hurt him," I said to her. "She was used to cover up his murder."

Katherine's mouth fell open. "What lie is this?" she demanded.

"It's no lie," I told her. "Cameron was murdered, possibly several days before our van ran over him. During that time he was frozen, then thawed and placed in the street directly in the path of the van. I believe Rigella's real target that night was Gilley."

Katherine appeared genuinely surprised, and I stared hard at her face to see if I could detect any theatrics, and saw none. "Someone *murdered* Cameron?"

"Yes," I said.

Katherine got up and began to pace. I knew she was withholding something, but what it was I couldn't say for sure. Into the silence Heath said, "And now the witch is killing other people. As you well know. That maintenance worker down in the close, we're pretty sure the witch scared him to death. And your landlord, Joseph Hill. We're also convinced the witch got him to hang himself."

Katherine's expression turned to a scowl. "That's no great loss, now, is it?" she muttered.

"Excuse me?" I asked.

She stopped pacing and regarded me. "Joseph Hill was a dodgy old bloke if ever there was one! He owned a great deal of property here in the village and was disliked by many people. He even turned against his closest friend, Fergus. The two had been chums since primary school, but in the past year, Joseph had become sullen and withdrawn and even avoided his oldest and closest mate.

"We had no idea what'd got into him until we learned that Joseph had a brain tumor and likely had less than a year to live. The cancer affected his mind, you see. He thought everyone was out to get him, so I wasn't surprised to learn he'd taken his life, what with that for a prognosis and a few screws loose in the ol' belfry."

"So what happens now that Joseph is dead?" Gilley wondered. "I mean, will you have to leave your home?"

Katherine smiled in amusement. "I suspect not," she said. "Fergus had told me privately after we learned of Joseph's terminal condition that when his old friend died, he'd step in and buy the whole parcel. He didn't want to see the property next to him be divided up into smaller sections with lots of noisy neighbors and his ghost tour has been a smashing success these past few months, so he can certainly afford it. I'm sure he'll honor my rental agreement once he's purchased the parcel."

We were getting off track again so I said, "The thing is, Katherine, we need to find the person who unleashed Rigella's ghost. You mentioned that you were part of a coven of women who used to worship her. If you didn't call her up, could one of the others have done it?"

Katherine wrung her hands. "No," she said. "Only one of that original group aside from me could have done that," she said, her eyes thoughtful. "But it's not possible that it was her."

"Why not?"

Katherine merely smiled and said, "She's not capable of that kind of malice, miss. Not capable at'all."

"Are you?"

Katherine's smile broadened. "Aye," she admitted, and I felt my shoulders tense. "But as I've said before, I did not call up the witch."

"Then it must be this other woman," I insisted.

But Katherine was shaking her head. "No," she said firmly. "'Twasn't her."

I sighed, exasperated by the conversation. We were going in circles. "Then who else could it have been?"

Katherine tapped her fingernails against the side of her teacup. "Rigella only communicates with her direct descendants," she said. "Only someone from her bloodline could have called her from the shadows."

My brow furrowed. "Hold on," I said. "How could Rigella still have a bloodline? I thought her entire family was murdered."

Katherine sat down again and lifted her cup. "One

sister escaped," she said. "Though just barely. Legend says that the youngest and fairest of Rigella's sisters, Isla, was ravaged by several villagers, then left for dead. But we know that the poor girl survived. She was found wandering about the forest by one of Rigella's loyal friends and taken to their home, nursed back to health, only to die eight months later in childbirth. The identity of the child was kept a strict secret and the babe was adopted into the family, which allowed Rigella's bloodline to continue."

"So who's related to this child?" I asked gently. "I mean, you know so much about Rigella, Katherine, you must know all the members of that ancestry."

But I could sense immediately that Katherine wasn't about to tell me, and I wondered whom she was protecting. "I'm sure I don't know," she said in a way that said there would be no further discussion about it.

"Can you tell us about the brooms?" Heath said next. "M. J. and I were chased through the woods yesterday by three phantoms riding brooms. Exact replicas of the one you have on your porch."

That seemed to trouble our host. "Chased?" she said, and her eyes fixed on Heath's bruised face and broken arm. "Did they do that?" she asked breathlessly.

"They did," I said. "And one of them very nearly took my life."

"I'm terribly sorry," Katherine apologized. Again I felt she was being genuine, but I also knew there was more to her than what I could immediately discern. "Rigella came to me in a dream several months ago," she confessed. "I hadn't seen her in decades. Since right before I disbanded the coven."

"Hold on," I said, putting my hand up in a stopping motion. "You dream about Rigella?"

"Often," she said. "She first appeared in a dream to me when I was only nineteen. She said that I was her sister reincarnated, and that I was to play a key role in her return. She was quite mesmerizing, you know. She had this presence, this almost regal quality, that I found quite irresistible."

"Oh, I know," I agreed. "But tell me about this most recent dream."

"It wasn't long after Cameron and I separated," she said. "I'd been having a rough go of it, and I'd just moved in here, liking the privacy afforded to me by living on Joseph Hill's property. Not many people would tolerate him after he became ill, and I knew no one would come round to stick their noses in my business if I lived here."

Katherine's eyes were staring far off again, and I wondered where she went, when she seemed to pull herself from her thoughts and continued. "So, one night I was fast asleep, and Rigella appeared at the foot of my bed. She called me sister again, and asked a favor of me."

"What kind of favor?" Gopher asked, his camera capturing the entire conversation.

"She asked if I would craft a series of brooms. She showed me exactly what they should look like, and I've always played with sculpture and such, so I found it quite challenging to try to reproduce them. It took some time and many prototypes to get them exactly right, but I think they're quite beautiful really."

"They look like something out of *Harry Potter*," Gil remarked.

Katherine appeared to take that as a compliment. "Yes, they do, don't they?"

"Yeah, they're great as long as they're not bashing

you over the head or chasing you through the woods,"
I grumbled.

Katherine blushed. "Right," she said. "Sorry."

"So you made more than one broom?" Heath said,
getting us back on track.

Our host nodded. "I made seven," she said. "And
six were stolen from my porch a fortnight ago."

"A fortnight?" I said, several things striking me at
once. "That's two weeks, right?"

"Aye," she said.

"What are you thinking?" Gil asked, knowing I was
putting something together in my head.

Instead of answering him, I looked at our producer.
"Gopher," I said, "when did Kim and John first come
here to scout Edinburgh as a location?"

Gopher lowered his camera. "Right around two weeks
ago."

"Someone knew we were coming," I said. Somehow we had triggered this series of events, I was sure
of it. But with whom still remained a mystery.

"All right," I said, placing my now-empty teacup
back on its saucer and getting up. "Thank you, Katherine, for the tea and cookies. We'll leave you to continue our investigation. But if there's anything else
that you decide we might need to know, would you
call us, please?" I quickly scribbled my new number
onto a piece of paper from my purse and handed it to
her.

She hesitated ever so slightly before taking it, then
smiled warmly. "Yes, of course."

We left her and headed outside to receive the last
shock of the morning. When we stepped onto the porch,
we all noticed that Katherine's one remaining broom
was gone.

* * *

It took us a lot of leg power to catch up to Gilley, who, upon seeing that the broom was gone, had bolted right back to the van at breakneck speed. In fact, I didn't think I'd ever seen him run so fast. Especially not weighed down by several pounds of magnets and a fire extinguisher.

"He can really run for a little guy," Heath panted beside me as we took off after Gil.

"He's motivated," I said, knowing Gilley was running on pure fear at this point. I'm not sure who'd eventually told him about our encounter with the brooms (although I suspected it was Gopher), but somewhere between the previous night and early that morning, he'd learned the truth about what had happened to me and Heath in the woods, and repeated the story back to me over breakfast, completely pissed that I'd tried to protect him from it. It'd been a relief when Heath had shown up to divert his attention.

Gil made it to the van but was left to wait for us, because Gopher had the keys. "Gil," I said when we reached him, and I had to double over to catch my breath. "You can't run away from us like that!"

Gilley was panting hard too. "Someone open the van!" he pleaded. "Come on, guys! Open the van!"

I looked over my shoulder. Gopher was walking with no apparent urgency and didn't seem particularly concerned that Gil was so rattled. I suspected he'd had enough of my partner's theatrics.

Heath, however, was more sensitive to Gilley's nervous condition, and he trotted off to intercept Gopher and get the keys. He came back shortly and opened the door. Gil practically shoved him aside as he dived into the van, pushing his way to the back and curling up in a small ball, hugging his extinguisher. I knew immediately that I'd never get him out of the van to go with us to investigate the ruins of the castle. "Great," I sighed. "That's just great."

"What now?" Gopher said, finally coming up alongside me.

"What time is it?" I asked, scratching my head as I struggled to think through how best to deal with Gilley's meltdown.

Gopher looked at his watch. "Ten minutes to noon."

I sighed tiredly. There was still a lot of daylight left, and I was already wiped out. Never a good sign. "Well, someone has to stay with Gil while we go back and search the castle."

Gopher looked from Heath to me, and back again. "I'm assuming I'm not included in that whole 'we' part."

"I need Heath," I explained. "It was his grandfather who told us to go looking, after all."

Gopher didn't look happy at the babysitting assignment. "Why don't *you* stay with Gilley and *I'll* go with Heath?"

"Because Heath needs me," I said, and was relieved when Heath backed me up with a vigorous nod.

"I do," he added. "I need M. J."

Something about the way he said that made my heart beat faster and the heat returned to my cheeks. Before either of them could notice, I turned away as if it were already decided and began to trek back toward the castle. "We'll be available by cell, Gopher," I called as I walked away. "And if we're not back in an hour, send the cavalry."

Heath caught up with me as I was making my way down the hill, and we walked in silence for a while, much to my relief. The castle was farther away than it appeared, and when I looked back well after we'd passed the cottage, I was surprised to find how small the house and guesthouse were. "It's a ways, huh?" I asked casually. Heath didn't answer me. He appeared to be lost in thought. "Yo, earth to Heath. Come in, please."

"Huh? Oh, sorry. What was that?"

"You okay?"

He smiled ruefully. "I was just wondering the same thing about you."

That took me by surprise. "I'm fine," I said quickly. "Why?"

Heath stopped and reached out with his good hand to stop me too. "What's going on with you and me?"

I was completely speechless. I had no idea how to reply, as I stood there with a thundering heart and scrambled thoughts. "Ah . . . um . . . wha?"

Heath sighed and looked away. Oh great, now I'd pissed him off. "Why can't you just say it?" he said.

My brow furrowed. "Say what?"

"Say that you don't want me around anymore."

I sucked in a breath. "Oh, Lord, Heath! Is *that* what you think?"

He turned back to me and there was real hurt in his eyes. "Well, it's obvious, isn't it, M. J.? For the past couple of days you walk away from me every time we're alone, and I can't get near you without you going all stiff and defensive."

I reached out and held the hand that had stopped me. "Honey," I said gently, working to hold his eyes. "That isn't it at all."

"Then what is it?" he asked. "I mean, why the cold shoulder? What've I done to deserve that?"

I closed my eyes and leaned forward, resting my forehead on his chest. "It's not you," I whispered.

"What?" Heath asked. He hadn't heard me, but I was finding it really hard to speak at the moment. He lifted my chin with his fingertip and repeated, "What did you say?"

"It's me," I told him. "I'm having a hard time being here, so far away from home."

"You miss Steven?" It was less a question and more an assumption.

I took a deep breath and answered him honestly. "No, Heath. I don't miss him. And that's troubling, don't you think?"

Understanding dawned in Heath's eyes and for a minute all we did was stare at each other. And then, very slowly, he lowered his lips to mine and kissed me. It wasn't a deep and passionate kiss, more soft and incredibly gentle . . . and somehow perfect. That is, until a terrible moaning broke the stillness of the early afternoon, causing me to jump at least a foot.

"What the *freak* was that?"

"A kiss, and then a moan," Heath said. I looked sideways at him and found him grinning.

"How can you joke at a time like this?" I demanded as I stood there with a hand on my chest to still my thundering heart.

"It beats running away like Gilley," Heath replied with a shrug. "Come on, girl," he added, reaching out a hand to me. "That sounded like a spook, which is right up our alley."

I steadied my breathing and took his hand. It felt warm and comforting and I refused to think about that when we had other things to tackle. "It came from the castle," I said.

"Yep," Heath said, and we'd taken only two steps forward again when another moan echoed out of the crumbling ruins. "Female," Heath whispered. "And in pain."

I had to agree. Whoever was making that terrible sound appeared to be in agony. "Injured?" I asked.

"Maybe."

We crept forward again and I let go of Heath's hand long enough to reach for a grenade. "Don't want to get caught unprepared," I said softly.

Heath copied me. "Good thinking. We can get in over there." He pointed to a large section of the main wall that had fallen inward.

I followed him there, listening closely and feeling out the surrounding energy. My sixth sense was definitely picking up some spectral action, and I silently cursed myself for leaving the two electrostatic meters behind with Gopher and Gilley.

We edged closer to the gaping hole in the side of the castle and were about to enter when I heard what sounded like footsteps clicking down stone stairs. I looked up and gasped, clutching Heath's shoulder. "What?" he asked.

I pointed straight up. There in the arched window of the central tower stood a male figure in period costume staring menacingly down at us.

"Someone's not happy to see us," Heath remarked.

"Yeah," I said, feeling the intense wave of angry energy wafting down to us. "I'm picking up the same vibe."

As a gesture of goodwill I raised my arm and waved at the figure. His scowl deepened right before he vanished into thin air. "Not too friendly, was he?" Heath said, a hint of mirth in his voice.

"Come on," I said, still gripping the cap of the grenade tightly. "Let's head in."

We had to help each other over the cascade of crumbling rocks into the main hall, which was dark and moody. I squinted in the gloom and turned around in a full circle. "Lots of spooks in here," I whispered, feeling the hairs stand up all along my arms and the back of my neck.

"I'm gettin' the same thing. Should we record?" he asked, lifting the camera Gopher had given him.

"Might be a good idea."

Heath handed me the grenade he'd been carrying in his good hand and tugged out the small camera from his tool belt. He had to work to get the viewfinder open, but eventually he had the camera poised and recording at shoulder level. "Where do you want to head first?" he asked.

An acute keening wafted through the musty halls of the abandoned castle. "I'd start by trying to find the source of *that*," I said.

Heath grinned. "I think it came from down there." He indicated with the camera down a hallway just off the main staircase.

"After you," I said with a slight bow.

Heath began walking and I kept close on his heels, peering around him as we entered the gloomy space. "Do you have a flashlight?" he asked.

I tugged the Maglite out of my belt and switched it on. It illuminated the hall fairly well, but sent spooky shadows all along the walls. We'd gone about ten paces when another keening cry reverberated down to us. We stopped in our tracks and listened. This time we could just make out the words, "Where's me babe?"

"Female again," I whispered into Heath's ear.

"And she's looking for a baby," Heath said.

"Let's keep going," I suggested.

We kept walking and made it another ten paces when loud, clomping footsteps thumped right over our heads. We ignored those and continued forward toward where we'd heard the woman's cry.

We made it to the end of that hallway without incident, only to discover that the corridor split off into two separate directions, one to the right, and the other to the left. There was also a room directly in front of us with an ancient-looking wooden door, covered in dust and listing heavily on rusty hinges. "Which way?" I asked softly.

Heath shrugged. "Not sure."

I was about to suggest we go left when that disembodied voice repeated, *"Where? Where is me babe?"*

"Right," Heath said, and turned right into the new hallway.

I was following so close to him that my head could have rested on his shoulder. Normally, I'm not so easily spooked, but this entire trip had been so far out of my league that I was a little jumpy, and felt the need to stick really close to Heath.

Okay, *and* I might have liked the way he smelled. Whatever. The point is, I felt the need to stick really close to him, and that was perhaps the cause of what happened next.

My foot accidentally caught his shoe, and that made him trip. I tried to catch him, but his larger size and momentum caused us both to pitch forward and tumble into a small room, where we fell to the ground on top of each other. The grenades I'd been clutching went spiraling out of my hands, as did the flashlight, but somehow, Heath managed to hold on to his camera. Still he sacrificed his bad arm to break his fall.

He let out a terrible groan, sat up, and hunched over to grip his cast tightly while rocking back and forth in severe pain.

"Ohmigod!" I gasped, trying to scoot around to help him. "I'm so sorry, Heath! I'm so, so sorry!"

His eyes were pinched closed and his mouth was set firmly in a grimace while he fought through the pain. "It's okay," he said in a very hoarse whisper a few moments later. "Just . . . give . . . me . . . a minute."

I hovered right next to him silently cursing my own clumsiness and trying to think of what I could do for him. "Do you need me to call Gilley or Gopher?"

Heath shook his head, but said nothing more. He just continued to keep his eyes tightly closed, hug his arm, and rock back and forth.

And the longer he did that, the worse I felt. "I think I should go for help," I said as the minutes ticked by. "I think you might have reinjured it."

Heath's eyes opened then. "No," he said, his eyes leaking tears. "Just zinged it pretty good."

"Do you have me babe?" asked a woman's voice right behind me.

I froze, and Heath's eyes became huge as he focused on something over my shoulder.

With great care I turned my head very, very slowly and nearly fell over when I found myself staring straight into the face I'd seen only in my dreams. The face of Rigella the witch.

# Chapter 12

On my hands and feet I scuttled backward, away from the woman hovering near us. She seemed to notice my reaction, and her hand went to her heart as one tear leaked down her cheek. "Please!" she begged me. "Someone's taken me babe away! You must tell me where!"

My heart was hammering in my chest, and as discreetly as I could, I began to feel around for a grenade. In that moment it didn't occur to me that I had several more tucked into leather loops around my waist; all I could think of were the two I'd dropped when Heath and I had fallen.

"Someone's taken your baby?" Heath asked gently. I didn't know if he knew whom he was talking to, but I wasn't taking any chances. The moment I got my fingers on a grenade, I was going to explode that ghost right out of the room.

Rigella nodded. "The child's come early," she gasped. "I tried to hold it inside a little longer, but the wee one wanted to come out." The witch's eyes darted about the room, as if she was searching for any sign of her child.

"Tell me about the baby," Heath offered just as my fingers closed on something metallic and cylindrical.

Rigella's eyes came back to him, and a look of pure joy overcame her face. "The most beautiful face you've ever seen!" she gushed. "Me sister would be so happy. She always loved children."

I eased my other hand over the top of the cylinder, gripping it tightly, and tugged. It held fast. "Your sister?" Heath asked, encouraging her to continue.

I risked looking down and realized I'd grabbed the flashlight, not the grenade, but my eyes also landed on one of them right at my kneecap. Taking great care not to make any sudden movements, I eased my hand to the grenade, lifting it off the floor and curling my fingers around the cap.

"Oh, Rigella would have loved the babe!" the woman said. "Me oldest sister was always such a caring woman."

"M. J.!" Heath hissed suddenly, and I looked up from the cap at the top of the grenade right before I was about to tug it free. "Wait!" he whispered.

I felt my brow furrow, and I glanced back at the woman hovering near us, who was the spitting image of the witch who'd entered my dreams. She was as real as any human being, although there was a bit of hollowness to her eyes that told me more than anything that she wasn't as real as she looked.

"What's your name, sweet lady?" Heath asked gently.

"Isla," she said distractedly while continuing to look about the room.

"That's beautiful," Heath told her. "I'll bet your baby also has a beautiful name?"

Isla fixed her hollow eyes on him. "Aye," she said. "Royshin. The tot's name is Royshin." Isla tugged at her woolen dress. "Have you seen where they've taken me babe?" she asked again, a note of desperation in her voice.

Heath shook his head slowly. "No, but I can help you look for Royshin if you'd like."

Isla seemed to brighten. "Oh, you're a kind sir, you are!"

But just as soon as she accepted Heath's help, a shadowy mist wafted into the room, and a sense of intense foreboding hit me hard in the solar plexus. "Um . . . ," I said, all my senses tingling in alarm. "Are you feeling that?"

"Something else is here," Heath said, and the moment he finished speaking, a door down the hallway slammed, and we both started.

"Look at the doorway!" I whispered.

The entrance to the room was thick with a gray fog that was starting to roil and swirl like an angry thundercloud before something parted it and began to emerge from the mist.

At first I had no idea what it was, just a small black circle edging its way out of the fog, but then the angle changed and I realized it was a long, black handle that I'd seen before. "Oh, no!" I gasped as the rest of it cleared the fog and came slowly into the room to hover right next to Isla, who was looking at it in confusion. In the next instant a smoky shadow grew out of the handle, and formed the willowy outline of a woman straddling the broom.

"Rigella?" Isla asked. "What are you doing here?" I held my breath as the spirit of Rigella must have answered her baby sister because the younger girl began shaking her head. "No, Rigella!" she said. "They're causing me no harm! They're going to help me look for Royshin!"

But apparently, Rigella wasn't willing to listen to her sister, and the broom reared up as if it was winding up for a strike and I had no choice. I uncapped the grenade, pulled out the spike, and held it right up to the broom.

Next to me, Heath dived for the other grenade, and faster than I would have thought possible with his injured arm, he got the cap off and tipped out the spike, also holding it out toward the two sisters.

For nearly five full seconds after I held up my spike, nothing happened other than Isla curling away from us. But once Heath's grenade joined mine, there was a terrible snapping noise, a burst of air so powerful that it pushed us both flat on our backs, and then silence . . . which was eeriest of all.

"You . . . okay?" I asked, panting heavily from the rush of adrenaline.

"Yeah. You?"

I sat up and looked around. Isla and the broomstick and the mist were all gone. The room was empty of anything but the two of us and some cobwebs. "Fine," I said, getting to my feet. "How's your arm?"

Heath sat up as well. "Throbbing, but I'll probably pull through."

That got me to smile. "What now?" I asked, helping him to his feet.

"Let's check out the rest of the castle."

We retrieved the magnetic spikes, placing them back in their canisters, before leaving the room. I followed behind Heath again, making sure to give him a little more space this time as we made our way back to the main hall, where we eyed the stairs. "What do you think?" he asked.

"As long as we don't find any more broomsticks, I'm game."

"At least we know that two grenades will do the

trick," he said, moving to the stairs and beginning to climb.

"Yeah, but did you feel her strength, Heath? There were a couple of seconds before she actually reacted. I think that spook is one of the most powerful we've ever encountered."

"And one of the most determined," he added, and then he stopped, as if he'd just thought of something. "Gilley," he whispered.

I felt a jolt of shock go through me, and immediately dug into my back pocket for my cell phone. With shaking fingers I tapped the contacts icon and scrolled to Gilley's number. I had to tap it twice to get it to dial, but after only two rings my partner answered, "What's wrong?"

I let go of the breath I'd been holding, but hesitated while I struggled to find the right words to say to him. "M. J.?" he said, his voice sounding concerned. "Are you okay?"

"I'm fine," I assured him. "But I wanted to let you know that we encountered Rigella's ghost here at the castle."

"Ohmigod!" he yelled, so loudly that I had to pull the phone away from my ear. "Should I send the police? An ambulance? Fire department?" He'd squeaked that last part, which caused me to let out a small giggle. "What's so funny?" he demanded, switching immediately to a defensive tone.

I struggled to hold in my laughter, and failed. Heath was looking at me curiously, so I placed a hand over the mouthpiece and repeated what Gilley had said. Heath also seemed to think it was funny, because he started laughing too. It was just so ridiculous that we should need to call any one of the public-safety departments he'd just named, but this bust had in fact required all three. I wondered whom we'd have to call next. "Do you by chance have Batman, Superman, or the Green Hornet on speed dial?"

"I'm serious!" my partner shouted into the phone.

And that made me laugh even harder. Here I'd been beaten, frightened, battered, and taunted by an evil spirit who clearly wanted to kill me, and everyone I held dear, and yet I was laughing. Somewhere in the back of my mind I considered whether I might be losing my mind.

When I had recovered myself, I simply said, "We're okay, honey. Just wanted you and Gopher to be on high alert. We chased her out of the room where she cornered us—but it took two grenades. So do me a favor: Take all the spikes you have and place them around the perimeter of the van until we come back, okay?"

Gilley didn't answer me right away, and I had the mental image of him gripping the phone with big wide eyes and nodding his head agreeably. "How soon will you guys be back?" he wanted to know.

I looked up the stairs. We were halfway to the first floor. "Soon," I promised. "We're almost done here."

It turned out I was a big fat fibber. The castle took Heath and me two more hours to explore and during that time we discovered at least a dozen more spooks. We could feel each energy that we encountered and took turns getting its information and documenting it for the camera. None of them were particularly malevolent, but all seemed to be greatly attached to that fortress, and almost all were active—in other words, they made a great show of displaying themselves by clomping along the stone corridors, or knocking, or moving pebbles and rocks, or making other sounds. And we were able to search every corner except at the very top of the highest tower, which was the last place we had to check, and by then we were really beat. So when Heath gave a halfhearted push on the old wooden door, which was warped with age and had rusted-out hinges, and it didn't give way, we left it and called it a day.

In all, the castle was a ghost hunter's paradise. "We should have shot here," I said wistfully as we left.

"I was just thinking the same thing," Heath agreed. "I mean, besides Rigella, not one of those spooks wanted to physically harm us."

"My kind of ghostbust," I said ruefully.

The day had turned gray and windy. I looked up at the thick black clouds hovering overhead and pulled the collar of my coat up around my neck. "Feels like rain."

Heath held up his cast. "It does," he agreed. "I think I need to get back to the hotel and take a pain pill. My arm's throbbing like crazy."

"I'm so sorry for making you trip," I told him, a wave of guilt washing over me again.

Heath surprised me by throwing his good arm around my shoulders. "Don't sweat it, M. J. It was an accident."

"I still feel bad."

"Make it up to me later?" I looked up to see a twinkle in his eye and he bounced his eyebrows playfully.

"Um . . . yeah . . . about that."

Heath tilted his chin and laughed. "Or not," he said, letting me off the hook. "But there is something going on between us, right?"

I sighed and took his arm off my shoulder, but still held his hand. "Heath," I said, trying to sort out my feelings as I talked. "I don't know what's going on. I will admit that I'm attracted to you, but I can't tell if that's just my reaction to what's happened to us in the past couple of days, or because Steven's not here and I really do want to get close to you."

"Ah, yeah," Heath said. "The *S* word."

I stared at my feet as I walked. "I'm sorry. I know I'm sending you mixed signals, but I've been seeing him for a while now and I genuinely care about him."

"It's cool."

"Don't be like that."

Heath cut me a look that was cold and hard and pulled his hand out of mine. "I'm not being like anything," he insisted. "Really, it's cool. Figure it out and get back to me, 'kay?"

He said that last part like he couldn't care less if I actually ever did get back to him, and part of me knew it was just Heath trying to salvage his ego, but another part really wanted him to care. "Okay," I said after a long pause. "Whatever."

"Whatever," he repeated.

I looked up at him again, but he was staring straight ahead, and he'd also quickened his pace to walk a few steps ahead of me. I sighed and let him go, wishing that just *one* thing about this ghostbust weren't so hard.

The moment I got back to the van, Gopher was all over me about leaving him with Gilley for over two hours. "The guy's driving me crazy, M. J.!" he hissed. "He's done nothing but jump and yelp at any noise, no matter how small. And when he's not doing that, he's complaining about how hungry he is. I mean, what am I supposed to do about that when I'm parked in some guy's driveway? Wave a magic wand over my hand and produce a hamburger?"

"Cut him some slack, Gopher," I muttered. "He's been through a lot."

"Can we go eat now?" Gilley moaned from the back of the van. I looked over my shoulder as Gopher pulled out of Joseph's driveway back onto the road. Both Gilley and Heath were pouting in their seats like dejected kindergartners.

"Sure, Gil," I said, then leaned over to Gopher and whispered, "Get us to the nearest burger joint you can find."

About twenty minutes later we were seated at a no-frills Wimpy restaurant awaiting our lunch order. Gilley was twirling his Pepsi with a straw while he wore one big frown. "This place sucks," he grumbled.

Like Gopher, I was quickly losing patience with him. "You said you were hungry. And I know you like hamburgers, so what's the problem?"

"I'm not talking about here," he replied moodily, tapping the tabletop. "I'm talking about Scotland. It sucks. And I want to go home."

I laid a hand on his arm. "Scotland doesn't suck, Gil. After all, this is where your ancestors came from, so there has to be something good here."

Gilley's mouth worked its way into an award-winning pout. "My ancestors *left* here, remember?"

"Maybe they just wanted to explore America."

"Or, maybe this place *sucked* and they wanted to go someplace *better*."

I leaned back in my chair with a heavy sigh and

looked up at the ceiling. I hated it when Gil got into one of his moods. And knowing him as I did, I knew that there wasn't much that could pull him out of it.

Except . . .

Maybe . . .

. . . a project.

I leaned forward again just as our waitress brought the tray with our food. "Say, Gil," I began nonchalantly.

"Here we go," he growled, clearly not in the mood for further chitchat.

Gopher looked at him before taking the plate the waitress was handing him. "Here we go what?"

"M. J. never starts a sentence with 'Say, Gil,' unless she's about to put me to work."

I smiled tightly, debating whether to give my partner a slap upside the head or just propose my project. I wisely decided on pitching my idea. "I need some intel," I said.

Gil picked up a fry and began to nibble on it, doing his best to look bored. I waited him out and he finally paused chewing the fry long enough to say, "Intel?"

I took a bite of burger, which was incredibly greasy, but in a good way, and waited to swallow before answering. "Heath and I encountered Rigella's sister Isla. I think she's the one the mob spared, well, after raping her and leaving her for dead, that is. Anyway, Katherine said that Rigella's little sister had died in childbirth, which fits with what Heath and I discovered when we met her, because she kept looking for her baby."

Gilley was working his way through the fries, one by one, listening to what I had to say but not appearing especially interested, so I kept going. "Anyway, Isla said that she named the baby Royshin."

"Roy who?" Gopher asked.

"Royshin."

"Weird name for a kid," Gil grumbled.

"It's probably Celtic or something," I said with an impatient wave. "The point is that Katherine said the only person who could call up the witch early would be someone who was within the bloodline. That makes me think that this Royshin lived. And if he lived, then I need to trace his line up through the past couple hundred years to find out who might have called up Rigella's spirit."

"How the hell am I supposed to find some dude from the seventeenth century named Roysomething? I mean, you don't even have a last name for me to run with, do you?" Gilley complained.

Normally, Gil would have been all over that challenge, but nothing about the last few days had been normal. Still, an idea occurred to me. "Oh, but I think we might," I said. "That castle on Joseph's property is where I believe Isla lived out her final days. She hasn't left it since the day she died, because she's still looking for her baby. That makes me think that whoever took her in had power and money, especially since they kept her son safe from the angry villagers who killed the rest of her family.

"I know I might be taking a leap here, but if we can trace the family of that castle back—we might actually find Royshin within the family tree, or at least perhaps on the servants' roll call. At the very worst they might have made him a stableboy or a farmhand or something."

Gilley scowled and took an angry bite out of his

burger. He chewed without saying anything, glower-ing at me. I merely smiled winningly back at him.

Finally after several heavy sighs and a long pull of his Pepsi he mumbled, "Fine."

"You'll do it?"

"Do I really have a choice?"

"Of course," I snapped, finally out of patience. "You can sit in your hotel room *hoping* it doesn't catch fire while we try to bust this case, *or* you can help us get the job done that much sooner by doing your part!"

Gilley lowered his lids at me and smacked his lips. "Well, when you put it like *that*," he muttered.

Gopher and Heath snickered and pretended to be really interested in their food, and that was the end of the discussion for a while.

When we got back to the hotel, Heath went immedi-ately to his room to take his pain pill and a nap. I was pretty exhausted myself, so I handed the camera over to Gopher to look at the footage we'd gotten from the castle, asked Kim and John to keep watch over Gil, and hunted down Meg and Wendell.

Meg was only too happy to hand Wendell over to me for some prime puppy love and a few z's. Half an hour later, I was fast asleep.

"M. J.," someone called to me softly. "M. J., can you hear me?"

I sat up and looked around. I was in my hotel room with Wendell cuddled up next to me; however, sitting in the corner was none other than Samuel White-feather.

"Hey!" I said, a little startled and still sleepy. "How'd you get in here?"

Samuel chuckled and I found myself smiling. "I climbed in through the window," he joked. For the record we were two floors up.

"Ah," I said. "Right. You're dead. You can go anywhere."

"One of the perks," he quipped. "That and you can get into any show or concert for free."

"No joke?"

"No joke."

I nodded. "Good to know." I rubbed the sleep out of my eyes and blinked a few times. "So what brings you by, Mr. Whitefeather?"

"I'm worried," he said. "And please, call me Sam."

" 'Kay, Sam. What worries you? The fact that your grandson had his arm broken by a spook-wielding broom, who then tried to kill me, or the three-alarm fire that nearly took my partner's life?"

Sam chuckled again. "Well, all of that, plus what I saw happen this afternoon."

I cocked my head, thinking back through the events of the day. "Which part exactly?"

"I think you missed something," Sam said. I opened my mouth to reply, but he stopped me by saying, "Don't get me wrong, M. J.—you and Heath make a great team—but there was a clue in that castle that I think you passed by."

"What clue?"

"There was a room that you never got to. Do you remember?"

I blinked a couple of times, trying to recall, and I had a hazy memory of a room at the top of the stairs that had a door that was still intact, and closed tight. "I remember," I said.

Sam smiled and folded his hands together in his

lap. "Excellent," he said. "What you're really looking for is in there. And you can't delay going back to find it. You must go later on tonight, or it could be removed and you'll never put it all together."

I didn't know what to say other than, "Can't you just tell me and save me the trip?"

"No," he said. "It's for you to discover. But I promise it'll be worth it. Oh, and Gilley won't find Royshin. But he might find Katherine. You'll tell him to look for her now, won't you?"

"Um . . . sure," I said, not really understanding what he meant.

"Wonderful. I have to leave now, but before I go, can I give you a bit of advice from an old man who loves his grandson?"

*Uh-oh.*

"Sure," I said with a gulp.

"Go easy on Heath. He likes you, and not just as friends. I don't want to see him get his heart broken again."

*Again?*

I felt my cheeks heat. "Sure, Sam. I can do that. And I'm trying to figure all this out, I promise. The last thing in the world I'd want to do is hurt him."

"I know, M. J. I know."

And with that, Samuel Whitefeather dissolved into a mist just as I heard three bangs on my door. Then Wendell barked, and I woke up with a start.

# Chapter 13

Still trying to sort out the dream from the reality, I pulled off the blanket I was lying under and stumbled to the door. When I opened it, I found Gilley standing there looking quite peeved.

*Quelle surprise.*

"Hey, Gil," I said, doing my best to sound upbeat and positive.

"I've been at it for *hours*," he yelled. "Hours and hours!"

I rubbed my face and shook my head, trying to get my brain to work. "What time is it?"

"Six."

"Okay, so you've been at it a few hours, and I'm guessing you came up with nothing?"

"Not. One. Thing," he growled, pushing his way into the room to pick up Wendell and go straight to the chair where Sam had been just a moment earlier. "I'm telling you this Royshin dude doesn't exist!"

"Did you look at the family that owned the castle?"

Gil's lids lowered—his look dangerous. "What do you take me for, an amateur?"

"Okay, sorry," I said, coming back into the room to

sit on the bed, remembering what Sam had told me. "But I might have given you the wrong name. I think that instead of looking for a Royshin, you should look for Katherine."

Gil's mouth dropped open. "You're *kidding* me, right?"

I sighed heavily. Gil could be so damn difficult sometimes. "I know I'm asking a lot of you to go back and look some more, buddy, but this is important."

Gilley sat forward and placed a squirming Wendell on the ground. The pup trotted quickly back to me, obviously scared of the testy guy who'd just entered our suite. "No, M. J., you don't get it. That's what I was going to say next. I've already found Katherine."

I shook my head again. "Wait. . . . What?"

"Katherine McKay of the McKays of Queen's Close. The woman living in Joseph Hill's guesthouse is a direct descendant of the clan of McKay—the same family that once owned that crumbling castle on Hill's property."

Gil pulled out a piece of paper that he'd scribbled his notes on and referred to it as he told me what he'd found. "The McKays have been residents of the village of Queen's Close for centuries. They were a very prominent family all the way up through the late eighteen hundreds, and they owned most of the property here in the close until they fell on hard times and had to sell off most of what they owned. That's when the castle fell into ruin, in fact."

"So the woman we met on Joseph Hill's property today was once related to the family that owned that castle?"

Gilley nodded. "Quite the coincidence, isn't it?"

"But, Gilley," I said quickly, "don't you see? She's a

direct descendant of Rigella's—she as much as admitted it to us this morning!" When Gilley cocked his head sideways like a confused puppy, I explained, "Remember? Katherine said Rigella only communicates with her direct descendants, and Katherine told us that Rigella came to her in Katherine's dreams! She said that the witch showed up the first time in a dream when she was nineteen, and then again recently when she asked Katherine to make the brooms."

"Okay," Gil said, still not following.

"Which means that if you can go back and follow her family branch specifically, it might lead us to who else has survived through the ages and would be in mind to call up the witch."

Gilley looked at his notes and said, "See, that's where things get really interesting. Katherine is one of seven girls."

*"Seven?"*

Gil nodded. "But only three sisters are still alive."

"What? Four of her sisters are dead?"

"Yep. Two were twins who died in infancy, one more was killed in an automobile accident in the late seventies, and the fourth died about two years ago. I found her obit half an hour ago. She had cancer."

"So where are the other two remaining sisters?"

"One is currently living in New Zealand, and the other you already know."

"I do?"

"Well, sort of. Vicariously. Through Wendell."

"Gilley," I said irritably, rubbing my temple." "Just tell me."

"Sarah Summers. She owns the animal shelter where Wendell was living."

I blinked, totally surprised. "You're kidding."

"I'm not."

"Then she must be the one," I said. "She must be the woman Katherine refused to tell us about, and she must have called up the witch."

"That's what I was thinking."

But then something struck me as odd, and I had to pause. "But why would Sarah want to kill Cameron?"

Gilley shrugged. "Why don't you go ask her?"

I leveled a look at him. "Yeah, great idea, Gil. I'll just walk right up and ask her why she murdered a man, froze his body, defrosted him, laid him in the road then cut your brake lines. I'll bet she'll share her whole life's story once I've broken the ice with that one."

"Beats sitting around here and speculating about it," Gil said, his own tone a bit testy.

I took a deep breath and pulled in my horns. "Okay," I relented. "We'll go talk to her. And see if we can't get her to cough up something incriminating."

"Now?"

I looked at my watch. "No. Now we go eat. Then I've got to borrow Heath to go back to that castle. So tomorrow we'll go talk to Sarah."

Gilley stared at me in shock. "You're going back to that castle? *Tonight?*"

I got up off the bed, stretching before I answered him. "There's something I need to check out, and Heath's grandfather said it was urgent."

"Wait," Gil said, looking at me oddly. *"Who?"*

"Never mind." I said, laying some water out for Wendell who'd gone back to sleep then grabbed my purse and motioned Gilley toward the door. "It's a long story. I just have to go back to the castle tonight and Heath needs to come too."

"But who's going to stay with me?" Gil asked anxiously as he stepped out into the hallway with me.

I shut the door, making sure it was locked, and began to walk down the hallway. "I don't know, Gil," I said, exasperated. "We can ask Gopher or one of the other crew to watch over you until I get back." My partner didn't look happy, so I added, "Or you could come with us back to the castle."

"Uh, no. That's okay. I'm sure one of the others will agree to sit with me."

"Where did you want to go for dinner?" I asked, trying to change the subject to something lighter.

"How about Greek?" Gil suggested. "I saw this really cool-looking Greek restaurant just down the street. . . ."

It turned out that going Greek was a big, BIG mistake. When you're with someone who is rightfully terrified of any open flame, having a bunch of waiters light cheese on fire and yell *"Opah!"* can cause more than just heart palpitations—it can elicit a rather embarrassing reaction from a scared little queen armed with a fully loaded fire extinguisher.

By the third ruined *saganaki* plate, we were asked to leave. Promptly.

"I'm still hungry," Gil moaned as he and I made our way back to the hotel. I'd called the other guys on our team to see if they wanted to join us for dinner, but Gopher, Kim, John, and Meg were already out to eat and Heath was likely still sleeping, because he wasn't answering his phone.

"Well then, you shouldn't have foamed up the restaurant, Gil," I snapped. I'd made it only partially through my spinach pie and I'd really been looking forward to some stuffed grape leaves.

Gil was silent for a minute, falling behind me as we walked, and then I heard him sniffle.

*Great. Just great.*

I stopped and turned around to look back at him. "Hey," I said gently. "Come on, Gil. Don't cry."

"I want to go home," he blubbered as big wet tears dripped down his cheeks. "I miss Doc! And I miss Steven. And I miss Mama Dell!"

I closed my eyes to gather my words carefully before speaking. When the waterworks started, Gil could be übersensitive. "Honey," I said, wrapping an arm around his shoulders. "It'll be okay. We just have a few more days to hang in there and then you'll have your passport back and we can get you out of here."

"But what if Rigella gets to me before we can get away?"

"I won't let that happen," I vowed.

"But how are you going to stop her, M. J.?" Gilley wailed. "I mean, she's already *killed* people, and she almost *killed* you and me in a fire, and Heath in those woods. How can you shut down something that powerful?"

I squeezed Gil in a firm hug and said, "The same way we always do, my friend. By finding her portal and shoving a whole mess of spikes into it."

"But if her portal is down in the close, how the hell are you guys going to get near it without her killing you?"

I didn't answer him because I honestly didn't know. And that was a major problem. I didn't know where the witch kept her portal, but I knew it had to be the location in which Rigella was likely killed over three and a half centuries ago, and then called up within the past two weeks by someone living in the village. That's why finding out who specifically had beckoned the witch forward was so important. We didn't just need to identify a local murderer; we needed to close up that portal and lock up this town's scariest spook forever.

"Don't worry," I insisted. "We'll work it all out."

Because I felt sorry for Gil, I agreed to attempt a meal at another restaurant and he pointed to the McDonald's right next to the hotel. We ran into Heath there, and he looked very tired and a bit out of it. "You okay?" I asked when I saw him.

He nodded dully. "These pain pills make me feel woozy."

"Are you feeling up to some ghostbusting tonight?"

"What'd you have in mind?"

"Your grandfather told me we should go back to the castle."

"Now?"

"After we eat."

Heath shrugged. "Sure, I guess." I had a feeling that if he hadn't been on Vicodin, he might have protested going back there at night, when the witch would be her most powerful. And that should have made me pause, but I trusted Heath's grandfather, plus we had plenty of spikes, so what was the worst that could happen?

We left Gil with Meg and Wendell, promising to return before midnight. Gilley looked extremely worried, and he'd made a show of making sure both our tool belts were stocked with extra magnets and the two remaining electrostatic meters. "Please be careful with these," he insisted. "I don't know where or when I can get them replaced if they get damaged or lost."

"Yeah, yeah," I said, kissing him on the forehead. "See ya."

Gopher surprised us by insisting on coming along. "If I don't have enough new footage to show the network, they're gonna to get antsy about fronting us the extra cash," he explained.

I was all too happy to have him along, more eyes and ears to keep a lookout for the witch. Kim and John had gone off to catch a movie, and on the way over to Joseph's property, I casually asked Gopher about them.

"They're totally boinking each other," he confirmed.

"Tactfully put, buddy."

Gopher smiled. "Oh, excuse me," he said. "I meant to say they are having *relations*."

"Well, they make a cute couple."

Gopher rolled his eyes. "Whatever," he mumbled.

I laughed, "Ho, Gopher! Don't tell me you're jealous!"

Our producer's cheeks turned a shade pinker. "Of who?"

I eyed him skeptically. "Of John. You're into Kim, aren't you?"

Gopher put on a good act, appearing aghast that I could accuse him of such things, but we had arrived at Hill's house just then and had to get back to business.

When we were well loaded down with grenades, flashlights, night-vision cameras, and such, we set off for the back of the house and the castle beyond. Heath glanced up at the sky and remarked, "Looks like rain again."

I looked up too. "Storm's coming," I said, feeling the atmosphere take on a charged energy.

The wind had picked up since we'd left the hotel,

and none of us talked much as we trudged down the hill, avoiding Katherine's cottage, and back up the other end to the crumbling fortress. "So, what are we looking for exactly?" Gopher asked as we carefully stepped around several stones leading to the large hole in the wall.

"I don't know," I admitted. "Heath's grandfather visited me in another dream and said we would find what we were looking for in here."

"Did he mention any specifics?" Heath asked.

I shook my head. "All he said was that we should make more of an effort to get into that room at the top of the tower."

"The one with the door that wouldn't budge?"

"Yep."

"Has anyone had any reservations about the fact that we're currently trespassing?" Gopher asked as we scrambled over the stones into the main hall of the castle.

"I doubt Joseph will mind," I told him.

"And if he does, we're the two people who can help him get over it."

I smiled. "Exactly."

Gopher held up his camera and turned it on, pointing it straight ahead as he turned in a circle while verbally documenting the date, time, and location for the television-viewing audience. The wind was making a show of howling through the halls and corridors, whipping stray bits of dried vegetation and litter all about.

"And with us on our ghost hunt tonight are our two mediums, Heath Whitefeather and M. J. Holliday." I yawned into the camera. "M. J.?" Gopher said, tilting the camera away.

"Yeah?"

"Can you *please* try not to look bored?"

I laughed. "Sure thing, buddy. But just for you."

"Thanks, I appreciate it."

"Come on, gang, let's get this party started," I said, motioning for my companions to follow me.

I led the way toward the staircase just as a tremendous crack of thunder shook the foundation and reverberated off the walls. "Whoa," I said. And before anyone else could respond, a bright flash illuminated the interior of the keep, followed two seconds later by another loud explosion, and then a torrent of water fell from the sky.

"Holy Moses!" Gopher exclaimed, moving up the stairs to one of the arched windows. "It is really coming down out there!"

"Good timing making it to the castle before we got soaked, huh?" Heath said.

I was about to agree when another flash of lightning lit up the landscape, followed by a virtually instantaneous crack of thunder that felt almost on top of us, then boomed its way all along the downs. It was so loud and went on for so long that I didn't immediately notice Gopher's stiff shoulders and trembling frame.

But Heath did. "Gopher?" he asked. "You okay?"

Gopher turned around and even in the dim light I could tell he was pale. I pointed my flashlight up to his face, which was a mask of fear. "What?" I asked. "Gopher, what is it?"

He lowered the camera and held it out to us. "Hit rewind," he said in a voice we could barely hear above the pouring rain.

Heath took the camera while I moved in to wrap a

comforting arm around Gopher, who was shivering even though he was wrapped snugly in a warm coat. I'd seen him mighty scared before, but never like this. This was a new level of fear.

Heath fidgeted with the camera, pressed rewind, causing the images to blur for a bit, then hit play, and out of the camera came the tiny voice of Gopher, telling the audience where we were etc.; then my yawning face came into focus, followed by us traveling up the stairs . . . the beginning of the storm . . . Gopher pointing the camera out the window . . . and then something that made both Heath and me suck in a breath.

The night-vision footage had gone bright green when the flash of lightning had illuminated the landscape, and something large and ominous had come into view. Fergus Ericson's massive oak tree was in the perfect position to be seen from the window Gopher had been shooting out of. And dangling from the boughs of that tree were the unmistakable figures of three hanging souls. "Jeeeeeeeesus!" I exclaimed, grabbing the camera and pulling it closer to get a better look.

"Did you *see* that?" Heath asked, clicking the rewind button again and almost immediately stopping it before hitting play. This time however, he advanced the footage frame by frame. And five button pushes later he landed on the most incredibly creepy footage we'd ever captured.

"There are people hanging from that tree!" Heath and I both looked out the arched window, but the landscape was pitch-dark and we couldn't see anything with clarity.

"Keep going," Gopher said. I took a quick glance over my shoulder as Gopher pressed himself close to both Heath and me, his shivering intensifying. "And get out your grenades," he added. "Now."

Just as he said that, I could feel the hair on the back of my neck stand up on end and I had goose bumps all along my arms. There was also an intense chill in the air, and as I exhaled, I could see my breath. "Uh-oh," I whispered, just as one of our meters started to make loud little bleeps.

"Is that yours?" Heath asked, handing me the camera before pulling his own meter out to check it. "Yeah, it must be. Mine was off." Awkwardly he turned his on as well and the needle immediately rocketed to the red zone and bleeped just as loudly as mine.

"Move it forward!" Gopher pleaded impatiently. "Advance the tape, M. J.!"

"Oh, sorry," I said, fumbling with the pause button. I advanced two more frames and saw something dark appear on the view screen. I squinted, advancing again, and the shape became larger.

"What *is* that?" Heath whispered over my shoulder.

It took two more presses of the button to make it register, but when it did, I nearly dropped the camera. Three shadows riding separate brooms were snaking their way around the castle just beyond the window. "Shit!" I gasped. "Shit, shit, *shit!*"

"Grenades!" Heath commanded. "Uncap 'em and keep 'em close!"

I gave Gopher back the camera and pulled the canisters out of the loops in my belt. I had two spikes out and exposed in less than ten seconds. Heath was having trouble managing his grenades with his cast, so I shoved mine at him and pulled his canisters free. I then handed those two to Gopher, who was just staring blankly into space. "Gopher!" I yelled, to get his attention.

He blinked and looked at me. "I think we should go."

Another flash and tremendous crash of thunder reverberated through the stone walls. And something else. Something with terrible, malevolent energy. "We're in trouble!" Heath said in my ear.

"We've got the grenades," I told him. "As long as we keep the magnets exposed, they can't get to us."

Heath set his jaw firmly and his posture defensively. At the bottom of the stairs we could see a mist form in the beam of our flashlights. If that weren't bad enough, something began to sound above the rain and the thunder—something like the angry voices of a mob.

From above and below we heard a cascade of noise that was like a group of people all shouting at once. Shadows came out of doorways to hover in the hallway below, swirling the mist and sending us wave upon wave of intense energy. My sixth sense felt overloaded and my vision became blurry. I felt queasy and sick to my stomach and I found myself trying to swallow, but my mouth had long since gone dry.

Above us, angry footsteps pounded up and down the corridors and then doors began slamming, one after another after another. "What the freak is happening?!" Gopher shouted above the cacophony.

"We need to get out of here!" Heath yelled, but I could barely focus on what he was saying. "M. J.!"

I felt a hand on my shoulder, but I couldn't respond. There was just too much input tunneling into my brain and it was all I could do to remain standing. I heard a *Ting, ting, ting!* and dully watched one of the metal spikes bounce down the stairs. I had the vague impression that I'd let go of it, but I hardly cared. I just wanted the assault on my sixth sense to stop, because my brain felt muddled and I couldn't even speak.

"Let's get her up the stairs!" I heard Heath shout before two hands hooked under my arms and lifted me slightly off the ground.

More noise and energy and chaos seemed to tumble all around us, cascading up and down the walls, the stairs, the ceiling, and the floors. Nowhere felt safe, and in the back of my mind I felt as if the entire castle had become one giant spectral creature, ready to swallow us whole. "Damn it!" I heard Gopher shout. "Heath! We've got broomsticks!"

One of the hands holding me let go abruptly and I sagged against Gopher. Closing my eyes and using every last ounce of concentration I possessed, I managed to say, "Throw the grenades!"

A moment later I heard that familiar *Ting, ting, ting!* followed by another set and another. I figured at least three of the metal spikes had been tossed down the steps.

"They're not stopping!" Heath gasped. I opened my eyes.

Below, in the main hall, three of the shadows and their brooms moved in and out over the cluster of spikes that had been tossed at them. And to my horror, the grenades appeared to have only a mild effect on the witches. In fact, Heath had to grab my shirt and pull me into a crouch when one of the spikes came zipping back up the stairway at us, and I realized we'd just given the spooks several lethal weapons.

"Run for it!" Gopher shouted when yet another spike slammed off the stair right below us.

I was roughly hauled to my feet again and pulled up the steps. My heart was hammering in my chest, which oddly helped to clear my head, and I was able to run without too much extra help from Heath and Gopher. We made it to the first-floor landing and Heath—still clutching my arm—tugged both Gopher and me right toward a hall that I remembered led to the central tower. "We've got to get to that circular staircase!" Heath yelled. "The brooms will have a harder time navigating it!"

I followed along behind, but winced and nearly went down when something struck the back of my thigh. "Uh!" I cried out as searing heat bolted up the back of my leg, and I could barely take a step forward.

"She's hit!" I heard Gopher yell. "Heath, she's hit!"

"Get her to the stairwell!"

My vision started to close in and my breathing felt ragged. "Can't . . . make . . . it," I gasped, but the boys just tightened their grip and Gopher pulled my arm over his shoulder.

"Hang in there, M. J.!" he encouraged. "We're almost there!"

I tried to focus, I really did, but the bobbing of the flashlight beams as we ran was like some sort of hypnosis, and the darkness seeped into the corners of my sight while small dancing stars appeared everywhere I looked. I was so out of it I had no idea when or how we got through the narrow doorway of the spiral staircase, but the next thing I was actually aware of was hanging between Heath and Gopher while we all stared at a wooden door. "This is the one that we couldn't get through earlier today!" Heath said, his own breathing sounding labored.

"Maybe they won't come up here," Gopher whispered. But I knew better.

"Get us in," I managed just as my head bobbed forward. I felt seasick and so out of sorts, and I had no idea why I couldn't focus.

"Here," Heath said. "Give her to me. You try and open the door."

I could feel the hardness of Heath's cast around my waist and he pulled my arm over his shoulder. "Stay with us, M. J.!" he commanded. "We'll be on the other side of that door in no time."

I closed my eyes and leaned heavily against him. He smelled so good! Like sage and musk and sharper spices I couldn't quite identify. And his heart beat rapidly in rhythm to mine, while heat from his body warmed me.

I wanted to sink right into him, to give in to the cloudy sensation that had taken over my mind since I'd been standing on the main staircase. But several loud thwacks below where we stood caused me to raise my head. Another flash of lightning lit up the tight enclosure and sure enough, one shadow-riding broomstick was making its way with slow determination up the spiral stairs. "Gopher! Get that door open *now*!" Heath shouted.

I could hear Gopher grunting and wood creaking, and finally, with one tremendous groan our producer managed to push open the door. "Get her inside!" he ordered.

Heath tightened his grip on me and half pulled, half dragged me through the doorway, where he very gently set me on the floor, butted up against a wall near a narrow window—one of the ancient arrow loops. Wind howled into the small, freezing room and rain pelted my face. It helped more than anything else to keep me conscious.

I looked over to where Heath and Gopher were struggling to close the door again. Outside, the raging storm kicked it up another notch; several lightning strikes flashed in a row—or maybe it was just one very long one strung out over a few seconds. I turned back to the arrow loop and craned my neck to look out the crevice.

From up here I could see the tree where the three figures had been. Its boughs were clear of bodies now, and I knew that I was supposed to connect a dot or two about that tree and those images, but the muddled feeling worsened and I felt close to losing consciousness. I closed my eyes, struggling with all my might not to give in to the darkness. My fingers fumbled with the belt about my waist. Something was poking into me and it was difficult to breathe. I tugged on the object and it came free. I held it in my lap for a minute, focusing on taking deep breaths. I knew what it was, a grenade. If I could just get the top off . . .

For long painful seconds I pulled gently on the cap and finally it came loose. I tipped out the spike and gripped it in my palm, but it had no effect. Chaos still bombarded my intuitive mind.

Gripping the spike and concentrating on the cool rain that pelted my face, I opened my eyes again. Heath and Gopher were throwing all their weight against the door, which looked like it was pushing right back at them.

The door was open only a few inches, but I soon

saw what they were struggling against when the handle of the broom edged its way through the opening and threatened to burst into the room.

Dully I looked around for something I could use to help them, and my eyes settled on a table near the center of the room. On the table was a large box that, as I squinted, looked like a speaker of some kind. There were wires running down from the speaker to another smaller box underneath the table.

*M. J.,* I heard clear as day in my head. *Turn it off.*

"Huh?" I asked, my head bobbing loosely on my neck. "Wha?"

*Turn off the box. It's the only way to stop them. Do it now! Right now!*

I recognized that voice. It was Sam Whitefeather. I took another series of breaths and flopped forward to the ground. Using my forearms, I crawled to the table, the pain in my leg making it incredibly difficult, but I made it. I felt around the small contraption that looked like a radio under the table. I could clearly see it was battery-powered and there was also something like a clock set into it. And an On/Off switch.

"They're going to get through!" Heath shouted, straining to push back the door. "Gopher! Shove that broom out of the way!"

"Dude!" Gopher practically screamed. "It's too strong! If I let go, they'll all get in!"

My head spun and I had to close my eyes again. *M. J.!* Sam demanded. *Flip the switch! Do it now!* Using the very last of my reserves, I lifted the hand still gripping the spike and felt for the switch. It took me a moment, but I finally got it just as the door was shoved violently open and three black shadows and their broomsticks thrust their way into the small tower room.

*Click*, I heard as I pulled down on the knob. The box turned off. Instantly my head cleared and I became fully alert.

The next instant there was a loud *WHOOSH* of air that knocked me backward, followed by the sound of three broomsticks striking the stone floor. Then, save for the wind and the rain, everything else was still.

# Chapter 14

"What the hell just happened?" Gopher said, his breathing ragged.

No one answered him. Instead, Heath ran to my side. Crouching down next to me, he asked, "Are you okay?"

I nodded, finally letting go of the spike in my hand and clenching my teeth against the terrible throbbing pain in my leg. "What's in my thigh?" I asked.

Heath's expression turned grim. "A spike."

"Christ!" I hissed. "Is it deep?"

He looked behind me. "An inch or two."

Swallowing hard, I reached back and felt the spike sticking right up out of my leg, and tried not to lose my cookies. Gripping it firmly with one hand, I grabbed on to the table leg for support.

Heath shook his head vigorously, knowing what I was about to do. "M. J., I don't think you want to do—"

"*SON OF A BITCH!*"

"—that."

My chest was heaving as I held up the bloody spike. Which was another mistake, because the sight of all that blood was not something I was prepared for. "Uh-oh," I said a moment before I lost consciousness.

I don't know how long I was out, but it was long enough for Heath to tend to my wounds with some cotton balls and antiseptic from the very small emergency kit we carried on our belts. He'd also made a bandage out of the tail end of his shirt, and tied that around my leg. "How you doin'?" he asked when I opened my eyes.

Gopher had set up one of the flashlights so that it illuminated much of the room. The tower was still chilly, but at least it didn't feel as cold as it had been earlier. "All things considered?" I told Heath in response to his question. "Okay, I guess."

"Take a sip," he said, offering me a bottled water.

I took it gratefully. "Thanks."

"And eat this," he added, shoving a granola bar at me.

"I'm not really hungry."

"Don't much care," he said, looking at me like he wasn't about to argue and I'd better eat the damn granola.

I took a bite, chewing thoroughly, and sipped a little more water. Heath then handed me one of his Vicodins. "For the pain."

I swallowed the pill quickly; my thigh was burning something fierce. "And you'd better finish the granola. That stuff is awful on the stomach."

I continued to eat the granola bar and look around thoughtfully. Even though I'd just fainted and was probably still bleeding, I felt far more conscious and alert than I had since first spying those spooks and their broomsticks. I noticed now that Gopher was summarily making the brooms into kindling, holding them at an angle while he jumped on them and broke them into several pieces.

"Something shifted," I said to Heath after wadding up the wrapper from my snack.

He pointed to the table. "Do you know what that was?" he asked me.

"No."

"Me either, but I saw you playing with it right before the broomsticks entered. What'd you do?"

"I turned it off."

"And the witches lost all power," he said. Pointing to the spikes on the floor he added, "And those seemed to work again."

I scooted painfully around to sit on my rump and lean in toward the contraption under the table. "I bet Gil will know what that thing is."

"That's what I was thinking."

"Okay," I said, working my way up to my feet. "Let's bring it to him."

Heath helped me stand up. "I think first we need to get you to the hospital. That wound's going to need stitches."

I sighed. "Well, that's a little inconvenient, don't you think?"

Heath smiled, holding his hands up innocently. "Hey, I don't make the rules, darlin'."

Heath and Gopher dismantled the contraption into three parts, but ultimately they decided taking the whole thing back to the hotel would be too much hassle with Heath's broken arm and my injured leg, so they settled for taking only the central box and leaving the speaker. "We can retrieve it later if we need to," Heath said.

I smiled ruefully at him. "Oh, I don't think we're coming back here anytime soon."

He laughed. "Good point. Come on, gimpy, let's get you stitched up."

I was at the hospital until three a.m. Unlike when Heath was brought in, because of the storm there had been two auto accidents and I had to wait in line behind more-critical-care patients. I didn't much mind as the Vicodin had by that time fully kicked in. In fact, I didn't much care about anything by the time the ER doc checked on me. "How did this happen?" he asked while I lay on a gurney with my bare butt on display under the bright lights.

"I slipped on some stairs, and a metal spike caught me just right."

The doctor grunted, but didn't ask any more probing questions. "Well, you're lucky it didn't strike your femoral artery," he said, squirting saline into my wound.

I laid my tired head down on my arms and closed my eyes, not really in the mood for conversation.

Once I was released, Heath and I took a taxi back to the hotel. Gopher had dropped the two of us off at the emergency room while he went in search of Gilley, and we'd told him we'd cab it back.

When we walked through the doors of the hotel, Heath caught my arm and showed me a text he'd just received from Gil. *Gopher fell asleep in M. J.'s bed. I'm beat too. Can she bunk with you tonight and we'll meet up in the a.m.? I've got a lot to tell you about your gadget.*

Before I could even fully register the text, Heath was tapping the screen and replying to Gil. "What'd you tell him?"

My companion wore a slightly wicked smile. "I told him it was no problem. I've got a king bed upstairs. Totally big enough for the both of us."

*Gulp.*

Heath lent me a pair of boxer shorts and a T-shirt to wear to bed. I tried to resist the urge to sniff the shirt outright—which smelled just as good as Heath. I also had to hand it to him—he was nothing but a gentleman, offering me either side of the bed I preferred, and keeping to his half once I'd crawled under the covers.

The back of my thigh throbbed as the local anesthesia wore off, but the Vicodin didn't allow me to dwell on it, and before long I was blissfully asleep.

Many hours later I woke up wrapped in strong, masculine arms. And bolted out of bed like a rocket. "Hey!" I yelped both from pain when I put weight on my right leg and from the shock of finding myself cuddled in Heath's arm.

"What's going on?" Heath mumbled, rolling over and burying his face in his pillow.

"You were groping me."

Heath lifted his head, squinting at me sleepily. "Was not."

"Then how do you explain how we woke up?" I snapped, completely flustered and desperate to find my jeans.

"*You* were groping *me*."

"I was *not!*" I insisted.

Heath sighed and pushed up onto his elbows. "I'm still on my side of the bed," he countered. "Which means you rolled over and tried to cop a feel."

I felt heat sear my cheeks while I tried not to look

at my appearance in the mirror over the dresser. My hair probably resembled a rat's nest. And my breath probably stank. And I was sure I looked completely ridiculous in blue plaid boxers and a brown T-shirt. Why hadn't I asked for something a little more matchy-matchy last night?

Heath shook the small vial of pills next to his bed. "Need more Vicodin?"

Ah, *that's* why.

"No thanks," I said, locating my jeans, sweater, and shoes and clumsily gathering them all before quickly moving into the bathroom. "I'll just get dressed in here and be out of your way."

"Take your time," Heath called. "There's no rush."

I got dressed in thirty seconds. Flat.

"Thanks again for letting me crash with you," I said, coming out of the bath to grab my coat and purse.

Heath chuckled. "M. J.," he said softly.

"Yeah?"

"I don't bite, you know. Well, that is, unless you *want* me to."

"Um. Okay." I had no idea what to do with that. So I turned and bolted from the room.

I found Gopher just coming out of my room looking fresh as a daisy. "Hey, M. J.!" he said when he saw me. "How's the leg?"

"Fine," I said, distracted. "Is Gilley in there?"

"He's in the shower. Might want to call up for more towels if you plan on taking one yourself, though."

I scowled and used my key card to step into the room. Steam wafted out of the bathroom and I closed the door to give Gil a little privacy, then tried to do something with my appearance, but it was no use. I needed a bath.

"Hey!" Gil said, looking pink from his shower, when he saw me sitting on the bed watching television about ten minutes later. "How's the leg?"

"It's fine. You done in there?"

Gil looked behind him. "Yeah, but we're short on towels."

I sighed. "I'll shake myself dry. I need a nice dose of cold water. Now."

Gilley gave me an odd look when I passed him on the way to the bathroom and then he burst into a fit of giggles. "Someone's in looooooove!" he sang.

"Shut. Up," I snapped. But Gil ignored me and opened his mouth to say something else, so I slammed the door in his face. Two minutes later I was standing under the spout, trying really hard not to get my stitches wet and attempting to forget about Heath, which, as the shock of cold water splashed down on my head, was somewhat easier than I'd expected.

My respite was short-lived, however. When I finally came out of the bathroom, all three of my ghost-hunting team members were in the room. "There she is!" Gil sang when I appeared.

"Can't a girl get some privacy?" I mumbled.

"Now that she's here, will you fill me in?" Heath asked, and he looked a little impatient.

I wondered why until I saw the tangled mess of wires and plastic on the table and remembered the small radio thingie we found at the castle. "Oh, yeah," I said, "you were going to let us know what you'd found."

Gilley sat forward with a sparkle in his eye. "You have found a really amazing little gizmo, M. J. Do you know that?"

I sat on the bed next to Gopher. "No. But I'm sure you're about to tell me."

Gil smiled winningly. "This little contraption is one heck of a device," he began.

"What does it *do*, Gil?" I said impatiently. I wanted him to cut the theatrics and get to the point.

"I suspect it drives the ghosties wild," Gil said plainly. "In fact, I'm sure of it."

"What does that even mean?" Gopher asked.

"It means that this thing revs up the atmosphere to a degree and frequency that ignites the electromagnetic energy and charges both positive and negative ions to a superfrenzied state!"

"In English, please?" I begged.

Gilley tapped his chin thoughtfully, as if he was searching for the best way to explain. "You know how anytime it rains, we have good conditions for ghost hunting?"

"Yes," I said. "The moisture helps the spooks travel around on our plane more easily."

Gilley nodded. "It does," he said. "So imagine if you could create an atmosphere that could not only make it easier for the spirit world to travel more easily among us but *merge* the two planes so that the spirit world was laying *right on top* of ours, making the two planes like one."

I blinked, looked at the remnants of the gadget on the table, blinked again, and gasped. "You're telling me that that little radio brings the spirit world right *into* ours?"

"Yes."

"Can someone please explain this to me in laymen's terms?" Gopher whined.

Heath seemed to be following because he said, "I think what Gilley is trying to tell us is that contraption creates an atmosphere which allows any ghost within hearing distance to easily interact with the world of the living."

Gilley nodded smartly. "Exactly," he said. "And it also supercharges them, allowing them not only to interact, but heightening their ability to affect physical objects. It would require very little energy for them to throw something or slam a door."

"Or make a broomstick fly," Heath said softly.

I looked sharply at him. "Oh . . . my . . . God!"

"Now we know how the witch became so powerful," Gopher said.

"Yes," Gil agreed. "When this little charmer gets turned on, it's like giving a shot of steroids to a spook. It makes them superintense, superpowerful, and nearly unstoppable."

I remembered the metal spikes and how they'd had little effect on the witch as long as the machine was on. "It altered the electromagnetic frequency," I said. "That's why when we uncapped the grenades, they only had a mild effect."

Gilley looked thoughtfully at me. "The spikes didn't work?"

I shook my head. "They only slowed them down a teeny bit, Gil."

"Whoa," he said, fiddling with one of the dials. "Cool!"

"And what about that speaker?" Gopher asked. "Remember? The box was hooked up to a speaker."

Gilley stroked his chin. "It would have enhanced the range of the box," he said.

"How far?" I asked.

"Depends on the size of the speaker, but I'd say at least a quarter mile. Plus, you should know that this puppy was on a timer. It was set up like an alarm, to turn on for two hours beginning at nine. Gopher told me that you had a hard time coping in the castle until you turned it off. I'm pretty sure it affected you just like it affected the ghosts. It would have pulled you out of the living world and more easily into the spirit world, and the effect would have been similar to when you have an OBE. You would have felt disoriented because your body would still be trying to hold you to the physical world, while your mind pulled you into the ghost's realm."

No one spoke for a few seconds and my mind went back to the footage we'd captured of Fergus's tree and those three swinging corpses. I now knew they were spooks, brought to life by the box, which must have been able to reach the tree. "So someone is purposely trying to harm us," I said, breaking the silence.

"And they're using this gadget to enhance the witch's power to do it," Heath agreed.

"Do you think this thing is the only one out there?" I asked Gilley.

He frowned. "Probably not, toots. I mean, the gizmo was configured out of an old ham radio and spare parts. It'd be really easy to put together another one." Something nudged at the edge of my memory, but Heath spoke to me and it flittered out of my mind.

"M. J., I don't get why you felt the effect of the gadget so intensely and I didn't."

"You'd taken a Vicodin, remember? That must have grounded you pretty solidly."

"I didn't take a pain pill and I felt okay," Gopher said.

"Yeah, but you're not a medium," I told him honestly. "Heath and I are affected by changes in electrostatic energy a lot more than the average Joe."

"So what now?" Gopher asked. "I mean, where does this lead us?"

"Down another rabbit hole," Heath replied with a sigh. "None of this stuff makes any sense! I mean, why would someone act so recklessly? That thing is really dangerous. You'd think someone would be concerned for their own safety being around that."

I smiled ruefully. "Ah, but they weren't around it, were they? They had plenty of time to set up the timer and get someplace safe before we walked into the party."

"But who would be out to get us?" Gilley asked.

"Someone who knows we can talk to spooks," I said, a tiny thought taking hold in my head. "And someone who must be afraid of having us around."

Gopher asked, "So, which spook do you want to focus on?"

I looked at Heath, knowing he was thinking of Cameron, but that tiny thought at the back of mind had taken seed and I wanted to follow it. "Joseph Hill," I said.

Gilley frowned. "Why him?"

"The gadget was found on his property, Gil. For all we know, he could have rigged it, set it on that timer, and gotten caught up in the heightened activity when the witch showed up. He could be more responsible for his own death than we've given him credit for."

"Do we know for certain that he's grounded?" Gil asked.

"No, but there's an easy way to find out."

"You want to go back to the tree," Heath guessed.

"I do."

Heath inhaled deeply, playing with the small vial of pills in his hand before pocketing them and saying,

"Okay. I guess I can live with the pain. Let's go see if Mr. Hill is interested in a little one-on-one time."

We made it back out to Fergus's and parked in front of his house. Heath rang the bell and I stood nervously behind him, keeping my eyes peeled for any spectral activity.

We'd had a short chat on the way over about how vulnerable that contraption from the castle made us. If we couldn't use our grenades, there wasn't much else in our arsenal that we could rely on should things turn ugly. About the best we could do would be to race back to the van and hope for the best.

"He's not answering," Heath said, ringing the buzzer again, which sounded like an angry hornet.

"Guess that means he won't mind if we head out back and check out the tree."

Heath nodded, but cautioned me by saying, "Let's agree to make this as quick as possible. If Hill doesn't show in fifteen minutes, we're outta here."

"Agreed," I said, and we set out for the back of Fergus's house.

In the daylight the tree didn't look nearly so ominous. The rainstorm that had blanketed the area with wind, rain, and electricity was all gone and sunshine beamed through partly cloudy skies. The day felt, if not exactly warm, definitely pleasant.

"One thing about all of this is bothering me," Heath said.

The corner of my mouth lifted. "Only one thing?"

Heath chuckled. "Okay, one in particular."

"And that is?"

"Why the timer?" I looked at him curiously, not understanding what he was talking about right away.

"Remember?" he asked. "The timer on the ghost enhancer. Why was it set for nine p.m.?"

"Obviously it was a trap," I said.

Heath nodded, but I could tell he wasn't really convinced. "But for who?"

"Whom."

"Huh?"

"Never mind," I said. "Someone set it for us."

"But who knew we would be at the castle at nine o'clock last night? I mean, we only decided to go there right before we left, right? It wasn't like we called ahead and told people we were coming."

"Who else could it have been set for?" I pressed. "I mean, you and I would have been the only two people around who would have been so adversely affected by something like that."

By now we were close to the tree and Heath paused to look up at it. "Yeah," he said. "Maybe."

I followed his gaze. The mighty oak was magnificent in the full light of day. "I wonder how old it is," I said.

"Several hundred years, I would think."

I edged closer to place a hand on the trunk. I love trees. I spent a lot of time as a little kid in the branches of one that grew right outside my parents' bedroom window. I would climb up there when my mother was very sick and dying of cancer and I was kept from her because my father felt she needed her rest. He never believed she wouldn't make it, and thought time spent alone and away from any form of distraction or noise would help her recover.

So, as a lonely little kid who dearly missed her mother, and who didn't understand why she couldn't see her, I would climb that tree and sit on one of the branches next to her window, close my eyes, and pretend I was sitting right next to her, holding her hand. It was the closest I could come to her at the time, and touching the trunk of the oak tree brought a huge wave of melancholy over me, and I began to tear up a little.

"M. J.?" Heath said, and I felt his hand on my shoulder. "You okay?"

I opened my eyes. "I'm fine," I said, hating that my voice trembled and more tears fell.

Heath's expression went from concerned to compassionate. "Your mom is hovering right over your shoulder, did you know that?"

I gaped at him. Those words were my undoing and I began to weep in earnest. Heath reached forward and hugged me fiercely. "Hey," he said gently. "It's okay, doll. It's okay."

But I couldn't stop crying. I missed my mother so much it physically hurt, and I'd never really gotten over her loss, even though it had been twenty years since she passed. It was the one great irony to my abilities: I could talk to the dead with ease, but never really trusted that the voice coming through to me specifically was my own mother's and not in my imagination—so after a while, she'd stopped trying to communicate.

But Heath had developed something of a rapport with her, and I knew that when he told me she was around—she really was. "I miss her," I blubbered.

"She knows," he said gently.

I took a deep breath and fought to regain some control. It felt really good to be hugged in the shadow of that tree. It even felt right. I leaned back from him and looked up into his handsome face. "Heath," I said.

"Yeah?"

"There's something I want to say."

"I'm listening."

I took a deep breath, looked up into his eyes, then over his shoulder, and said, "Joseph!"

"I don't get it," Heath said, his brow furrowed.

I pointed over his shoulder. Heath turned around and jumped a little. Standing under the very branch we'd found him hanging from was Joseph Hill.

Heath and I both stared at Joseph for several seconds and the poor man looked terribly distraught. "Could you lend me a hand?" he asked, plain as day.

Heath was the first of us to recover from the shock of seeing him in full form. "Of course. What can we do for you, sir?"

"I'm afraid that I'm having a bit of trouble," Joseph said. "Someone's broken into me home, and I can't seem to get the police on the line."

Thinking fast, I pulled out my phone and pretended to dial. "I'll call them right now, Mr. Hill." I then held the phone up to my ear, paused for effect, then asked, "I've got the police on the line. What would you like me to tell them exactly?"

"Tell them someone's in me house!" he snapped impatiently. "And tell them not to dawdle this time like they did the last time! If they don't come quickly, I'm likely to take matters into me own hands!"

My eyes swiveled sideways to Heath while I pretended to tell the police exactly what Hill had said. He gave me an encouraging nod to keep up the ruse.

"They'd like it if you could give a description of the intruders," I told Mr. Hill.

He opened his mouth to say something, but paused, then looked confused. "I must not have got a good look at them," he confessed, scratching his head. "But I thought I had," he added. "Yes, I thought I had. So why can't I remember?" he mumbled, and then, without warning, his hands went to his throat and he began making choking sounds. He then began to struggle, and flail his arms, and that's when we saw what looked like a length of electrical cord appearing out of thin air and held by unseen hands wrap around Joseph's neck. The scene went on for only a few seconds more before poor Joseph disappeared into thin air.

"Oh . . . my . . . *God!*" I nearly shouted, turning to Heath. He was staring at me with big round eyes.

"It wasn't the witch!" he gasped, and I nodded vigorously in agreement. "Joseph Hill was—"

"Murdered!" I cut in. "He was murdered in his own house!"

We simultaneously looked up at the branch where Hill had been cut down. "So someone strung him up here to make it look like a suicide, or like the witch had taken over his body and killed him!" Heath guessed.

I had goose bumps running all along my arms and a chill shivered down my back. "Come on," I said to Heath. "We need to get the heck out of here before someone sees us."

"And by someone, you mean the murderer," Heath said softly as he and I both looked around suspiciously.

"Yep," I said, limping quickly away from the tree.

We reached the van shortly thereafter and both of us shuddered before buckling ourselves in. "We have to tell the police," I said.

"Tell them what?" Heath asked, starting the van

and checking the mirrors before pulling away from the curb.

"About what Joseph said! That someone broke into his home and strangled him!"

"And how would we tell them we know this?" Heath said, looking at me pointedly. "I mean, they've treated Gilley and Gopher with such warmth and respect, I'm sure they'll be *more* than happy to take our word for it."

I frowned. "Right," I said, picking up on the sarcasm. "Okay, but we . . . hold on."

"What?"

"You missed the turn," I said, pointing at the road. "I think we were supposed to go left back there."

Heath focused on his driving and glanced at an approaching street sign. "Crap!" he exclaimed, hitting the brakes hard.

"Whoa!" I yelled, putting a hand on the dash and looking over my shoulder. "Heath, be careful! There could have been someone behind us."

"Did you really want me to turn onto that street?" he snapped as the tension got to both of us.

I leaned forward again and looked at the street sign. It read BRIAR ROAD. My heart thumped hard in my chest. "I'm so sorry," I said as he tried to do a U-turn in the narrow street hampered as he was by his cast while holding up traffic on both sides of the road.

"It's okay," he said, grimacing as several cars honked at us. "I just didn't want to get stuck there again."

I shivered for the second time since getting into the van. "I'm with you."

Heath finally made the turn, punched the accelerator, and got about half a block before I yelled, "Stop!"

Heath stomped on the brakes again while shouting, "What?! What?!"

"There!" I said pointing to his right. "Across the street. Do you see that storefront?"

Cars began honking again, so Heath put on his turn signal and found a space to pull over and park. "You want to follow that lead about the witch's descendant?" he asked.

"I do," I said, getting out of the car. "I really do."

We walked across the street to the small storefront with the words A PAWS SANCTUARY. The sign in the window said the place was open.

Heath held the door open for me and I went in, immediately spotting a pleasant-looking woman with round cheeks, pale blue eyes, and wispy gray hair. "Good morning to you," she sang as we came forward, her voice competing with the yips and the barks from somewhere in back.

"Hello," I said pleasantly. "We're looking for Sarah Summers. Is she in?"

The woman behind the counter beamed at me. "You'll look no further to find her," she said. "I'm Sarah."

I blinked. She looked *nothing* like her sister. "You're Sarah?" I pressed, wanting to be sure.

"Aye," she said, her eyes taking me in quizzically.

"And your sister is Katherine McKay?"

"Aye," she said again, and her face became concerned. "What can I do for you now that I've identified myself several times, lass?"

I smiled again. "I'm sorry. It's just . . . we met your sister yesterday, and well, you two look so different."

Sarah laughed and the sound was light and full of mirth. "Oh, you're not the first person to wonder about that. I'm afraid that in our family when the good looks were handed out, Katherine got well more than her fair share."

I blushed and I tried to apologize again for the awkward conversation, "Oh, I didn't mean to imply—"

But Sarah waved her hand and said, "Now, don't worry yourself over it. After fifty years of walking in my sister's shadow, I'm more than a little used to it."

I had to admit that as suspicious as I wanted to be of this woman, her easy manner, her kind eyes, and the way her brogue turned "it" into "eht" all but charmed me. So I decided not to beat around the bush, and dive right in and introduce us. I thrust my hand forward and said, "I'm M. J. Holliday, and this is my friend, Heath Whitefeather."

Sarah shook our hands warmly. "Would you two be part of that American film crew that's here looking for ghosts?"

"We would," I said.

"Oh, then you're the one who adopted the wee darlin' pug from us!" she said, recognition dawning in her eyes. "I've got all the paperwork filled out for you. You'll need it to get him through customs. All it needs is a signature, Miss Holliday, and he can be your little love for good."

I'd forgotten all about the paperwork, so when Sarah spread it out on the counter for me, I began scribbling my John Hancock on all the dotted lines.

When I was done, I handed the documents back to Sarah, who put them into a neat little folder for me. "There ya are now," she sang happily. "And thank you for the very generous stipend you've committed to, Miss Holliday. You're helping our cause, you know."

I smiled and took the folder from her. "It's my pleasure, Sarah," I said.

"And I never have to rent out another poor pup to that dreadful ghost tour ever again. Oh, but it tore up me conscience to do that! Though I suppose there was no way around it—we really needed the few quid we got to keep this place going."

I wanted to ask her about Rigella's spirit being called up early, but her chatter was making it difficult to get a word in edgewise. I got my lucky break when someone from the back yelled, "Ma!"

Sarah jumped and held up her finger. "Excuse me one moment, would you? My youngest daughter's in back helping with the pups, and her condition makes it difficult to move the heavier cages."

Before I could ask her what she meant, Sarah ducked through a door and disappeared. Heath and I were left to stare around the front of the shelter, which was actually a store filled with all sorts of doggy supplies. I took advantage of the lull and started to sort through some of the toys that Wendell might like.

"M. J.!" Heath said in a loud whisper to get my attention. I looked over at him and saw that he was pointing to a framed collage of pictures. At the top of the collage was a nice photo of Sarah, and below that were several photos of young ladies with varying styles of hair that I would have judged ranged from the midseventies to the late eighties.

"What am I looking at?" I asked, crossing the room to him to get a better look.

"I think these are Sarah's daughters," Heath said, and even though he was speaking quietly, I could tell he was getting excited.

"Okay," I said, still not following why this was cause for celebration.

"Count them," he urged.

I did. There were seven. And the last girl looked really familiar to me. There was a name underneath each photo. The name listed under the last girl read *Roisinn*, which didn't ring any bells. I was about to comment when the door opened again and Sarah bustled back out. "So sorry to have kept you waiting," she said. "Rose is due any day now and I keep telling her to go sit and put her feet up, but she's a restless lass."

I whirled around, openly gaping at Sarah. "Your daughter's name is Rose?" I asked.

"Aye," Sarah said, then seemed to notice we were standing under the framed photograph of her family, and she laughed. "Oh, you're not looking at that old thing, are you?" And she came over to us. With a sigh she pointed to the first girl. "That's Marie," she said. "My oldest and the bright light of my life, if truth be told. She died about two years after that photo was taken."

I bit my lip. "I'm so sorry."

Sarah touched the photograph with her fingertips lovingly. "Marie was the reason I started this shelter, in fact," she confessed. "She had such a love for the animals, and she was always bringing home a stray here and there and finding homes for them. When she died, I felt such terrible sorrow, and I needed a purpose, something to get myself out of bed in the morning, so I opened this wee little shop and took in a few strays and it gave me back my life."

My heart went out to her. She seemed like such a lovely, kind woman. "And your other daughters?" I asked gently.

Sarah chuckled. "Well now, let's see," she said, pointing to the next photo over. "This is Katherine, named after my sister, and the two couldn't have turned out more alike. My Katie moved to London and she's an artist now, restoring works for the Victoria and Albert Museum. Next there's Heather, ah, such a lovely girl. She married an Irishman named Paul and they live just outside Dublin. They're expecting their second child in a few months' time. Then there's Millie, she's my bright one. She studied law at one of your schools in America and now she's living in Hong Kong. I hardly hear from her anymore.

"Next up is Beth. She's more like me, a nurturer at heart. She went off to join the Peace Corps and she just sent me a postcard from Nigeria, where she's nursing sick children back to health. And second to last is Christina; she's in school at Cambridge right now. She wants to follow in Millie's footsteps, and I suspect she'll do it, because she's every bit as bright. And last is my darlin' lamb," Sarah said with a sigh. "Roisinn."

"Excuse me?" I gasped. "Did you say Roy-shin?"

Sarah looked a bit startled by my reaction but explained, "Aye. It's her given name. It's Celtic for 'baby rose.'"

I wanted to slap my forehead. Roisinn wasn't a boy's name. It was a girl's. I'd totally sent Gilley in the wrong direction both with how to spell the name and what gender to look for.

Heath and I exchanged a meaningful glance, just as the door to the back room opened up and the very girl we were discussing stood there looking sweaty and uncomfortable. "I need your help again, Mum."

"I'll be right there, dear," Sarah promised. "Did you want to purchase those, Miss Holliday?" she asked me, indicating the toys for Wendell still clutched in my arms.

"Um . . . ," I said, caught off guard by Rose's appearance. "Sure."

I followed behind Sarah as Rose gave Heath and me a disapproving look and disappeared into the back again. While Sarah was ringing me up, I mentioned casually, "We saw Rose at Cameron's funeral. I'm so sorry for her loss."

For the first time since we'd come into the shop, Sarah's genteel demeanor changed. "Oh, that cad," she said with a flip of her hand. "Our Heavenly Father might not approve of what I'm about to say, but I'm not sorry he's gone."

"Why not?" Heath asked, again sneaking a pointed look at me.

Sarah placed the toys in a bag. "He was a horrible match for my Rose," she said. "Horrible. He chased after her, you know, seduced her right under me nose. I didn't come to find out about it until the poor thing was already with child. And even though my sister had already left the sorry sot, it still caused terrible problems between us."

"Have you mended fences with your sister?" I asked, hoping that Sarah wouldn't feel I was overly nosy.

She handed me the package and nodded. "Aye," she said. "And she's revealed a lot that's helped me make sense of what my poor Rose has been through."

"You mean Cameron's death?" Heath said.

Sarah shook her head and leaned forward. Speaking low, she said, "No, that Camey was having *another* affair. He was cheating with a girl on the other side of town. And it was no wonder to me then why he wouldn't marry my daughter, given her condition, the lying oaf. He wanted his cake and to eat it too."

I held a hand to my mouth, shocked by all that Sarah was revealing to us. If she knew why we were interested, she'd never tell us so much. "Did your daughter know about the other woman?"

Sarah was about to answer when Rose stuck her head back out of the door again. "Mum!" she snapped. "Are you comin'?"

Sarah's cheeks tinted and she looked rather guilty as she bade us a good-bye. "Sorry to cut our chat short," she said, bustling over to her daughter in the doorway. "Give that pug of yours a right big hug, if you would?"

"I'll do that, Sarah. Thank you."

She smiled broadly. "He was one of my favorite rescues," she said. "Such a good pup. I just know he'll make a wonderful addition to your own family."

I knew it too. "Thank you again, Sarah," I said, waving my good-bye.

When we got out to the street, I told Heath, "Let's get back to the hotel and call an immediate meeting!"

Heath was already sending text messages. "I'm on it," he said. And we were off.

# Chapter 15

We made it back to the hotel and hurried to the bar. Gilley, Meg, and Gopher were already there, but John and Kim were still missing. "They're on their way," Gopher explained with a hint of irritation. "They were in line buying tickets or something."

Heath frowned. "Sounds like they're enjoying their vacation."

"I know, right?" Gopher replied. "I swear, if we didn't need every member of this crew right now, I'd fire their asses."

"Fire whose asses?" Kim said as she and John joined us.

Gopher was caught off guard. "Uh, the waitstaff," he said. "They take forever to get your drinks."

Kim smiled and set down a pink flyer she'd carried in. The color caught my eye, so I read the large caption. *Take a tour of Scotland's most haunted locations!*

I squinted at the paper. "Is this Fergus's tour?"

Kim smiled and smoothed her hand over the paper. "Yeah," she said. "It's the talk of the town ever since rumors of the witch being back cropped up. John and I wanted to take the full tour last night to check it out for research—you know, to maybe see if there was anything on the tour that might help you guys out. Fergus only took us to the first part of his tour when we first came here to scout out locations. Anyway, we thought we'd pick his brain along the way and maybe get something that could assist us with the bust."

"But the tour was canceled due to the weather, so we caught a movie instead," John said.

I nodded and caught Heath staring at me impatiently. He wanted to discuss Rose and our theory. I got straight to the point. "We know who called up the witch," I said.

Gopher, Gilley, Meg, Kim, and John all stared at us with mouths agape and said, *"Who?!"*

"Rose Summers."

No one seemed to recognize the name. *"Who?"* Gilley asked again.

"Sarah Summers's youngest daughter," I clarified. "She was Cameron's girlfriend."

"How could she have called up the witch?" Kim asked.

"Sarah Summers and Katherine McKay are the witch's descendants," Heath explained. "Only someone blood-related could have called up the witch, and Sarah Summers was the seventh daughter of Allister McKay. A few centuries ago the McKays owned a castle where Rigella's baby sister was taken after she was raped by the mob. She gave birth to a little girl who must have been adopted by the McKays and given their name to hide her from anyone still angry at the witch."

"It gets even better, Gil," I said. "Rose's Celtic name is pronounced Roy-shin, but it's spelled R-o-i-s-i-n-n."

"No way!" Gil said, digging into his messenger bag

for his notes. "I found that name early on in my research, but I didn't think that's how you pronounced it and I thought I was looking for a boy!" He showed me the small chart he'd drawn from the research he'd done that traced everyone back to the year the witch had died. "See?" I said, pointing to her name. "Roisinn is listed here. She married Peter McKay seventeen years after the witch was killed!"

"So the McKays *did* bring her up," Heath said.

"And if we follow this thread," I said, moving my hand carefully through the marriages and finally landing on Katherine and Sarah's line, "we can see that these guys really are related to the witch!"

"Tell him about the seventh daughter of the seventh daughter!" Heath encouraged. "You know the myth about how the seventh offspring of the seventh offspring is supposed to have magical powers?"

By now, Gopher had gotten out his video camera to record our conversation, and I ignored him while I focused on Gil. "Sarah is the seventh daughter of her parents' children, and Rose is Sarah's seventh daughter. Rose is the seventh daughter of the seventh daughter!" I said, which won me another surprised look from the group.

"That is *freaky*!" Kim said, leaning over my shoulder to look at the chart. "Oh, hey, Gilley! Your family intermarried with the McKays too!"

Gilley frowned distastefully. "Yes, I know," he said. "The traitors."

"And so did the Ericsons," she added. "See? Right here. Pheona Ericson married Gabriel Gillespie! Then, their daughter Clementine married William Hill! I'll bet that means you and Fergus are distantly related!"

Again, that tiny, niggling thought at the back of my

mind began to creep out of its hiding place, but I became distracted again by what Heath was saying. "We also learned that Cameron was cheating on Rose," Heath said. "The poor woman is ready to give birth and her boyfriend is sleeping all over town."

"So she called up the witch to get even with him?" Gopher asked.

I shook my head. "No, she called up the witch to cover up his murder."

"You really think she murdered Cameron?" John asked.

I nodded. I knew it in my gut. "Yes," I said. "I'm sure of it. You should have seen her at the funeral—she just looked totally guilty, like someone realizing they've done a terrible thing, but there's no way to repair the damage."

Heath scratched his chin thoughtfully. "Something about her as the murderer doesn't add up, though, M. J.," he said.

"What?"

"Well, you saw Rose. She's nine months pregnant. How did she kill Cameron and get him into the freezer, then pull him into the street so that Gilley's van could run over him? Plus, how did she know where the brake lines were to cut them? Most girls I know barely know how to check for oil."

I decided not to take offense at that and focus on the question. Before I could answer, however, Heath added to the debate by saying, "And for that matter, how did she know we were coming? Cameron was killed over a fortnight ago, before Kim and John got here to scout out the location. Did you guys visit with a pregnant lady and discuss our plans to come here?"

Both Kim and John shook their heads.

"How'd you find out about this village anyway?" I wondered.

John said, "All we did was plug *European haunted locations* into Google and came up with some choices. We hit on Fergus's Web site, came here to check it out, and only stayed one night before we left early the next morning."

"So Rose couldn't have known ahead of time that a Gillespie was coming to the village," Heath concluded. He then offered another fly in the ointment. "Also, if Rose is responsible, why did she also murder Joseph Hill? I mean, the two murders have to be related, don't they? I think she could probably have strangled him if she caught him by surprise, but there's no way she alone could have strung him up in that tree."

"She must have had help," Gilley said.

"But what about Jack McLaren?" Gopher asked. "You know," he said when everyone looked curiously at him. "The maintenance worker who died down in the close. Do you think he was murdered too?"

I thought about that for a minute, wondering about that poor man, caught down there in the throes of a heart attack, dropping his little radio as he stumbled down the close . . . and just like that, all those pieces came together. "Holy freakballs!" I said, slapping the table with my hand, causing several of my colleagues to jump.

With trembling fingers I reached for the pink flyer and held it up as evidence. "It's been right in front of us all along!" No one in the group seemed to understand what I was talking about, so I took a breath and tried to calm myself to explain my theory to them. "When Heath and I were down in the close for the first time, I remember stumbling over what I thought was a small transistor radio. At the time I believed that Jack had dropped it when he felt his heart attack coming on. Then, later, when we were chasing the van where Gilley was trapped, I remember seeing another small radio lying broken in the street!"

Gilley's eyes widened as understanding bloomed. "They weren't radios!" he said. "They were miniature ghost enhancers like the one you found in the castle!"

I nodded vigorously, turning to Heath. "Remember the energy on Briar Road?" Heath's brow furrowed. "Remember how intense and overwhelming it was?"

"You think it was being enhanced?" he asked.

"I'm sure of it!"

Heath's eyes darted to the flyer. "Fergus," he said. "Fergus has been using the gadgets to enhance the energy for his ghost tour!"

I nodded again and pointed to the flyer. "This ghost tour starts at nine p.m.! The same time we felt the effects the other night in the castle!"

"But what about the woods?" Heath asked. "We weren't there at nine."

"If Fergus is controlling the devices, he could have a remote control or just flip a switch. He had to have seen us following him into the woods, and flipped one of his gadgets on. My thinking is that there's another device hidden somewhere near where we saw the first broomstick in those woods."

"So Fergus called up the witch?" John said, clearly confused.

"No," I told him. "But somehow he convinced Rose to do it."

"But what's in it for him?" Kim asked. "Why kill Jack McLaren and Joseph Hill?"

Heath and I exchanged glances, and I knew, like me, he was remembering that conversation in the car we'd had with Fergus. "I think Jack was simply an unexpected casualty," I said. "But I know why Fergus would want Hill dead."

"Why?" Gopher asked.

"He wanted the castle," I said, knowing it in my gut. "With all the competition of ghost tours in Edinburgh, his business was suffering so to lure tourists in, he needed to purchase that old ruin. And I bet he didn't want to wait the year or two for Joseph to die, so he took advantage of the witch's reappearance and Joseph's depressive state of mind to kill him and make it look like a suicide."

Gopher eyed me skeptically, so I pointed back to the bottom of the flyer where a small map was drawn. "Look where the tour goes, Gopher! It starts on Briar Road, heads into the close, comes back up here, right next to the woods we got smacked around in, continues on to the giant oak tree where we found Hill, and *ends at the castle*!"

"Holy cow!" Gilley shouted. "Why didn't we see that before?"

Kim and John looked at each other guiltily and then Kim said, "We overheard someone gossiping about Ericson yesterday," she said. "One of Joseph Hill's neighbors was saying that she believed Joseph was driven to suicide by Fergus. She said that Fergus tortured him constantly by vandalizing his home and that Joseph had even called the police on Ericson, but no charges were ever brought."

To cement my theory, I turned to Kim and John and asked, "When you guys first came here to scout the location, did you tell Fergus anything about our show?"

The couple looked guilty again. "We did," John admitted. "We even gave him your Web site, M. J."

I looked at Gilley. He was featured almost as prominently as I was on the Web site, because Gilley had a bit of an ego and he'd designed it, after all.

"So he *knew* a Gillespie was coming to town," Heath mused. "And our visiting the village was the last ingredient for this perfect storm. I'll bet he was the one on the video the night of the accident caught sneaking along the side of the van and the one responsible for cutting the brake lines."

"He probably also placed one of the gadgets right under the van while he was at it," I added.

Heath nodded. "So, if he helped Rose kill Cameron, he would have wanted her quid pro quo help to call up the witch as a cover to kill Joseph Hill, purchase his property, and create the scariest ghost tour on record by using his gadgets. All he had to do was set the timers to nine p.m., wait for something really spooky to happen, and enjoy all the publicity Rigella's reappearance was creating for him."

I nodded and beamed at Heath. He'd just given me a brilliant idea.

"So what do we do now?" Gopher asked.

I locked eyes with Gilley. "I have just the plan," I said, reaching for Fergus's flyer again.

"Uh-oh," Gil said. "I never like it when she says that."

At a quarter to nine p.m. that night most of our crew was gathered at the base of Briar Road. I'll admit that I was pretty nervous, even after Gilley and Gopher had discovered and dismantled all of Fergus's gadgets and Gil had worked feverishly to increase the magnetic field of each of our spikes. Our grenades were now supercharged, and we had to be careful getting them too close to the zippers and snaps on our clothing, and especially careful not to open up the canisters near any car or large metallic object. "If you get one of these near a car, you'll never get it off," Gilley had warned. "And I don't think you want to carry your iPhones around with these babies. You'll cause irreparable harm to the touch screen if you do."

Still, we'd had no time to test their increased power when the ghost enhancer was powered up, so I could only hope they worked better than before. Either way, there was no going back now.

I looked around as the wind kicked up, blowing leaves and debris in small swirling circles. "Are you sure they're coming?" I asked John.

"They promised," he assured me, but as he glanced at his watch again, he seemed a little unsure.

"Is Gilley in position?" I asked Meg.

She tapped the headphone that was all but hidden by her long hair. "He sounds like he's in position."

"How's his mental state?" I asked, still worried about the risk to my partner.

Meg placed a finger over the hidden microphone by her cheek. "He's a little frantic, but I think he's okay."

Kim and Gopher were with Gilley. I'd wanted at least two people to guard my partner while he worked the ghost enhancer, which was repositioned back at the top of the castle. I knew Gil was as safe as he could be, with both Gopher and Kim to look after him while they all hid behind the sturdy wooden door with several fire extinguishers, flame-retardant clothing, and a bucket of magnets. But I was still terribly worried. "Let's just hope this works," I muttered.

Heath moved over to huddle next to me in the biting wind. "Wonder where our host is."

"He'll make a dramatic entrance," I predicted. "At least, that's what I'd do if I were him."

At five minutes to nine the rest of our party arrived: the barrister representing Gilley and Gopher, along with the inspector assigned to Cameron's murder. They did not look happy to be there, but at least they'd come.

Another couple I didn't recognize hurried over to our group too, shivering but excited and flashing toothy grins. "Uh, Meg!" I whispered harshly, nodding toward the couple.

"They bought the tickets before I had a chance to buy up all the rest!" she said defensively.

I frowned. The last thing we needed here was innocent bystanders. "Okay, but keep your eye on them, all right? This could get ugly."

At that moment, Fergus Ericson stepped out of one of the local shops, looking smug and full of himself. In his arms he carried a small, rather sleepy-looking mutt. "Good evening!" he announced, looking round at us. For a moment I caught the look of confusion, and then disappointment, when he realized how few people were here, versus how many had purchased tickets. His eyes drifted skyward—the forecast had called for more rain that evening—and he seemed to make up his mind that the turnout was due to the weather.

I hid a grin when I glanced at my own ticket, which clearly read, *No refunds if weather permits the tour to continue.* By my estimate, he'd made over a thousand pounds for just this one tour. Fergus was pulling in a pretty penny for an hour's work.

I pulled the hood of my jacket a little more over my head. I knew I was well disguised, but still, I wanted to be careful. Heath was also well hidden in a long raincoat that covered the cast on his arm, a pair of glasses that he had on hand when he wasn't wearing his contacts, and a ski cap that hid his black hair.

Fergus smiled pleasantly at all of us, rocking back and forth on his heels. A clock nearby chimed nine times, and Fergus's eyes swept the streets, searching for more ticket holders. When none appeared and the time ticked to nine oh five, he called us forward to collect our tickets. Heath and I gave ours to Meg so that Fergus wouldn't see us up close and John did the same for the inspector and our barrister. Fergus then walked us over to the corner of Briar Road and Waverly, and gestured dramatically before going into the same speech he'd given on the DVD recording we'd seen of him a few weeks ago. He then placed the mutt on the ground and began to walk forward onto Briar. The dog followed obediently behind as if it didn't have a care in the world. I couldn't help it; I smiled.

"It's working!" Heath whispered excitedly.

"It is," I agreed.

As we watched, Fergus kept eyeing the dog, as if he was waiting for it to react or do anything other than follow obediently behind. Finally, the man paused and ordered the dog to sit. The dog sat, looking up at him and wagging his tail. The unknown couple who'd purchased tickets on their own began to laugh, and the inspector and the barrister kept eyeing each other like they didn't understand what was supposed to happen.

Fergus tried to cover his embarrassment by waving us forward. "The dog is old and frail," he said with a forced laugh. "It's obviously having trouble detecting the restless spirits who haunt these cobbled streets. But if you still yourselves, I'm sure you'll feel the terrible energy that lingers here!"

I kept my intuition purposely reined in, which was difficult because even though there wasn't a gadget enhancing things, I could still feel the energy radiating off the walls as hundreds of grounded spirits begged for my attention. I'd hate to live in this part of town, and doubted highly if I could manage much more than to simply walk down this street, but somehow I held my senses intact and focused on appearing like any other tourist.

"I'm with the dog," John said loudly and right on cue. "I don't feel anything,"

The couple snickered and Fergus darted a menacing look at them. I only hoped that when the time came, I could protect them.

Fergus then walked us to the middle of Briar, talking about the thousands who'd perished from fire and plague and how along this street there was regular poltergeist activity. Ever so subtly his gaze shifted to the small ledge along one window where what looked like an old radio with a red light was resting.

Gilley and Gopher had discovered it earlier, and Gilley had disarmed it in under five minutes, but he'd left the timer alone and the power switch on so it would appear to Fergus to be working.

At the end of Briar, Fergus placed the dog on a pillow inside his car parked at the curb, retrieved an electric lantern, and motioned for us to follow him to a nearby stairwell. We descended the many stairs and waited for him to open the door to the close. "Through these doors lies unspeakable terror," Fergus was saying, the light from his lantern making his face look spooky. "Many are those who have come here only to be driven slightly mad by what they see and feel. Keep alert, my friends, for the Witch of the Village of Queen's Close is said to lurk in these caverns, searching out her next victim!"

With a dramatic flourish, Fergus threw open the door and quickly descended into the close. We gathered very near the spot where the poor maintenance worker had died and I could see Fergus's eyes flashing with anticipation.

"If you hold very still," he whispered loudly, "and listen very carefully, you will hear the approach of the mob!"

We all held perfectly still. Heath reached over and held my hand. I knew what he was thinking; down here it was especially hard to keep the spooks at bay without reacting to their energy. I knew they had the sense that we could hear them, and in the back of my mind I heard their pleas, and on the edge of my energy I felt them knocking against me. But we couldn't show Fergus any sort of reaction. We had to keep up the ruse that we were just another bored witness to his tour.

"This is lame," Meg said, her voice carrying in the confined space.

I gave her the smallest nod of approval. She'd said that really convincingly.

"Yeah," said the man who was part of the couple. "I agree. I thought we were going to see real ghosts," he complained. "I mean, we paid, like, fifty pounds to see something scary."

Fergus Ericson looked near the boiling point. He kept glancing up and down the cavern, as if he was expecting someone. I knew exactly whom he was waiting for, but I was careful to keep my facial features neutral.

"Let us continue!" he snapped, motioning everyone down the close to the opposite end.

We followed behind him back to the surface and cut through two streets while he coaxed us encouragingly along, promising us many terrors within the haunted woods just ahead.

I recognized the street we were walking down. It was the same one where we'd followed after Fergus the day of Cameron's funeral. Gilley hadn't wanted to go into the woods to locate Fergus's ghost-enhancing gadget, but John had been willing, and he'd discovered it after only a short search and brought it out for Gilley to work on; then he'd kindly put it back in the birdhouse where he'd found it.

I tried to remember that as we got close to the woods. "I'm cold," the woman next to me muttered. She and her companion were about to become a liability if I couldn't convince them to abandon the tour.

"I know," I told her in confidence. "It is freezing and this thing is totally lame. I think we got ripped off."

"We heard about this tour and how scary it's supposed to be, but so far, you're right, it is lame." I was about to suggest that she and her partner ditch the tour, but she cut me off by pointing to the woods and saying, "Oooh, those look totally creepy! Maybe we'll finally see something good in there!"

I could only hope we didn't. Those woods scared the crap out of me, but I marched forward anyway. Heath continued to hold my hand and press close to me, and that really helped. Otherwise, I didn't think I could go in.

Fergus walked us to the very spot where Heath and I had first seen the witch's broom—the exact spot

I'd sent John to in order to search for Fergus's little gadget. I now saw the birdhouse that our guide stood right next to. And up in the house I could see a small red light.

Fergus saw it too. I caught him looking up at it while he waited for the crowd to gather close. With a confident smile he told us the history of these woods. How many people reported being followed by strange dark shadows, while others reported disembodied footsteps chasing them from one end of the woods to the other. And recently, how several locals had reported seeing the witch, riding her broom through the trees, always searching out her next victim.

Heath wrapped an arm around me and squeezed me tightly. Bending low to my ear, he said, "She's in here."

My heart began to pound in alarm. "We're not at our spot yet!" I whispered, my eyes darting around the woods.

The atmosphere was getting to everyone else in the crowd too, because I could see their heads swiveling to look all about the woods, and their faces appeared nervous and concerned. Somewhere in the woods off to my left we all heard a noise that was rather indescribable. It wasn't a scream per se, more like an outraged cry. And it was terrifying.

There were collective gasps among the small crowd, and Meg and John both moved in closer to Heath and me. "I thought Gilley had dismantled that thing!" John hissed.

"Meg," I whispered. "Ask Gilley if he's sure he disarmed the enhancer."

Meg put her hand to her ear and turned her head discreetly away so that Fergus couldn't see her. She then turned back to me and said, "He said, and I quote, 'What does M. J. take me for? An amateur?'"

I grinned, but any humor was short-lived, because in the trees right behind us were some aggravated rustling sounds. "What was that?" someone yelled.

"I believe it is the witch approaching," Fergus said, his creepy smile spreading wide.

Very slowly and as discreetly as possible I reached into my raincoat and uncapped a grenade. Using Heath and Meg as a cover, I tipped out the spike and held it behind Meg's back.

The rustling stopped.

We all waited quietly and were rewarded a few seconds later with another aggravated scream, but much farther away. "She's a powerful one," Heath muttered.

"And quite dangerous," I said. Then a thought struck me. "Heath," I said. "If she's that strong without the enhancer, then we must be close to another source of power for her."

Heath turned to face me and mouthed, "Her portal?"

I nodded. "We've always just assumed her portal had been near the place where she'd died—in the close."

"But what if she'd didn't die in the close?" Heath said, and something in the back of my brain ignited.

I recalled the image Gopher had captured on tape at the castle of the three figures hanging from the huge oak in Fergus's yard. I gasped, "The tree!" and unfortunately, I said that a little too loudly because Fergus snapped his head in my direction.

And our ruse was nearly up until a quick-thinking

Meg pointed to a nearby elm and said, "I saw it too! A shadow! Right over there behind that tree!"

Fergus held his lantern up toward the elm, his expression triumphant. "She approaches!" he said.

Nearby I could hear the inspector and the barrister murmuring together. I was especially grateful that they hadn't walked out on us, but we had made rather bold promises of revealing Cameron's killer if they would just take the tour. It'd been risky, but so far, it seemed to be paying off.

"Jeff!" the girl next to me squealed when a nearby twig snapped. "Let's get out of here!"

I held my breath, hoping they would leave. "Are you kidding?" he exclaimed. "Shelly, this is awesome!"

I exhaled with a sigh. Shelly and Jeff were the one fly in this ointment, and I didn't have it worked out yet how I was going to do what I had to do and protect them at the same time. I didn't even feel confident that we could keep the other members in the party safe. "We don't have enough grenades," I whispered worriedly to Heath.

"I know," he said. "But we're too far into this to turn back now."

When the woods became quiet again, Fergus waved to us. "Shall we continue?" he asked.

"Yes, if it'll get us out of these woods!" said Shelly

Fergus laughed wickedly. "This way, then, me lady," he said. Shelly hurried up to Fergus's side and Jeff went with her. I bit back my irritation. They were just making it harder and harder.

As we walked, I became aware that Heath was looking this way and that. "We're being followed," he said.

I'd felt it too. The witch was with us. I didn't know if her two evil sisters were also in attendance, but I sort of hoped so. It would make things just a little easier if they were.

We got clear of the woods and approached that tremendous oak tree. I could feel my heart rate tick up a bit and reached for Heath's hand again after tucking the spike back into its metal container.

His palm was a little sweaty. He was nervous too. "Meg, and John," I whispered, and they edged closer to me. "I'm going to have to split you guys up. On my signal, Meg, you'll have to cover the odd couple up there, and get them away from Fergus. John, you're on your own to cover the inspector and the barrister."

Meg looked really nervous. "What if the grenades don't work?"

"They'll work well enough," I assured her, and I hoped I was right. "They won't go after you with easier targets so close. The one thing you cannot do is let anyone get too far away from the grenades. Keep your groups contained, and close to you. Lock arms with them if you have to, but cover them no matter what you see or what comes out of these woods."

"Okay," they both said.

"And Meg, make sure that Gilley flips the switch on and off only on my signal. You're the one in constant contact with him, so make sure you're watching me at all times."

"Got it," she said.

I felt butterflies in my stomach as we got closer and closer to the tree. Looking east, I could just make out the top of the tower where Gilley, Gopher and Kim were. I'd chosen not to wear a headset because I couldn't concentrate with Gilley shrieking in my ear—as I knew he'd be doing on this bust—so I'd given the communication over to Meg, who'd been a champ about volunteering for the post.

We walked another hundred yards and the misty atmosphere turned slightly drizzlier. It wasn't raining outright, but it was definitely wet. Fergus stopped under the bough of the great tree and turned to address us. Heath let go of my hand, and I moved in toward Fergus's right, while Heath edged over to his left. Meg put a hand to her ear, and I knew she was telling Gilley to get ready, while John angled over to the inspector and the barrister.

So far, Fergus hadn't noticed our sudden jockeying of position, and he began his speech. "For several hundred years throughout the Middle Ages, this mighty oak has seen a torrent of death. Dozens, perhaps even thousands, were brought here under suspicion of witchcraft or heresy and hanged right above my head."

I pulled the hood of my raincoat off my head and I heard Meg say, "Now, Gil!"

I opened my sixth sense and closed my eyes. The atmosphere changed in an instant as it became charged with ions and electrostatic energy. "What's happening?" Shelly squeaked, her voice high-pitched and frightened. She was right next to me.

"Go stand over there," I urged, opening my lids and looking her directly in the eyes. "Next to my friend Meg."

Meg stepped forward and reached out her hand. "You can get a better view over here," she said, her face friendly and encouraging.

Shelly looked from me to Meg, thoroughly confused,

and then something creaked right overhead. "Crap," I whispered, just as Shelly screamed loud enough for Meg to cover her ears.

I looked up and ducked low, in spite of myself. Behind me there were gasps and even Fergus seemed surprised. Dozens of people were swinging back and forth from the tree, all of them looking wretchedly blue. Three of them I recognized quite clearly—Rigella and her sisters hung from the largest bough, only Rigella's eyes were open and staring menacingly down at us.

"Jesus Christ!" I heard Heath shout. "M. J., I think Gilley's using too much juice!"

I'd assigned Gilley to put the gadget we'd found in the tower room back together, and I'd told him specifically to amp up the power. I needed to make a point with Fergus and for a minute or two I needed things to get a little intense. What I hadn't counted on was how many people had actually died in that tree.

Nor, apparently, how many had died in the woods. Shelly was still shrieking her head off, and her boyfriend, Jeff, joined her in creating some chaos when Fergus lifted his lantern, illuminating the bodies for everyone to clearly see.

Shelly took off then, with Jeff hot on her heels. My eyes darted to the woods and the faintest shadows that I could make out swirling now in and around the trees. "Don't let them get trapped in the woods!" I cried.

Meg nodded and took off after then. "Use the grenades!" I added. "Meg! Pull out your grenades!"

I had no idea if she'd heard me, but John at least was on the ball. He stood right in front of the barrister and the inspector with arms crossed and at least three magnetic spikes gripped firmly in each hand. "What's going on?" Fergus demanded, and I could tell he'd finally taken a good long look at who was on his tour.

I turned to face him. "Your little ruse is up," I told him. "We know what you've done, Fergus."

He actually laughed at me. "Oh, Miss Holliday!" he said, appearing delighted to find me here. "I see you've decided to sample my tour. Are you enjoying yourself so far?"

"I'll be enjoying myself a little more in a few minutes, Fergus, when you're taken away in handcuffs for your part in the murder of Cameron Lancaster!"

Ericson looked around and his eyes sparkled in the lantern light. "We'll see about that, Miss Holliday," he said, and nudged the lantern first toward the tree, where Rigella and her sisters no longer appeared, and then toward the woods.

From out of the trees came three black shadows, exactly like the ones we'd caught on camera in the close and later attacking the van. They came with blinding speed straight at me, Heath, and Fergus—who was the only one of us who appeared unfazed by their approach. "And where is your friend?" Fergus asked wickedly. "Mr. Gillespie? I believe the Witch of Queen's Close would like to invite him to a barbecue."

I didn't take the bait; instead, I shouted out to Heath, "Brace yourself!" A second before they got to us, I closed my eyes and crossed my arms over my chest, protecting myself as best I could. It was to no avail. Rigella was one of the most powerful spirits I'd ever encountered, and she knocked me flat on my back and stomped on my chest for good measure.

Instinctively I pushed back against her—but she was stronger than I was in this melding of both planes. I opened my eyes and I could see her face hovering above me. "Where do you hide the Gillespie?" she demanded. "I'll find him, you know!"

The weight of her was pressing so hard against me that it was hard to breathe. Out of the corner of my eye I could see Heath, also on the ground while two shadows pounded him with blows. John made a sudden movement, lowering his crossed hands as if he was about to go help Heath, and I shouted, *"Stay where you are, John!"*

"Tell me where he is!" the witch shrieked, and Fergus laughed.

"It's impossible to deny her," he said. "She must claim a victim tonight, and if it isn't your friend, then she might be satisfied with you."

I struggled to take a deep breath and then I focused directly into the witch's black, hollow eyes. "You want a Gillespie?" I snapped. "Why not go for the closest one?" Working to get my arm free, I finally managed to point an accusing finger at Fergus. "His great-great-great-grandfather was Gabriel Gillespie!"

The witch's head snapped in Fergus's direction. "Lies!" he roared, but I could see the panic in his eyes.

"I'm not lying," I told the witch, recalling the extra bit of research I'd had Gopher do in preparation for tonight. What he'd discovered had sealed our advantage. "You have access to Gabriel, witch! He died in that very tree! He was hanged for high treason when he came out against the king!"

And sure enough the witch's eyes traveled to the tree, and one man swinging there, who suddenly opened his eyes. Even I could see the resemblance to Fergus. "Leave my family be, witch!" he shouted at her.

But she merely waved her hand and he vanished with a thin pop. She then released me and called to her sisters. They pulled back from Heath and came to her side. I got sorely to my feet and looked at Heath. He groaned, but managed to get up too. With a pang I could see he was cut and bruised but otherwise okay.

"Stay back!" Fergus warned as the sisters crept toward him.

The witch raised her right hand, her thumb and middle finger pressed tightly together before she snapped them loudly. A small flame burst from the ground right by Fergus's feet and he leaped back with a squeal. "Stop this!" he begged me. "I know you can stop this!"

Heath moved to my side. "The woods, M. J.!"

I glanced quickly toward the woods. They were alive with shadows. Somewhere in their interior we heard a woman scream, and I couldn't tell if it was Shelly, Meg, or some spook. "I can stop this," I said, "but you'll have to confess your sins, Fergus!"

Rigella gave another snap of her fingers, and a small flame to Ericson's left sparked from the ground. He stomped it out with his foot and kept edging backward, away from the approaching sisters.

"I . . . I . . . I . . . ," he stammered. "It was an accident!" he cried. "I swear! And I was only trying to help Rose after all. Cameron was cheating on her, and I thought if I told her, then she would have the sense to leave him. But she confronted him and they argued and then he hit her. I heard them from outside, and when I went in, she had taken a frying pan to his head. He died from the blow and there was nothing I could do!

"She begged me to help her. So we placed Cameron in the freezer and came up with a plan. As the seventh daughter of the seventh daughter, she'd always had the power to bring forth the witch, and I'd been working to expand my ghost tour, and invented a small device to help Rose call Rigella forth. But that's all I did!" he shrieked. "I merely helped her cover it all up! It's her you should be questioning!"

The witch raised her hand again, and this time, so did her sisters. "We'll definitely talk to Rose," I assured him. "But none of that explains why you killed Joseph Hill."

There were three loud simultaneous snaps, and the cuff of Fergus's pant leg caught fire, along with two more patches on the ground. He cried out and slapped his leg, snuffing out the flame and hopping over another, in his effort to get away. "I killed Joseph because he wouldn't sell me that parcel with the castle!" he said. "The sorry sot was dying, after all, and his illness was making him suffer! I needed that castle for my coup de grâce! I planned to turn it into a haunted bed-and-breakfast. It would have made me a very rich man!"

At that moment, Joseph Hill appeared. He walked right into the middle of our group and pointed an accusing finger at Fergus. "So you broke into me home, strangled me, then strung me up in this tree to make it like a suicide, Fergus? Why would you do such a thing to me? I was your best mate from primary school!"

Fergus was shaking from head to toe and his complexion was ashen. "I'm sorry, Joseph! Truly I am!"

"And what about the likes of me?!" shouted another voice and instantly a man in a green workman's uniform appeared at my side. "Your gadget gave me a heart attack, it did! I was down in the close, mindin' me own business, just needin' to change one last bulb before me shift ended, and I find your little radio. I was thinking what a fancy bit of luck, and I turned it on and before I knows it, the witches are comin' for me! I starts to run, and me poor heart gave out, just like that!"

Fergus's hand rose to his mouth as he stared at the new stranger. "Jack," he whispered. "Oh, Jack, I never meant for you to get hurt!"

"Admit it, Fergus!" I yelled. "You murdered these people for your own gain!"

"Yes!" Fergus cried pitifully as the witches continued to close in. "Yes, yes! I'm guilty! Take me away, but don't let them kill me!"

I looked at the inspector. His eyes were wide as saucers and his expression was one of utter disbelief. Under any other circumstance I might have laughed at his reaction, but we were risking a lot by pushing the envelope this far. "Okay," I said to John. "Tell Gilley to turn it off."

John shook his head. "Meg's wearing the headset," he reminded me.

"Call him," I ordered, stepping forward to the oak tree.

John lowered his arms long enough to pat down his coat. "Oh, shit!" he swore. "M. J., I don't have my cell! Gilley told us not to carry them on the bust!"

I looked at Heath. He shook his head. "Back at the hotel."

I quickly grabbed for mine and pulled it out of my back pocket. I was the only one in the group apparently who didn't care if a stupid cell phone was damaged. Handing it impatiently to Heath, I said, "Call him now and get him to turn it off!"

Heath took the phone as Fergus yelled at us, "Why aren't you helping me?!"

"I'm working on it!" I snapped, focusing back on the trunk of the tree.

"M. J.!" Heath said. "All the power just drained out of your cell! It's dead!"

I snapped my head at him. "Son of a . . . !" There was no way to get to Gilley and tell him to turn off the gadget, and that meant that there might be little I could do to stop the witch from hurting Fergus. "John!" I said. "Head into those woods and see if you can find Meg and get her to tell Gilley to turn off the enhancer!"

John looked doubtfully toward the trees. "Which direction should I head?"

The night air was broken by yet another bloodcurdling scream. "I'd try there," I told him, then turned to Heath. "I need you to get to the castle. If John can't get to Meg in time, you're the only person fast enough to reach Gilley before it's too late!"

Without another word Heath bolted for the castle. John shoved half the magnetic spikes he'd been holding at the two men he was guarding and took off like a rocket. I pulled out a grenade and said to the witches, "Back off right now, Rigella, or I'm going to lock you into purgatory for good."

The three black shadows were nearly on top of Fergus now. He was bent over and curled into as small a target as he could make himself. Rigella turned her shadowy form back to me and I heard her hiss menacingly. "Do not threaten me, lass!" she commanded.

I eased backward to stand right next to the tree as I held up my spike for her to see. Feeling my way along the bark I began hoping against hope that I was right. If Rigella and her sisters had died hanging from these branches, then Rigella's portal was likely somewhere along the tree's trunk. "It's no threat," I said. "It's a promise."

Her reaction was exactly what I was hoping for. Her eyes became large and wide and she and both her sisters charged me. As fast as I could, I pulled out another grenade and frantically began feeling around the trunk. About a second before her energy slammed into me, I found a cold spot on the tree—the distinctive mark of a portal—and jammed one of the spikes directly into it.

Rigella screamed and fell to the side as if I'd physically punched her. Her sisters stopped long enough to hover over her and that bought me a little more time. I began feeling around the base of the tree again and found another cold spot. I thrust the second spike deep into the trunk and the second sister cried out in agony. I felt for my belt as the third sister growled low and began to charge. I knew I didn't have time to get a canister free and pull out a spike, so I yelled at the inspector, "Throw one to me!" He hesitated and I shouted again, *"Now, man!"*

He tossed it, but he overshot the throw and the spike hit the tree way above my head then fell somewhere to the ground. In the dark I couldn't find it and just as I was about to fall to my hands and knees to search for it, the spook hit me.

I flew backward, somersaulting over and over, my head hitting the hard ground and stars filling my vision. The ghost of Rigella's sister was incredibly strong, and fueled by rage, she lifted me off the ground again and tossed me several feet away.

I landed in a heap, sputtering and coughing as the wind got knocked out of me. There was another raging scream and I looked up to see Rigella, getting to her feet again and eyeing me with deadly intent. Behind her Fergus was running as fast as his legs would carry him, and to my great dismay, both the inspector and the barrister were running after him . . . leaving me alone to face the Bitches of Eastwick.

# Chapter 16

There is a time to fight and a time for flight, and this time, I knew without a doubt, was a time to head for them thar hills.

I took off like a bat out of hell and didn't stop, even after I felt the searing pain of all my stitches popping out, or the hot molten heat of the injury in my thigh being ripped open and the liquid sticky feeling as blood trickled down my pant leg.

For several tense seconds, I had no idea where I could run that could possibly be safe, but then an idea came to my panicked mind and I prayed that I'd make it there ahead of the sisters.

While I ran, I managed to tug loose one of the grenades, which would have less of an effect the closer I drew to my target, so I popped the top and held it above my head, hoping it would give me just enough of a magnetic field to make me a slightly less viable target.

I swept down the hill racing as fast as I'd ever run in my life, willing my feet to move faster and faster while my free arm pumped for all it was worth. I leaned slightly to my right and through another set of

thin woods I could see a light shining like a beacon—
as if it were calling me home.

Out the corner of my eye I could see a black shadow,
edging closer and closer. I lowered the arm holding
the spike and swung it toward the shadow. I heard a
slight squeal and it peeled back a little.

"Get away from me!" I cried as I surged into the
woods, narrowly missing a low branch and dodging
the trunk of another tree. Branches scraped my hands
and face, but I didn't slow down. In fact, if anything, I
think I was so scared I actually sped up.

Something clawed hard at my shoulder, but I tore
free while a searing pain raked across my collarbone.
"You bitch!" I yelled, and kept going, finally bursting
through the trees. The little house was only a hundred
yards away, but I was breathing hard and my pace
had finally slowed. Another shadow appeared on my
left and I switched hands holding the spike and swung
out at it right before something grabbed my hair and
nearly pulled me to the ground.

With all the remaining strength I could muster, I
lurched forward, feeling several strands yank out, and
I managed to keep running. My breath was so loud
and so heavy that I realized I was gasping, but I had to
keep going. I had to make it!

I took two more gulps of air and shouted, *"Katherine!"*

Nothing happened and I strained to see in through
the window with the light on.

*"Kaaaaaaaatheriiiiiiine!"* I cried for all I was worth.

An instant later the door burst open and she stood
there along with someone else. Both figures appeared
quite startled as I sprinted toward them. *"Help me!"* I
pleaded.

And just like I'd hoped, Katherine held up her hand as I approached, and shouted, "Stop!"

I of course kept running, but the shadows next to me peeled off. I reached her porch in four more strides and collapsed on the ground at her feet, panting hard and totally out of breath. "What is going on?" she demanded when I hugged her leg.

I pointed behind me, and stared up at her. "Send . . . them . . . back!" I rasped.

Katherine looked over my head, and I knew she could see the three distantly related ancestors. "I did not call them forward," she said simply. She then turned to the woman at her side and asked, "Will you end this now, Rose?"

I turned around and sat up, trying to catch my breath and barely able to do much more than that. Rose stood next to Katherine looking terrible. Her face was ashen and her eyes were huge and there was such guilt in her eyes. "I don't know how," she cried.

I held up a finger to get her attention. "I . . . might . . . know," I said, pausing as I took two more heaving breaths and called out, "Isla! Isla McKay! I command you to appear!"

In the wink of an eye a mist formed about ten feet from us, and through that mist we could clearly see the white outline of a woman. "Have you seen me babe?" she asked.

I nodded. "She's right here." I pointed up to Rose. "This is Roisinn," I told her, struggling to my feet.

Isla looked terribly confused and shook her head. "She's not me babe."

I turned to Rose and asked, "What's your name, honey?"

Rose hesitated, but a nod from her aunt seemed

to convince her to play along. "My name is Roisinn McKay," she said.

By now I'd gotten command over my breathing again and said calmly, "You missed her growing up, Isla. Roisinn has become a young lady now."

Again, Isla looked terribly confused. "I don't understand," she said to me, and turned to her sisters for an explanation.

Before they could communicate anything, however, I said, "You died giving her life, Isla. That's why you missed her growing up. She's lived her life and moved forward in this, the world of the living, while you've been looking for her all these years."

"I've . . . *died*?!"

I nodded firmly, and was grateful that Katherine did the same. "Your restless spirit has been wandering these hills for some time, love," Katherine said. "And your pain has kept your dear sisters restless and in search of vengeance."

Isla gasped anew. Turning an accusing stare at the three dark shadows hovering nearby, Isla asked, "Is this true, Rigella?"

If there were words exchanged, we could not hear them, but we could all watch Isla's reaction, and to my great relief she appeared horrified. "You must stop!" she demanded. "Rigella! Dera! Firtha! You must *not* continue this!"

Behind the three sisters, over two dozen new silhouettes appeared. There were a little over thirty souls gathered and three of them I recognized: Joseph Hill, Jack McLaren, and Cameron Lancaster. When Cameron appeared, I heard Rose emit a small cry, and I looked up to see tears leaking down her face and she whispered, "Oh, Camey! I'm so sorry!"

Isla also caught sight of the souls behind her and she stepped away from her three sisters, recoiling in horror. "Rigella!" she shouted accusingly. "This is not our way! You've *murdered* these poor souls?! It's against everything we stand for! Everything *you* stand for! Our mission has never been for ill! It has always been for healing! For *preserving* life!"

Rigella's shadowy face became more humanlike and her expression showed uncertainty for the first time. Rose must have caught it too, because she said, "Aye, me aunts. Me mum is right. I've learned what terrible things can happen when you're consumed with vengeance. It's time for you to undo this wretched curse, and let the blood you've taken be penance enough for those lives of your clan taken by that mob."

I watched the witches carefully. Either the three sisters were going to listen, or they weren't. And if they didn't, then we'd all likely pay for it. I felt a hand then on my left shoulder and I turned my head to see Sam Whitefeather standing right next to me. I was far too stunned to do anything but gape at him, and he merely smiled and nodded toward Isla.

A light, bright and pure, appeared above her head, and I knew exactly what it represented. And beyond her thirty-one more lights appeared and hovered over the lost souls on the grass behind the sisters. Slowly they lowered toward each individual, and Isla seemed to be aware that she was running out of time, because she pulled her hands up in a prayer and begged her sisters, "Please! I don't want to leave here without you! Make peace with these souls now and move along with all of us!"

And then, something in the ether shifted. The black shadows lost their inky richness and lightened to a more gray appearance. Rigella spoke, and her voice rang loudly across the grass. "We shall consider it penance enough, Isla, and we ask for peace among those against whom we've taken our vengeance." An instant later, three balls of white light appeared above Rigella and her two sisters, and in the next moment all the figures on the lawn disappeared in an intense burst of light, and the shadows that were zipping through the forests vanished, and the night became still and calm and oddly peaceful.

I got up and limped over to a nearby chair where I eased myself down. I was exhausted and the back of my thigh hurt something fierce. Heath, Gilley, Gopher, and Kim showed up a few minutes later as Katherine was bringing me a hot cup of tea. "Are you okay?" Heath asked, squatting down next to me. I could see he carried spikes in both hands, and Gilley still held tightly to his fire extinguisher.

"You know," I told him, "all things considered, I'm just ducky."

Fergus Ericson was apprehended by the inspector shortly after running into his house and trying to hide under his bed. Meanwhile, the barrister we'd hired for Gilley and Gopher assured me that they would both have their passports returned to them in the morning.

Meg finally called Gilley to see what was happening. She'd lost her headset in the woods, and she'd also lost sight of Jeff and Shelly. We had no idea what'd happened to them, but I had an intuitive feeling that they'd made it out of the woods okay and they were probably done checking out the local ghost tours.

We also made sure to retrieve the dog from Fergus's car, which happened to belong to one of his neighbors. He'd taken it without her permission from her backyard. Luckily, the old mutt hadn't experienced anything more traumatic than a car ride, a short walk and a nap on a lumpy old pillow.

Rose went into labor that very evening. In fact, she'd been having contractions most of that evening, and before she went to the hospital, she wanted to confess all to her aunt and apologize. That's why she'd been at Katherine's.

Early the next morning, Rose gave birth to a baby girl she named Camille. We heard later that, given the fact that Fergus admitted to hearing them scuffle and finding her a moment later with a bruised lip and holding a frying pan, she was unlikely to spend any time in jail for his murder, as it was a clear case of self-defense.

Fergus Ericson would not be that lucky. While we were on another bust some months later, Gilley read that he got forty years to life for killing Joseph Hill.

Heath and I spent a little time cleaning up the area, going back for several nights in a row to help those grounded spirits we'd found hanging from the tree and in the woods cross over. It was exhausting work, but it was worth it, and we got some really fantastic footage out of it for *Ghoul Getters*.

Gilley calmed down as well, and I finally got him to go to sleep without a fire extinguisher for a binkie. And while Heath and I cleared the tree, castle, and woods of the spooks, Gil continued to play with Fergus's gadget, telling me it might come in handy one of these days.

Gopher was all for that.

Katherine also took an interest in our work, and came out with us on the ghost hunts, revealing that

Cameron had never changed his will after they split up and he'd left her a sizable sum. She planned to buy Joseph's place, rent out the main house, then work on renovating the castle. She liked Fergus's idea of turning it into a bed-and-breakfast—sans ghosties.

The day before we were set to leave Scotland for good, a message arrived for me at the front desk that there was a package awaiting my signature. I passed Heath in the hallway on my way down to see what it was. "Where're you headed?" he asked, bumping me with his elbow. He and I had been making goo-goo eyes at each other for days now, but we'd always stopped just short of doing anything other than hold hands.

"Down to the lobby. Someone sent me a package."

"A package?" he said with a smile. "I wonder who could have sent you something."

He said it so coyly that I thought he might be up to something. "Want to come with me to see what it is?" I asked flirtatiously.

"Sure," he said.

I rolled my eyes and laughed. "Yeah, right," I said.

"What?"

"Nothing. Come on, let's see who sent me a sweet nothing."

We made our way down to the first floor and over to the front desk, and I continued to smile and poke him in the ribs while we waited behind some other folks checking in. "Come on," I prodded. "What'd you get me?"

Heath laughed and wrapped his arms around me, pulling me tightly into him. I was surprised by his sudden boldness, but I didn't fight him off. "I didn't," he said, but there was a twinkle in his eye.

I giggled. "Sure, sure."

"Can I help you?" the desk clerk asked.

I held Heath's hand, tugging him with me to the front desk. "I was told I had to sign for a package?"

"And you are?"

"M. J. Holliday."

"Ah yes," said the clerk, disappearing into a little room and coming back a moment later with a huge bouquet of flowers. "These just arrived for you."

I squealed with delight and poked Heath again. "Ohmigod! Heath, they're gorgeous!"

His eyes were huge and I had to hand it to him, because now he looked convincingly surprised. "I didn't," he said.

"Yeah, right," I said, snatching the card and ripping open the envelope. With great happiness I read aloud, "Turn around." That made me blink. "What does that mean?" I asked him. But Heath was only staring at me blankly. "Heath? What does 'turn around' mean?"

"It means turn around," said a deep baritone that froze me in place and sent a shock wave right down to my toes.

Slowly I swiveled in place to face the gorgeous brown eyes of my current boyfriend. "Steven!" I squeaked.

"Surprise," he said levelly.

*Oh boy.*

"Um . . . ," I said, trying to think of something to say. "What are you doing here?"

"Gilley sent me an e-mail and said you'd been in a fire. So I got on a plane and came here to make sure you were all right."

I attempted a smile in the awkward silence that followed. "Maybe we should talk?"

"Maybe we should," he agreed. "Are you free now? Or do you two have plans?"

*Oh boy times ten.*

"I've got time," I said quickly. "Tons. Let's go some-place and talk." I took Steven by the hand, trying to lead him away from Heath, who did not seem at all pleased that Steven had shown up out of the blue.

We'd only gone a few paces when Steven called over his shoulder to Heath. "Are you coming?" he asked.

"Me?"

Steven nodded. "I believe your name will likely come up, so it's only fair for you to be included."

*Oh boy times infinity.*

I had a feeling this was going to be a very long night. And the truth is, that wasn't even the half of it.

But that's another story. . . .

Read on for a sneak peek at
Victoria Laurie's next Ghost Hunter Mystery,

# GHOULS, GHOULS, GHOULS!

Coming soon from Obsidian.

For the record, I am not a morning person. Especially not the morning we were about to depart Scotland, because, technically, I believe it was so early it still qualified as the middle of the night. However, the hour did nothing to dampen my producer's enthusiasm for our next shooting location for our new cable-TV ghost-hunting show. "I know you guys don't want to hear too much about the history of the place we're investigating next," Gopher was saying as the entire cast and crew were seated around a table at a small café in the airport. "But in this case, I really think it's necessary."

I felt something heavy hit my shoulder, and when I turned, I saw my business partner and best friend's head, resting near my collarbone.

Gilley Gillespie and I have known each other since the first grade. After high school, I followed Gil to Boston, where he attended MIT and I did readings for clients, connecting them with their dearly departed.

From there, Gilley and I became partners in a rather unprofitable ghostbusting business. Last year, in search of other funding, Gilley had signed us up to participate in a cable-TV show that investigated haunted pos-

sessions, and that was where we'd met another medium, Heath Whitefeather, and of course our producer,
Peter Gophner, or Gopher for short.

Gopher had shown the film from that original
haunted-possessions show to some bigwigs at Bravo,
and they'd signed me, Gilley, and Heath up for thir-
teen episodes of a production called *Ghoul Getters*.

Since filming began, we'd solved a big mystery or
two, and had our lives endangered on a regular basis.
All in a day's work when you're a ghostbuster, I suppose. And did I mention that the schedule Bravo had
us on was exhausting? Hence, why we were at the
airport so early, ready to depart to our next shooting
location, and why Gilley was now unconscious with
his big heavy head resting on my shoulder.

"Gil," I whispered, nudging him with my elbow.

"ZZZZZZZZZ . . . ," he snored.

Heath laughed quietly. "He's out cold."

"ZZZZZZZ . . . ," Gilley agreed.

I sighed, yawned, and tried to focus on the map
Gopher was laying out on the table. "As you know from
your tickets, we're heading to Belfast, Ireland. From
there we'll travel by car to Portrush and check in to
our hotel. Once we get some rest, we'll head here."

Blearily I followed Gopher's finger, which had zipped
over the map to rest on a small X that seemed to be in
the middle of the channel that ran between Scotland
and Ireland. I vaguely remembered approving some
ruins along the Irish coastline back when we were still
planning this excursion to Europe, but my brain was
so foggy that the details were lost.

"Are we going scuba diving?" I asked.

Gopher smiled and for the first time he seemed to
detect the rather cranky mood of those of us still awake

at the table. "Ha," he said, flashing a toothy grin. "No. This is actually a very small island just off the Giant's Causeway."

"The whose what?" Heath asked.

"The Giant's Causeway," Gopher repeated. "It's a narrow strip of water that cuts into the coastline of Northern Ireland."

"'Kay," I said. "I'm following you."

"Anyway, right here is Dunlow Castle. And that's the spot for our next investigation."

Gopher looked around at us with an expression that suggested he was really excited and we should be too.

The only one who said anything was Gilley. "ZZZZZZZZZ . . ."

"Gil thinks that's great," I said, hiding a smile. Next to me Heath ducked his chin and snorted.

Gopher glared at us. "*Any*way," he continued, "Dunlow Castle comes with a pretty rich history and is said to be very haunted."

"Hopefully not quite as haunted as Queen's Close," I muttered, referring to the rather dicey bust we'd just come off.

Gopher ignored me and laid out a set of blueprints on the table. "Legend has it that in the late fifteen hundreds a ship from the Spanish Armada came close enough to Dunlow to become a prime target for Ranald Dunnyveg—the lord of the castle. He sent a flotilla of ships against the Spaniards, sank the vessel, and traded the crew back to Spain for a tidy ransom."

I yawned again. So far, I wasn't that impressed, but I knew that Gopher wouldn't be this excited about something unless he was working a specific angle, so I waited him out.

After taking a sip of coffee, he continued. "So, from

that conquest, a legend grew. It seems that many believe the Spanish vessel was carrying more than just soldiers. It was carrying gold bullion."

I sighed. This was getting complicated and I was getting hungry. "Anyone want a muffin?" I asked, ready to gently transfer Gilley's head onto Heath's shoulder.

"Hold on, M. J.!" Gopher snapped. "I haven't gotten to the best part yet."

"Oh, sorry," I said, hoping he'd get there really, *really* soon.

"Legend has it that Ranald kept the bullion a secret so that he wouldn't have to pay taxes on it, and he snuck it off the Spanish Armada and hid it somewhere in his castle." Again, Gopher looked around at us to get our reactions, but we all just stared blankly back at him. "Don't you get it?" he asked us.

"Clearly we don't," said Kim, one of our assistant producers.

Gopher tugged on the brim of his ball cap and said, "The ghost of Ranald is one of the spooks said to haunt the castle! If M. J. and Heath can find him and talk to him, maybe he'll tell you guys where he's hidden the bullion!"

That got my attention. "Hold on," I said, putting up my hand in a stopping motion. "You mean to tell me this bust isn't about documenting spooks as much as it's about sending us on some sort of ghost treasure hunt?"

Gopher beamed at me. "Yes!"

"ZZZZZZ . . . ," said Gilley.

I eyed Heath over Gilley's head and saw that he was looking at me to gauge my reaction. Something unspoken passed between us, and he and I both smiled at each other. I then turned back to Gopher and asked, "If we find the bullion, can we keep it?"

"Yes," Gopher said, a twinkle in his eye.

"We're in," Heath and I said together.

Gopher let out the breath he'd been holding. "Really? You guys think this is a good idea?"

"Dude, if we find a lost treasure of gold bullion, then it's a genius idea!" I said.

Heath was equally enthused. "This could open up a whole new industry for us. Instead of ghostbusters we could be ghost treasure hunters!"

"We could retire early," I agreed.

"There's just one catch," Gopher said softly.

I snapped my head back in his direction. "What'd you say?"

Gopher smiled nervously. "It shouldn't be any big deal," he assured us.

"A time to worry," Heath said.

"What's this catch?" I demanded.

Gopher sighed. "The castle's supposed to also be haunted by a particularly nasty phantom."

My brow furrowed. "A phantom?"

Gopher nodded. "Some supernatural being is supposed to lurk around the ruins in search of trespassers. He's so scary that none of the locals will go near the place."

"What's he done to make everyone so scared?" I asked.

Gopher swallowed and wouldn't meet my eyes.

"ZZZZZZ . . . ," said Gilley.

"Come on, Gopher, out with it," Heath insisted.

Gopher took a big breath. "Supposedly, he's responsible for throwing a few people off the side of the cliffs."

*"What?"* Heath and I said in unison again.

"But he hasn't attacked anyone in a few years now,"

Gopher added quickly. "The last victims were thrown over the side well over six years ago."

"Who were they?" Kim wanted to know.

Gopher smoothed a hand over the papers on the tabletop. "A group of paranormal treasure hunters. They lost three crew members."

"*WHAT?!*" Heath and I exclaimed again. It was freaky how many times we said the same thing at the same time.

Gilley woke up at this point, probably from all the yelling. "What'd I miss?" he asked.

"Gopher's trying to kill us," I snapped.

Gilley rubbed his eyes and looked around blearily. "So, nothing new, huh?"

"Seriously, guys," Gopher said calmly. "This thing is nothing you can't handle! I mean, you two are the best at busting the worst demons and spooks the underworld has to throw at you. I've seen that firsthand!"

I eyed our producer skeptically. "Someone's got gold bullion on the brain."

"Want to pull out?" Heath asked me.

I sighed, thinking about the pros and cons for a minute. Finally I looked at him and said, "I'm in if you're in."

Heath's smile returned. "Then we're both willing to go for it."

"Awesome!" Gopher exclaimed. "Guys, that is awesome!"

At that moment the call to board our plane was announced, and we all got up and shuffled toward the gate. And while I tried to appear enthused as we moved to the plane, in the back of my mind I couldn't help but wonder if by agreeing to this bust, I'd just made the biggest mistake of my life.